THE SCENT OF DANGER

Fiona Buckley

**SEVERN
HOUSE**

First world edition published 2020
in Great Britain and the USA by
Crème de la Crime an imprint of
SEVERN HOUSE PUBLISHERS LTD of
Eardley House, 4 Uxbridge Street, London W8 7SY.
Trade paperback edition first published
in Great Britain and the USA 2021 by
Severn House, an imprint of Canongate Books Ltd,
14 High Street, Edinburgh EH1 1TE.

British Library Cataloguing in Publication Data
A CIP catalogue record for this title is available from the British Library.

ISBN-13: 978-1-78029-133-8 (cased)
ISBN-13: 978-1-78029-679-1 (trade paper)
ISBN-13: 978-1-4483-0383-0 (e-book)

Typeset by Palimpsest Book Production Ltd.,
Falkirk, Stirlingshire, Scotland.

For Anne and Alan, Liz and William, Anne and Ian,
The best friends anyone could have.

BRISTOL LIBRARIES
WITHDRAWN
SOLD AS SEEN

Please return/renew this item by the last date shown on this label, or on your self-service receipt.

To renew this item, visit **www.librarieswest.org.uk** or contact your library

Your borrower number and PIN are required.

A selection of recent titles by Fiona Buckley

The Ursula Blanchard mysteries

* available from Severn House

ONE

One Small Cloud

'Why is it,' I said brightly to Joyce Frost, my twenty-year-old ward, 'that when there's just one small cloud in an otherwise clear sky, it insists on covering the sun?'

'It will pass,' said Joyce prosaically. 'One can't expect much sunshine at the beginning of February.'

'But why did that wretched cloud have to go near the sun at all?' I persisted. 'There's the whole sky to choose from and it's so cold; we long for sunshine! That cloud is positively wilful.'

'It's moving away now,' said Joyce patiently, as the cloud drifted on and the sun came out.

'So I see,' I said shortly. I had only mentioned it for the sake of making light conversation to Joyce and the effort had fallen flat as usual.

Joyce and her twin sister Jane had become my wards just over three years before. Their mother was dead and their father had lately been imprisoned in the Tower, and although I had been instrumental in sending him there, he had nevertheless, for his own reasons, asked me to take care of his daughters. He had now been released but he was a merchant who would often travel abroad, and the house he and his daughters had once called home was no longer theirs. His girls needed a home and, he felt, a woman's guidance. He knew well enough that I was justified in what I had done and Jane, sweet-natured and sensible, knew it too but Joyce would not forgive me. She was polite, obedient, prepared to learn from me (I had first met her and her sister when I was engaged to teach them the finer points of embroidery), but I could engender no warmth between us, try as I might.

I had tried to find her a husband, but so far, my attempts had all failed. Jane had been married very soon after coming to live with me, but Joyce was not impressed by any of the gentlemen to whom I introduced her although they were all personable and young, with prospects. So here she was, beside me at the window of the great hall in my Surrey home of Hawkswood, making dull answers to my attempts at brightness. She was more depressing than any amount of aggravating little clouds.

I supposed that I ought to be used to it by now but instead it had grown more and more exasperating. How could she keep this campaign of coldness up so long? The twins had come to Hawkswood shortly before Christmas in 1582 and now it was the February of 1586. I turned away from the window, quelling a desire to shout at her: *Say that little clouds can't really be wilful and I'm foolish to imagine that they can, say you hate Hawkswood and detest me and why did your father ever abandon you to me, but say something, anything, with some sort of passion or enthusiasm or LIFE, can't you? Just stop giving me those flat, dead, ladylike answers that don't mean anything!*

Instead, I said: 'I'm having our horses saddled. It's a good morning for a ride. I dare say Dale is brushing our riding skirts at this very moment.'

Dale was my waiting woman. Her real name was Frances Brockley, for she was the wife of my manservant Roger Brockley, but I still used her maiden name, out of habit. 'Let's go upstairs,' I said, 'and change.'

I would enjoy a ride and I knew that she would, too, though she wouldn't say so to me. She was fond of her dappled Patches, just as I was fond of my bay gelding, Jaunty. I had had Jaunty now for several years and had grown so attached to him that to the amusement of my household, I went to the stable on most evenings to say goodnight to him. I let them laugh. I liked to see him content and comfortable in his stall, his coat glossy with grooming, pulling at his hay rack.

Joyce said: 'A ride would be nice,' in her best polite voice but then added, with just a little more animation: 'But what about those Withysham accounts that Brockley fetched for you two days ago? Didn't you say yesterday that you must look at them this morning?'

Withysham, in Sussex, was my second house. I moved my

household there sometimes, though not often. It was in the hands of a competent steward, Robert Hanley, though on principle I sometimes examined the accounts at unexpected moments. I had just done so.

I had a third property, Evergreens, which had been granted to me because of some work I had done for the queen the previous year. It was just south of Guildford and consisted of a small house and a smallholding. I had however rented it out and its day to day expenses were the business of the tenant and not mine.

As I led Joyce towards the stairs, I thought to myself that I had plenty of things to think about which had nothing to do with accounts. One, obviously, was Joyce herself. But I also had a problem with the maids.

Phoebe, my senior maid, was feeling her years and that came hard on Margery, the second maid. Margery was young and brisk but she had already had to take on more work because a very young maid we had formerly had, Lucy, had been so homesick that she finally went back to her parents, while Netta and Tessie, who were both married to grooms of mine and worked as maids in between having their children, now had four children apiece and came only for an hour or two now and then. It wasn't enough.

I must find at least two new maids and probably another groom as well, since the senior groom, Arthur Watts, was becoming old before my eyes. Even Adam Wilder, my steward, was visibly ageing. Soon I would have to pension him off – which he would hate – and find a replacement. I had much to do besides the Withysham accounts. I had passed those on to others.

'I changed my mind,' I said. 'Wilder and Harry are going through the ledgers. They're working in the east parlour; there's plenty of room there to spread out ledgers and notes. Master Dickson says that Harry has no gift for figures but he needs to learn. He's fourteen already. He is my heir and one day he'll need such skills.'

I tried not to sound despondent but I felt it. In the midst of this busy household, I was often lonely. My companion of many years, Mistress Jester, had gone to live with her married daughter in Edinburgh, and Jane, dear Jane, was with her husband – and now her two babies as well – in London. I missed Hugh, my late husband, too, even though he had been gone for many years. I lacked company of my own generation.

But in the midst of this happy, busy household, I had no right to be despondent. As we started up the stairs, I glanced over the banister to a window that overlooked the courtyard and there was Roger Brockley, who was a groom before he became my manservant, and still helped out in the stables, just leading Jaunty out. Patches was already saddled and waiting in the yard. Upstairs, I could hear Harry's tutor Peter Dickson, practising his lute. He was musically gifted and was teaching Harry. And – this did make me smile – I could hear Gladys Morgan grumbling.

Gladys Morgan had no official place at Hawkswood and she was no ornament to it, either. She was old, lame and ill-tempered, with a disgraceful line in curses when she was really roused. She had a nutcracker profile and her few remaining teeth resembled brown fangs. She had attached herself to me, limpet-like, after Brockley and I had rescued her from a charge of witchcraft. Later on, because her imaginative curses had outraged more than one vicar and her skill with medicinal potions had outraged nearly every physician she encountered, we had to rescue her from another and that time we nearly failed.

Secretly, I sometimes wondered if she really did have mysterious powers, for she sometimes prophesied danger and she was usually right.

Danger was familiar to me, far more familiar than it usually is to dignified widowed ladies running households in Surrey. In bygone years, needing extra money, I had let myself become an agent for the queen. At first I worked for money; later I learned that though I was illegitimate, I was a half-sister of the queen and from then on I was inexorably bound to her service. I usually took instructions from her principal councillors, who were now her Secretary of State, Sir Francis Walsingham, and her Lord High Treasurer, Sir William Cecil, otherwise Lord Burghley. Their assignments, often presented to me as safe and harmless, had frequently led me into danger. Gladys always seemed to see it coming.

Though it was true (and I had made a point of telling Gladys so), that I had lately carried out an assignment which led me into no danger at all, and been paid for by the grant of Evergreens. There had been increasing fears that Mary Stuart of Scotland, who was in England, half as a guest and half as a prisoner, had been trying to plot with Philip of Spain with a view to getting the Spanish to invade and put her on Elizabeth's throne. I had been asked to recruit some new agents, especially in the West Country, which was one of Philip's likely landing places, should he ever come. I had done so, successfully.

I hoped now to give up my secret work. I was over fifty. My hair was still dark and my hazel eyes still saw clearly, but I was no longer young. Looking after things at home was more than enough to keep me occupied. Not to mention, safe. The desire for safety had grown on me through the years. Here at Hawkswood I *was* safe and I had nothing to be depressed about.

We were halfway up the stairs, when below us, a door opened, releasing a flood of sunlight into the vestibule. Harry's voice called: 'Mother!' and was at once echoed by Wilder calling: 'Madam!' I stopped and peered over the banister. 'What is it? What's the matter?'

'It's these accounts from Withysham!' said Harry excitedly.

'What about them? Wilder?'

In a solemn voice, as though he were announcing a death, Wilder said: 'There's something far wrong with them, madam. Will you come?'

I looked at Joyce. 'There goes my ride! But you can have yours. Your horse is ready and Brockley will go with you. Have a pleasant outing.'

'May I not help you look at the Withysham ledgers? I used to help our steward with the accounts at home, when Father was away at sea. In fact, I miss them. They exercise the mind,' said Joyce.

In all the three years she had spent with me, except for such minor things as *please pass the apple sauce* she had literally never asked me for anything before. 'Of course you may,' I said warmly. 'We'll both go. Harry, make room for us at the table in there and then go and tell Brockley that we're not riding this morning after all. Then come back.'

When we were all seated shoulder to shoulder on a bench at the table in the sunlit parlour, with the two Withysham ledgers set out before us, Wilder did some explaining for Joyce's benefit.

'I expect, Mistress Frost, that you already know that Withysham just has the one small home farm?' Joyce nodded. 'This ledger with the blue leather binding is for the farm. This with the red binding is for the house. Madam checks them every quarter but also at occasional unexpected moments in between. This is one of those moments.'

'How does Master Hanley keep his accounts while the ledgers are here with Mistress Stannard?' Joyce asked.

'He has a second, identical, set,' Wilder told her.

Harry, who had just returned at a run from transmitting my orders to Brockley, pushed the farm ledger eagerly towards me and jabbed a forefinger at a recent entry. 'Mother, look at this order for the farm horses' oats! And this one!' He turned back two pages and pointed out another entry. 'If the horses have really been eating all those oats, they must be jumping out of their skins! Over the fences and over the moon!'

'It's the same pattern for the three horses that count as household expenses,' Wilder said. 'Oats were ordered for them at the same times. Far in excess of what they need.' He flicked over pages in the household ledger and showed me. 'It makes no sense,' he said.

'No extra horses have been bought?' Joyce questioned.

'No,' I told her. 'I used to keep our stud of trotters at Withysham but as you know, I have moved them here.' Trotters, the light harness horses with high action and a remarkable turn of speed, were becoming very popular and I had begun a stud, as an extra source of revenue and an extra inheritance for Harry. 'There are only five horses at Withysham now,' I said. 'There's Hanley's own cob, and two general purpose animals that draw light carts and are ridden by anyone who needs them. And there are two heavy horses for the Withysham farm, for the plough and the harrow and the heavy carting. That's all.'

'It isn't just the oats,' said Wilder. 'That extra order for them warned me that something was wrong and as soon as I really looked for trouble – God's teeth, I found it! New saddles for our two Withysham horses! Madam, when the last three-monthly audit was made, you went to Withysham yourself, with Master Harry and Mistress Frost here. I'm sure you all saw the tackroom. Did any of the horses need new saddles?'

'No, they didn't,' said Harry decisively. 'I looked round the tackroom to see if anything new was needed. I didn't find anything. All the tack was in good condition.'

'And why so much new linen – these towels and sheets?' asked Joyce, who was scanning the ledger intently. 'There was plenty of linen in the house four weeks ago! We didn't sleep between patched sheets!'

Joyce was becoming positively animated and she was asking very sensible questions. This pleased me so much that just for a moment, the dubious Withysham accounts seemed no more important than the little cloud that had briefly covered the sun.

I should have known better. There is a saying about the ominous nature of clouds no bigger than a man's hand.

Wilder was leaning past Joyce to study the household ledger and running a forefinger down the entries. 'There are things here that I never noticed before because they're small. Though I should have noticed them . . . madam, I feel I must apologize . . .'

'We have been too trusting, both of us,' I said. 'Me as much as you. I just skim the books sometimes. I think to myself: Hanley is reliable; why peer and pry and check up on every entry? Harry, when I am gone . . .'

'Mother, please don't say that!'

'When I am gone,' I repeated firmly, 'and you are the master here, always check every single entry in the ledgers, even if it bores you, even if it gives you a headache, even if you would much rather be out riding or playing the lute or dallying with the beautiful wife I hope you will one day have. Remember!'

'But if Hanley has always been so reliable,' said Joyce, 'why isn't he reliable now?'

'That's what we're all wondering,' said Wilder. 'Now that we're looking for oddities, well, here are some more. How can Withysham possibly have used up so many candles!'

'It's a shadowy place,' said Joyce doubtfully. 'Those narrow windows don't let in much light.'

'I still know how big the candles order ought to be, and this is much *too* big,' said Wilder. 'And this purchase of salt. There's always extra salt needed in November, of course, when the surplus animals are slaughtered and the meat is salted, but this entry is still inflated.' He raised troubled eyes to mine. 'I don't like this at all.'

Joyce said gravely: 'Even small falsifications, added together over time, could amount to a considerable sum.'

'But why?' My momentary elation over Joyce had passed. Something at Withysham must be seriously wrong, but what in heaven's name could have made Robert Hanley behave like this?

'In all these years,' I said, 'there has *never* been any suspicion about Hanley's honesty, and I think, if this falsification has been going on for long, we would have noticed it before. What has happened?'

No one answered. I rose to my feet. 'I must speak to Dale and Brockley. I shall leave for Withysham today. Harry, you and Wilder will take charge here while I'm away. Joyce, do please come if you would like to. You need not be present when I talk to Hanley, of course; that could be embarrassing for you both.'

'I would like to come. I should enjoy the journey,' said Joyce.

Was there, at last, a trace of softening? The visit to Withysham would be serious business, so I didn't smile but I nodded, and said: 'I shall welcome your company, Joyce.'

TWO

Bygone Sins

In recent years, Dale had been finding horseback travel more and more difficult. The very idea would make her prominent blue eyes bulge, and the old, faded pockmarks left by a childhood attack of smallpox would somehow become more noticeable. They always did when she was upset.

But it didn't matter because although Brockley and I, and now Joyce too, preferred to travel on horseback, a stay away from home meant luggage. I always equipped myself with at least one fairly formal gown and of late years, even moderately formal dress had become so elaborate that just one gown could occupy an entire hamper. It certainly couldn't travel in a saddlebag.

I possessed a coach, which Hugh had used when his joint evil became too bad for riding, but it was big and unwieldy, requiring two horses and sometimes four, depending on the number of its passengers. I had therefore had a small carriage made which could be drawn by one horse. Dale could travel in this, along with the baggage, and Joseph, one of my grooms, could drive it while the rest of us rode alongside. Even so, Dale grumbled, saying that she couldn't abide these sudden journeys; she'd woken that morning in her own bed and she hadn't expected to find that she'd be going to bed that night in Withysham.

'Where you and Brockley have a pleasant chamber on the west side and well you know it,' I said, laughing at her. Fran Dale had been with me for years, and had been through much with me, even into serious danger. She was welcome to grumble if she liked. I still needed her help to get in and out even of a semi-formal gown. Some brocades can almost stand up by themselves.

We took an early dinner. My tall, broad-built cook John

Hawthorn shook his head over that but as ever, he and his contrastingly short, bald assistant Ben Flood, provided an excellent meal, with fresh caught trout from our own lake, baked with almonds and accompanied by beans in a dark meaty sauce, with preserved plums in a spiced custard afterwards. Then Brockley and Joseph together put a placid horse called Rusty into the shafts of the carriage, put the baggage inside and saddled the riding horses. Brockley handed Dale in and then Joyce and I and Brockley mounted, Joseph jumped into the driver's seat and away we went.

'This is a strange turn of events, madam,' Brockley said as we started out. Brockley had a high polished forehead strewn with a few pale gold freckles, very steady grey-blue eyes and a general air of calm dignity, but at the moment he looked worried. 'We have never had trouble with dishonesty like this before, and I can hardly believe it of Robert Hanley.'

'Nor can I,' I said. 'That's the reason I want to know *why.*'

We made the best speed we could but February roads are usually muddy and it was past nine o'clock when we arrived, according to the little timepiece, another gift from the queen after my efforts at recruitment, that I carried at my girdle. As we rattled through the gatehouse tunnel and into the courtyard, Hanley came out of the house to meet us. He looked much as usual. He was a stocky, quiet mannered man, not striking in any way. He greeted us in his usual courteous fashion, called to the two Withysham grooms to help Joseph and Brockley with our horses and told me that our rooms had, as always, been kept in readiness. Had we taken supper on the way? If not, it would be set in hand at once.

Everything seemed normal. But I knew Hanley well. He should have been surprised to see us so unexpectedly, and he should have been smiling. He didn't look in the least surprised nor did he smile and in his indeterminately coloured eyes, there was fear.

It was too late that day to start an inquest into financial irregularities. We accepted some supper and then retired. But next morning, I had us all up betimes and personally took the disputed ledgers to the room I used as a study when I was at Withysham.

'As I've already said,' I told the others, 'I'll see Hanley on my own at first. There may be some simple explanation. I hope so!'

'I can't imagine one,' said Brockley candidly.

Before King Henry the Eighth, the father I had never known, disbanded all the monasteries, male and female alike, Withysham had been a house of nuns. It was an old grey stone building on the northern edge of the Sussex downs, and many of its windows were the original ones, almost as slender as arrow slits, an echo of the times when only the wealthier houses could afford glazing and to let in light was also to let in the cold. Withysham had never been wealthy. It had had no cloisters, no guest-house, no separate lodging for its abbess. It was so unobtrusive that it was a wonder that King Henry's officials had noticed its existence.

I had had the windows glazed and some of them exchanged for modern mullions. The atmosphere of the house, which was one of serenity, the result, no doubt, of the centuries during which prayer had soaked into the walls, remained unchanged. The main hall, though, where we had eaten supper, was not so much serene as austere. I had tried to temper this with new mullions, and by hanging lively tapestries on the walls and flinging an eastern carpet, all azure and vert and rose, over the long table, but austere it unconquerably remained.

The study also had new windows and I ordered a fire to be lit in its hearth. It was far more comfortable than the hall. Brockley drew the square oak table that did duty for a desk near to the warmth and pulled a couple of stools up to it. I set out the ledgers and asked Brockley to tell Hanley that I wanted to see him. Then I waited.

Hanley came promptly, but his unhappy face was enough to tell me that he knew why I had come. I asked him to be seated and he obeyed. His hands were tremulous and he looked at me with hangdog eyes.

'I have been expecting you, madam,' he said. 'Ever since Master Brockley arrived here to collect the ledgers, saying that you wished to do an unexpected audit.'

'And if I had not done so?'

'Master Brockley glanced at the ledgers, saw that one set seemed to be complete, while the other one had no entries after last summer, and took the complete one. If I had had time, I would have filled in the other set with . . . with the extra expenditure more widely spread and hope that it wouldn't attract attention. Those ledgers are the ones I would have handed over for inspection. I knew I had done it too roughly, in the set that Master Brockley took. I am not used to these deceits. I . . .'

He ran out of words. His expression was agonised.

'So you know why I'm here,' I said. 'You've been expecting me, in a state of dread, I fancy. I am glad to hear that you're not used to deceit, but why did you do it at all?' I was more bewildered than angry. For years, Hanley had been a byword for trustworthiness. If he had been falsifying his accounts, it wasn't because of innate dishonesty. He had a reason. And then I saw that he was crying.

'Hanley!' I said. 'Please don't. I want to know why you have been doing this. And for how long.'

He found a napkin under his black woollen doublet and wiped his eyes. 'Since last summer. At first it wasn't noticed.'

'My fault, and Wilder's,' I said candidly. 'We've grown complacent. I'll repeat my first question. Why?'

He looked straight at me, gathering some shreds of dignity about him. 'I have been desperate, madam. I have an uncle . . .'

He stopped, which made it sound as though an uncle were some kind of disease or deformity. 'Most people have uncles,' I said. 'What is wrong with yours? Hanley, this is like drawing teeth. Please explain properly.'

'His name is Crispin Hanley and he lives somewhere in south Devon, I think, probably not far from Plymouth. I don't know exactly but all the couriers he sends say they come from around there. I make a point of asking them! But none of them know just where he lives. The same man never comes twice.'

'And they started coming last summer?' I queried. 'Asking you for money, I take it? How often?'

'Every six weeks or so, madam.'

'Why do you send it? Is your uncle very poor?'

'I don't know. But he . . . he knows something about me, madam,' said Hanley wretchedly.

'Go on.'

'He's told me – written – that he tried for a long time to find me but up to last year, he couldn't. Then he did. I don't know how. I don't know whether he's rich or poor. Madam, he . . . says he will tell everyone what he knows about me, tell you, the people here, unless I pay him. Only I can't afford what he asks, not out of my wages, so . . .'

'What is it that he knows about you? Are you wanted by the law?'

Hanley shook his head. 'No. Not that. When I was a boy of sixteen, I was a fool, that's all.'

'Boys of sixteen frequently are,' I told him. 'Did you steal something? Or was it to do with a girl?'

I knew at once that I had put my spade into a buried hoard. His eyes flashed. 'I was so *stupid*,' he said bitterly. 'And so ignorant.'

'All right, what happened?'

'I couldn't – I can't – bear anyone to know. I . . .'

'Did you murder the wench?'

'No, no, of course not!' I had hoped for an outraged denial and here it was. But then he added, cryptically: 'Well, not exactly . . .'

'Hanley, I find it difficult to understand how anyone can *not exactly* commit a murder!'

'I was born in a Hampshire village. My father was a steward to a big house there. I was walking out with the daughter of one of the tenants. I was sixteen, she was fifteen, and one evening we were in an empty barn and . . . and . . . cuddling . . . oh, God . . .'

'And it went too far?'

'She cried *stop* and I couldn't. . . well, I didn't. Afterwards, she hit me and said she never wanted to see me again but she wouldn't tell anyone; not ever. She said I'd taken her virtue from her . . . God's teeth, how she wept.'

Hanley's voice was bitter but he was no longer hesitant. He had embarked on his tale and it was carrying him forward by its own impetus. 'It was only the once,' he said, 'but it got her with child. Eventually, she couldn't hide it so she had to tell her parents and they came after me. They found me working in the fields and said I was to come to their house.

They said they'd tell my father if I refused. So I went. When I got there, there was such a scene; the wench and her mother weeping . . .'

'What was the girl's name?' I asked.

'Marion. Does it matter? Her and her mother howling; her father raging and saying I'd raped her and brandishing a great whip and telling me I was to put things right or he'd half kill me . . . it wasn't rape!' Hanley was crying again. 'I didn't jump out at her from behind a bush. She wanted me to . . . to pet her. I think she . . . she wanted the other only she didn't dare to but she let me get so near it that I couldn't . . . couldn't . . .'

'All right, you needn't go into details. I know what happened. You couldn't stop. You were told to put things right. You mean you were told to marry her?'

'Yes. I had to tell my parents but they weren't so bad. These things happen, they said. My Uncle Crispin said that too. He lived with us; he was a groom at the place where Dad was a steward. So Marion and I were married. We were far too young. We were given a cottage to live in; my father arranged that somehow. Marion did her best, I suppose. She could cook quite well; she tried to keep our home clean and tidy; she tried to make me love her. But I didn't. I couldn't. I said, I was stupid and ignorant at that age; I almost blamed her for getting pregnant. I knew it wasn't her fault but I wasn't reasonable, and she got fat and bloated and kept on being sick and I was disgusted . . .'

'Go on,' I said relentlessly.

'Her time came. The baby was stillborn and Marion died. That's what I meant when I said it wasn't exactly murder. But in a way I killed her. I am still so ashamed.'

His voice dropped and he would not meet my eyes. 'I got away from Hampshire after that,' he said. 'I found my first post as an assistant to a steward in Berkshire. I never went back. My parents died. Uncle Crispin sent word to me about that. He's my father's brother. He's much younger than either of my parents were. He's still very much alive. It's all more than twenty years ago and ought to be forgotten but no. I changed my post and I lost touch with my uncle. I heard nothing from him for years until he found out where I am and he's been demanding money and now, I suppose, you will dismiss me without a character. Well, it's just as well that I never married again. I've no family to be flung into despair. I will take my leave as soon as I can pack up and give some instructions to whoever replaces me. I ought to replace the money and I will try but I don't know how, what with my uncle . . .' He ran out of words.

I suppose most people in my position would have dismissed him without a second thought and ordered him to repay me or be arrested – or possibly be arrested anyway. Perhaps my curious career, which had frightened me nearly to death at times and also widened my horizons far beyond the norm, had something to do with it. Instead of doing what most people in my position would have done, I said: 'No, Hanley. You will stay put and not, ever again, falsify your accounts. We – Wilder and I – will notice if you do and that will indeed be the end for you. I will also remit the debt. But you will never pay your uncle another penny. I will deal with your Uncle Crispin. I will visit the West Country myself and try to find him and if I succeed, I will make it very clear to him that he is to cease plaguing you, and that extortion is unlawful and we are being merciful in not going to the law about this.'

'I wouldn't want you to go to law about him,' said Hanley, looking horrified. 'Not my own uncle! And my past would come out! That's what I've been trying to avoid! I'm so ashamed of it . . . so ashamed.' His eyes were the pleading eyes of an injured dog. 'If only,' he said, 'he would let me be, perhaps I could . . . not think of it so much. I didn't mean to hurt Marion but she's dead and nothing can change that and it's all my fault. But what he is doing is cruel and . . . what if there are others like me?'

'If I find him,' I said grimly, 'I will answer for it that there will not be others like you. He will never trouble anyone in such a way again. It may even be my fault that he traced you,' I said ruefully. 'You say that he suddenly found you last year. I was in south Devon last year on a family visit, to my daughter's in-laws. I met many people and sometimes talked about Hawkswood and Withysham. I probably mentioned

my stewards. Meanwhile, I repeat, don't pay your uncle a
farthing more. Understand?'

'I am not dismissed, then?'

'Hanley,' I said, 'what you did is what thousands of foolish
boys, and men too, do all too often. It is very wrong, but it
isn't always a disaster. Many marriages begin that way, but turn
out well and at the end of their lives, the pair are adoring
grandparents and devoted to each other. You were unlucky. No,
you are not dismissed, though you will be if you ever do this
again, and in future both Wilder and I will, as I said, be much
more watchful.' I stood up. 'I must now prepare to travel to the
West Country.'

First of course, I had to return to Brockley and Joyce, waiting
in the hall, and tell them my decision. I expected them to argue
but they didn't. 'Boys of sixteen . . . no need to brood about it
for ever. Poor old Hanley,' said Brockley, quite kindly. Joyce
said: 'You mean to keep him on? Are you sure? I don't think
my father would have been so merciful.'

'I am not your father,' I said and that appeared to be that. I
added: 'We must go home now, and do some extra packing.
We will probably make quite a stay in Devon.'

One of the drawbacks of being half-sister to the queen and also
one of her agents was that Lord Burghley and Sir Francis
Walsingham (very likely at the queen's behest) felt it necessary
to keep me under observation. They said it was for my own
good, my own safety. It was probably a wise precaution but I
disliked it.

I was well aware that Laurence Miller, who was officially
the chief groom at my stud of trotters, was also Cecil and
Walsingham's current watchdog and would report my
intended journey and its purpose to his employers. I wasn't
surprised therefore when a message came from Sir Francis
Walsingham. Since I would be in the right area, the message
said, it would be a good chance to see how the two agents
I had found in that district were performing. Their last reports
had both said they had heard of money being collected,
possibly for Mary but neither could be definite. No further

reports had arrived. Please would I find out if they had discovered anything more.

'I was going to talk to them anyway,' I said crossly.

'Oho,' said Gladys Morgan. 'Trouble. That's what this is. Trouble.'

THREE

A Stone in a Still Pond

Because I did want to talk to the two Devonshire agents while I was about it (I didn't need Walsingham to remind me, I said grumpily to Brockley) I naturally wished to make my visit look as harmless as possible. My married daughter Meg's Devonshire in-laws were her husband's cousin Bartholomew Hillman and his wife Thomasina. The previous year, when I did my recruiting, they had let me stay with them. Perhaps they would do so again.

I therefore despatched my youngest groom Eddie with a letter, explaining my wish to find my steward's uncle and saying I would be glad if they would let me make another short stay with them. I would be bringing only the Brockleys, my ward Joyce Frost, and one groom.

I was entitled to use the royal remount network and I gave Eddie the badge that would entitle him, too. With fresh horses available at frequent intervals, he managed the three-hundred-mile ride to Devon in six days and was back with the reply in a fortnight. Yes, we would be very welcome; Thomasina and Bartholomew would be glad to see us.

Our departure was delayed for a week by a spell of bad weather, first with snow and then with a thaw in the shape of downpours and a thunderstorm. We finally set out at the end of February, taking Eddie, who now knew the road, to share the driving with Brockley. With placid, plodding Rusty in the shafts, there was no question of us doing the journey in six days. Rusty and our small carriage weren't catered for by the remount service. We took three weeks to get there.

The weather had settled to being cold and overcast, with occasional rainstorms and the roads were deep in mud. The carriage got bogged several times. It had to be freed by putting sacks under the wheels, asking Dale to get out and then taking out the luggage too. Brockley, always one to think ahead, had put some spare harness in, and more than once we harnessed Patches to the carriage as well as Rusty, using their double strength to get our transport free.

The worst patch was when we were crossing a part of Devonshire where the earth is as red as sunset and has the consistency of cream cheese. Our wheels just sank into it. Joyce, who had never seen such earth before, marvelled openly and turned to me to express her wonder. Was the ice really breaking at last? I made no comment, however. Let it come naturally. If I remarked on it, Joyce might freeze up again.

The soil was browner and lighter on the last stretch to the village Bartholomew and Thomasina lived. It bore the unusual name of Zeal Aquatio. There were other villages in the area named Zeal this or that. My daughter Meg had said she thought that Zeal had something to do with willow trees but Aquatio meant that the Romans had had a bathing place there, presumably in the river that ran past the village on the western side. The river must have silted up since, for it was too shallow for bathing now, at any point.

It was actually the tail end of an inlet from the sea, which was fed from the inland side by a stream. It was tidal and Thomasina had said, laughing, that the poor thing was never quite sure whether it was supposed to be salt or fresh.

Many streams ran into the area from the higher ground that surrounded it, and there were other inlets, as well as the wide mouth of the combined rivers Plym and Tamar. It was as though the land had been clawed by a gigantic cat. It was these waterways that made Cecil and Walsingham nervous.

'If I were Philip, bringing an invasion fleet,' Walsingham had said to me once, 'I would be interested in Plymouth and its surroundings. It's about the first bit of England I would encounter. It might be worth landing a force to seize Plymouth and send vessels up the rivers and the inlets, while the rest of my fleet sailed on up the Channel for a landing at the nearest point to London. I'd have a major port in my grip and vessels laden with men, hidden under Devon willows, a claw plunged into the west of England, awaiting a pre-arranged time to burst out, subdue their surroundings, and march towards London across southern England, putting down resistance as they came. The rest of the fleet would land its soldiers as near to London as it could, and they would march on the capital. It could work if he had enough soldiers.'

He added: 'In the West Country, there is considerable affection still for the old religion. There are those who might help the Spaniards – give provender, turn a blind eye to craft hiding under the willows on their property, that sort of thing. We want a few agents there, on the watch.'

I had done my best to supply them and now, like Walsingham himself, wondered what if anything they had discovered. Well, I hoped I would soon know.

For the moment, we had left Okehampton and Tavistock, the last notable towns on our route, behind us. We were now concerned with getting ourselves safely over the fords and bridges we had to cross before Zeal Aquatio came in sight. The floor of the carriage was awash twice, when a ford turned out to be deeper than a ford ought to be, and some of the bridges were rickety.

Waterways apart, we were travelling now through a country with two aspects. To our left was a tame world of gentle hills, draped with fields. On our right was wild heath stretching away to the foot of the Dartmoor hills, whose heathery shoulders, crowned with rock outcrops, made harsh silhouettes against the sky, or else jutted into the clouds.

We had taken care of our horses all the way, never overtiring them. It was one of the reasons why the journey took so long. But at last we were somewhere I recognized, travelling alongside a streamlet which had suddenly begun to run faster, down a gentle slope, and there ahead of us at the foot of the slope was the village.

Zeal Aquatio lay in a valley, no doubt carved by the same sluggish river that now formed its western edge. Appropriately, it was overhung by willows. The village itself consisted of a strung-out line of cottages and small houses, mostly thatched, on either side of a single narrow street with the square tower of a small church at the far end. Some larger houses, one of which was the home of Bartholomew and Thomasina Hillman, were scattered along the higher ground to the east.

'Their house is called Ladymead,' I said to Joyce, as I pointed it out to her. 'About a hundred years ago a very charitable and much respected widow lived there and everyone knew her as the Lady. Hence the name.'

'And let's get there as soon as we can,' said Brockley. He patted his horse. 'Even Firefly's beginning to wilt after this long journey. Take heart, my friend. You'll soon be in a comfortable stall with deep straw, a warm bran mash, and a haynet.'

Another half hour and we were clattering into the courtyard of Ladymead and a crowd of people had come out to welcome us. The dignified steward, Stebbings, tried to announce us formally but was completely overwhelmed. Bartholomew and Thomasina were there along with their children, like a flock of chattering sparrows, with their tutor and governess smiling benignly at their excitement. The eldest was a boy aged fifteen and the youngest was a little girl of five, but I noticed as Thomasina seized me in an affectionate embrace, that she was once more expecting, and that the birth might well be soon.

'Yes, I know,' she said, her warm brown eyes beaming, when I commented. 'And I'm forty-six now. There I was, thinking it would never happen again but wonders never cease, do they? I am not far from my time. Come in, come in, all of you. You too, Master Brockley, you know quite well that our grooms will take good care of the horses. We have ponies now for the elder children and the fuss they would make if their ponies weren't glossy and well fed! Our eldest, Tom, thinks his Bay Hillman must forever look as though he was ready to carry the queen in a procession.'

'Very well, Mistress Hillman,' said Brockley, steadying me as I dismounted, and then turning to hand Dale out of the carriage. 'Eddie, you are to go with the grooms and be my representative. The grooms here have perfectly comfortable quarters. I know!'

Eddie, who was not one for parlours and polite society, said that suited him, and went to Rusty's head. Thomasina laughed and marshalled the rest of us indoors.

The front door opened straight into the hall. Ladymead, being an old house like Hawkswood, possessed a great hall. It wasn't actually all that big but it was traditionally furnished, with an oak dining table, several pairs of antlers to decorate the walls, and a minstrels' gallery, albeit a small one that wouldn't accommodate many minstrels.

'You can have the room you had before, Ursula,' Thomasina said. 'It's big enough for Mistress Frost as well, and the Brockleys can be next door. We haven't any more spare rooms at the moment; Tom is studying – he hopes to take up the law as a profession – and we have had to let him have a room to himself; the others are so noisy.'

'But you have plenty of space, or you had last year!' I exclaimed. 'You had that new guest wing on the east with four bedchambers over a music room . . .'

'There was a fire,' said Thomasina. 'Just before Christmas. There was a thunderstorm one day, at midday. Do you remember that tall fir tree that used to be at the far side of the courtyard?'

'Yes, I do. Was it struck?'

'It was, and it caught fire and crashed down on to the roof of the new wing. The whole thing was burned down though the wall between it and the rest of the house is made of stone and is three feet thick and so the rest of the house was saved. We did manage to rush into the music room and rush out again with a couple of lutes, a guitar – and two of the stable lads came staggering out, just in time, with the spinet. But we are now short of space.'

'Oh dear,' I said helplessly.

'Well, you can still have the rooms you had before and Mistress Frost can share with you, if that's all right.'

We assured her that it was.

'I'll send a maid up to help you all unpack. Now I must make sure that my cook is adjusting dinner for you – we didn't know when to expect you, you see. We've been on the alert for a week, laying in supplies of extra ham and bacon from the pigman in the village . . .'

'What's happened to Peter Gray who used to supply those things for you?' I asked, surprised.

'Oh, that's a sad story. He had an accident and he was killed. It was a wretched business, but as I said, there's a pigman in the village who can provide anything in the pork line. He's a happy man,' said Thomasina. 'He's got all of poor Gray's pork business. And his pigs! He bought them when Gray's stock was auctioned.'

'But Gray was so young!' I was startled. 'What kind of accident was it?'

'Had one too many in the Castle Inn in Okehampton,' said Thomasina. 'Staggered out for a breath of fresh air just as a team of horses pulling a heavy cartload of something or other decided to bolt. They ran him down. Yes, it was dreadful. I don't like to imagine it. He was only in his twenties. He'd taken over the business two years before, when his father died, and he was doing so well. Who'd have thought it?'

'No one,' I said, shocked.

Thomasina wanted to talk to her cook and I knew the way to our rooms, so we parted from her and I led us all upstairs. The rooms had once simply led out of each other but they had been good-sized rooms, so Bartholomew had made them a little smaller, thus providing a narrow passageway, with a separate door for each bedchamber.

'This one's ours,' I said to Joyce, as I laid a hand on the latch.

'And ours is here to the right,' said Brockley, also remembering. 'It seems like yesterday.'

When Joyce and I went into our room, I immediately sat down on the bed. Something must have shown in my face, for Joyce said: 'Is there anything the matter, Mistress Stannard?'

'I'm tired,' I said. 'I'm feeling my years.'

Peter Gray had been one of my agents. He was young and active, very willing to take the task on and I thought him a good choice, for he met many people and heard all the news. He went about in the course of his work, doing deliveries to customers, even going inland as far as Okehampton, which was a crossroads for traffic to and from both Plymouth and Exeter. He also enjoyed a pint of cider now and then in public houses, which provided more good opportunities to hear what was afoot round about. But he had fallen victim to this unlikely accident. No wonder Walsingham hadn't received any further reports from him.

Hadn't received any further reports from either of them, apparently. Had Walsingham been implying something that I should investigate?

I thought about it. Gray's accident sounded extraordinary. And it had happened in Okehampton. That was where my other agent for this area, Gregory Reeves, lived. Or had lived.

I sat quite still, and a cold snake of fear coiled in my stomach. What if Gregory too . . .?

No. Unlikely accidents do happen. Gregory was probably quite all right. But if he too had died by mischance, then it would be plain that their accidents weren't accidents at all. And I was responsible, for I had thrown them into the path of danger. I was angry as well as afraid. Gregory and Peter had been young, strong, alive . . .

Pray God that Gregory still was. For investigating them might put me in the path of danger too.

No one in this house knew anything about them. In the eyes of Thomasina and Bartholomew, they were merely among the people I had chanced to meet last year, while I was in Devon.

If it came to the point, I didn't think I would be able to hide what I was doing from Thomasina and Bartholomew, nor ought I to do so. This happy, normal house, with a baby in prospect, was entirely the wrong base for such a thing.

I remembered Gladys croaking *trouble* in that maddening way she had, and here it was. Or might be.

I had landed here like a stone cast into the middle of a quiet pond. I would make ripples and – I would try to keep everything as quiet as I could but my ripples had on occasion become tidal waves. Please, Gregory, be still alive.

FOUR

Improbable Coincidence

J oyce was still looking at me doubtfully. It was time to stop
pretending. If my fears were realized, I wouldn't be able to,
anyway. 'It's not just that I'm tired,' I said. 'Will you find
the Brockleys?'

When the Brockleys were with us, I told Dale to leave the
unpacking to the maid. 'I have things to explain,' I said.

I moved to one of the basket chairs with which the room
was provided, and explained, firstly about my plan to see my
agents, secondly that they hadn't been sending any reports to
Walsingham of late and thirdly, what a strange coincidence it
was that a quite extraordinary accident had befallen a young
man who happened to be one of them. In the eyes of any
conspirators, of course, one of her majesty's spies.

'It really was extraordinary,' I said. 'So he had too many
ciders and tottered outside for some fresh air *just* at the exact
moment when the horse team pulling a heavy cart chooses to
bolt. What do you think, all of you?'

'It's looks funny,' said Dale. Brockley snorted and said: 'More
than funny, something like that happening to an agent.'

Because the Brockleys knew about my agents, I felt free to
tell Joyce as well. She now said: 'What about the other agent,
Mistress Stannard? What's his name?'

'Gregory Reeves. He's the son of Andrew Reeves, who is a
well-known weaver in Okehampton. Where Peter Gray was
killed.'

Joyce was perceptive. 'Is Gregory Reeves still alive?'

'I don't know. I'll have to find out. I am sorry to drag you
all into this but it must be done and if Gregory has also had a
fatal accident, then I must find out who was responsible.'

'And we still have to find Crispin Hanley,' said Joyce.

'Yes, we do,' I agreed. 'He traced his nephew, by the sound

of it, when I was visiting Devon last year. Another coincidence. I am wondering if any of the people I met here last year know him. They may have told him where to find my steward! They could have learned that from me in casual conversation. It could have happened so easily. Robert Hanley's predicament *could* be my fault!'

Indeed it could. I could have been strolling round a garden, or talking across a dinner table, being asked where I lived, describing Hawkswood and then remarking that I had a second house as well. *Oh no, Withysham is no trouble; it has an excellent steward, Robert Hanley.* Uncle Crispin just might have found his nephew through me.

Joyce was thinking. 'About Gregory Reeves,' she said. 'Even if something has happened to him, too, surely you don't have to go finding out things yourself. Couldn't you just report your suspicions to Sir Francis Walsingham and let him do the investigating?'

'He may not take it up,' I said. 'Agents are very much on their own. Or he might ask me to do it. "Don't take any risks, Ursula, but you are in the right place with a perfectly good reason for being there and I don't want it to seem as though anyone is officially interested in their deaths. After all, we shall need to replace them and secrecy is their best protection." I can just hear him. Anyway, I was the one who recruited them,' I said. 'I wasn't lying when I told you I was tired, Joyce. I am. Very.'

There was a pause, until Joyce said: 'How did you find the two of them – Gray and . . . Reeves, is it?'

'I met Gregory Reeves last year at the weekly market in Tavistock – that little town we came through, between here and Okehampton. I was with Thomasina and Bartholomew. The Reeves family have a regular stall there, to sell their cloth, and Thomasina is forever buying. She always says that to keep a growing family clothed takes cloth by the furlong. Gregory was in charge of the stall that week, and we got into conversation. He struck me at once as a likely prospect for an agent. He was young – tough and healthy looking, with bright eyes and a bright brain, too. You only had to talk to him for a minute or two to find that out. I turned the conversation towards Mary

Stuart and the danger that she poses, and I got a strong response. He didn't like her! At a moment when Bartholomew had wandered away and Thomasina was out of earshot, examining rolls of cloth at the other end of the counter, I hinted to him about a possible source of extra income, simply for being on the watch for anything questionable, and reporting it. We arranged to meet privately. Gregory, his eyes dancing, said he knew the right place.'

'I remember!' said Brockley. 'Fran and I didn't go to the market but I escorted you to the meeting afterwards. You met Reeves on the edge of the moor, not far from Tavistock, under a dead oak tree that had been bleached by lightning.'

'Yes. There, I explained to Gregory what I wanted him to do. God forgive me, I said it wasn't dangerous. He was to keep his ears and eyes open, try to identify people who supported Mary or the old religion and if he heard any whispers of people who might join an insurrection or provide billets for Spanish soldiers if there was an invasion, or if he heard of any attempts to collect money for Mary's cause, anything like that, he was to report it. He would be paid an annual retainer, on a certain date. He would collect his retainer, and despatch reports to Walsingham, by calling at the office of a royal messenger service based in Okehampton. It was his own town and he was a young man who was often here and there about the place; he could step into the office at irregular intervals without anyone noticing. I gave him a medallion to show, so that the messengers who carried his reports would be paid at the other end. He seized on the chance! He loved the idea of the retainer! And he and Peter Gray both seem to have reported hearing talk of money being collected for Mary, though they didn't know any details. Gossip overheard in a tavern, I suspect. But Walsingham has received no further reports. From either of them.'

'How did you find Gray?' Joyce asked.

It was Brockley who answered. 'He keeps – no, used to keep – chickens and pigs and supplied customers including Mistress Hillman with eggs and hams and bacon and so forth. They don't have poultry or pigs here at Ladymead.'

'I don't think Master Hillman is interested in such things,' I said. 'They own a tin mine in Cornwall, and three of the cottages in the village here, as well. There's no lord of the manor now in Zeal Aquatio. The family died out in the last century and people like the Hillmans – some of the others in the big houses up here – bought the cottages. Never mind all that. I met Peter Gray here when he was making a delivery. I talked to him a couple of times and things developed as they did with Reeves except that we settled it here, not under an oak tree on the moor. For his reports and so on, he could use a royal messenger service in Plymouth. Most towns of any size have one. He was his own master; he could come and go at will, even more freely than Gregory! I warned him about the need for discretion. I warned them both but . . .' I made a helpless gesture.

'They may not have taken me seriously enough. Somehow, they must have drawn attention to themselves. That is, if what I fear is true. Perhaps it isn't! Perhaps Gregory is still selling cloth at Tavistock.'

Dale, reverting to my earlier remarks, suddenly, and sympathetically, said: 'Ma'am, you ought not to feel unhappy about accidentally telling people that you employ a man called Robert Hanley. You couldn't have foreseen that it would do any harm.'

'But I may have done harm, by mistake,' I said. 'I was looking out for likely recruits to her majesty's service and I was oh so sociable last year! There were the Smithsons – they're at the other end of the village; the Fullers out on the Plymouth road . . .'

'There were the Hannacotts, too,' said Dale, and chuckled. 'I don't think, ma'am, that you gossiped much to them.'

'No, I didn't,' I said with feeling.

Brockley was grinning too. Because it was my custom to treat the Brockleys as friends rather than servants, they had accompanied me on some of last year's sociable outings. For Joyce's benefit, I said: 'The Hannacotts are a couple with four children and a passion for backgammon, shared by the whole family but not with me. Thomasina and Bartholomew go there now and then to play, but I dislike backgammon and play it very badly, and my one visit there wasn't a success. They play very earnestly, in silence. When they realized what a poor player I was, it became a grim silence. There was no conversation to speak of.'

'Nor at the Ingles,' Brockley said.

'Not what you would call conversation,' I agreed. 'They did all the talking; we just listened. I don't think I ever mentioned my home; I never had the chance. Joyce, they are two sad old widowed ladies, with no living children and few friends. When they do have company, they talk without stopping, about all their daily doings, their new recipe for pickles, their argument about the colours for a tablecloth they're embroidering, the cold in the head that one of them had last week and their troubles with maidservants. No, I need not visit the Ingles. If it becomes necessary, if anything really has happened to Gregory, then I must ask Thomasina to arrange for me to see the Fullers and the Smithsons. And I will have to go to Okehampton. I must think of a good reason.'

We were interrupted by a clanging gong, which we knew meant supper. Bartholomew, who had been out when we first arrived, was now home and joined us at the table. He was a tall man, very dark and inclined to be silent, except when he gave way to a concealed and sometimes weird sense of humour. He was always, though, very aware. Last year, when I was searching for agents while staying in his house, he had apparently known nothing about it. My daughter Meg and my son-in-law George Hillman had been staying as well and it was George, on one occasion, who tactfully made the study available to me so that I could interview a prospect (not Gray or Reeves, and as far as I knew, still alive and functioning in another part of the West Country).

But Bartholomew was the master of the house and not a man to be unaware of whatever was going on under his own roof. This time, although his conversation over the supper table was harmless, concerned with our journey from Surrey, the shocking business of my steward being blackmailed, the doings of his children and his hopes for another healthy chick, I noticed that he was watching me.

Sooner or later, I thought, he was going to ask awkward questions.

FIVE

No Escape

I slept badly that night. Beside me, Joyce slumbered peacefully but I continually surfaced, to lie worrying about Gregory Reeves, and how, if my fears were realized, I could possibly go about tracing those responsible. I also fretted again over whether I ought to pursue such enquiries from within this house. And I wondered how a perfectly reasonable attempt to free my steward from his uncle's grip had somehow turned into all this.

But one must keep up an appearance of being normal. In the morning I rose, washed and dressed and made commonplace conversation with Dale and Joyce before we all joined the family in the hall for breakfast. The Hillmans – both in my daughter's household and this one – were well acquainted with the fact that the Brockleys were friends, not servants.

Bartholomew was present, and once more seemed to be watching me. And then, just as we were all getting up from the table, he leant forward and said to me, very quietly: 'I must talk to you, Ursula. Come to my study,' and walked off, leading the way as it were, and showing that he meant *now*. Obediently, I followed.

The study was quiet and secluded. There was a small hearth, in which a fire had been kindled in readiness for us, a table, draped fashionably with a striking Turkey carpet, a desk with papers and a writing set on it, a couple of cushioned chairs. I remembered it well.

'Last year,' Bartholomew said, as he sat in one of the chairs and waved me to the other, 'I recall that you had a long interview in here with one of your fellow guests. My cousin George showed you both in and left you together. But I knew about it, Ursula, and what you were after and at whose bidding. I am the owner of this house, after all, and George respected that. He told me of the game that was afoot under my roof. He told me that you were recruiting agents hereabouts because of the strengthening threat from Mary Stuart, and said that you had asked for assistance.'

'I always thought you must have known,' I said.

'Perceptive of you. And now,' said Bartholomew, coming suddenly to the point, 'what is your purpose here this time? Yesterday, Thomasina saw your face and heard the tone of your voice after she told you that Peter Gray, who used to provide us with eggs and hams and the like, had died in an accident.'

'I see,' I said.

'You hardly knew him, so why should the news so startle you? And it did startle you. Thomasina is very perceptive. My dear Thomasina,' said her husband fondly, 'seems cosy and serene and devoted to her household, but she is no fool. She told me what she saw. She is . . . wondering. I have wondered from the start.'

He was deadly serious and there was no trace at all of his hidden sense of humour. 'You say you are here for your steward's sake,' he said, 'but such a thing would be a convenient cover for other business, would it not? So, Ursula, is there any other business, and if so, what?'

I wasted no time on evasion. Indeed, this direct challenge was a relief. Bartholomew could decide whether or not I could stay in his house and if not, might suggest some other haven. 'Gray was an agent,' I said. 'I recruited him. And now I'm afraid he . . . did not die by accident.'

Bartholomew looked grave. 'You're not the only one to puzzle over that accident. It caused quite a stir – news travels, you know. I don't like our one village inn but it's the only one we have and I drink there sometimes. I met a fellow who was at the inquest. He was telling everyone about it who wanted to listen! The verdict was misadventure but the coroner himself apparently said that it was an odd coincidence that Gray should blunder out of the Castle at the very moment when those horses bolted. But there, he said, coincidences do happen. That was it, it seems. You aren't satisfied with that?'

'Not in view of the work he was doing. I'm also wondering about a young man called Gregory Reeves,' I said. 'He lives in Okehampton. He's the son of . . .'

Bartholomew cut in. 'Thomasina and I know the Reeves family in a way – they have a regular stall at the Tavistock market and Thomasina buys there quite often. Also, I sometimes have business in Okehampton and I stay at the Castle Inn and hear the local gossip. Was Gregory another of your recruits? Yes? I am sorry to tell you that he too is dead and that his death was as strange as Gray's. Early in January, Gregory for some reason rode out onto the moor alone, with dusk falling and a frosty night ahead. The sky was full of glittering stars and that's a warning at this time of year. He didn't come home that evening. He was found next day lying in the shelter – the very poor shelter – of a pile of rocks. He had died of the cold. Why he went out on to the moor like that, no one knows. He didn't tell anyone. He should have been safe enough on horseback, but was presumably thrown. The horse came home to its stable without him and it's dangerous to be caught on foot far from home out there on the moor, on a freezing winter night. He very likely lost his way and crept or stumbled to the rocks seeking shelter from the wind. There was a bitter-edged east wind that night. I don't imagine that anyone has connected his death with Gray's – why should they? Gray was a smallholder near Zeal Aquatio; Gregory from a well-to-do weaving family in Okehampton. But now you imply that they are linked, and the inference is that those two accidents weren't accidents at all. You now seek to discover what really happened. That is your intention, I take it?'

'Now that I know that Gregory has also died in an extra-ordinary accident, it's my duty,' I said.

'If they were murdered,' said Bartholomew bluntly, 'then you are likely to encounter dangerous men. And in that case, you will draw danger to you.'

He stopped and I helped him out. 'Do you want me to leave?'

'It would be best. Ursula, I am sorry to be inhospitable, but I have a houseful of children and another due very soon. I have to put my own family first.'

'I'll move out to the inn, if they can take all four of us.'

'That means the Marchers' Arms. Named for our long-gone lords of the manor. The ale is all right but otherwise it's atrocious.

Bed bugs and appalling food. I must try to think . . .' He fell silent, frowning.

'Tell me,' I said, 'is there really much sympathy hereabouts for Mary Stuart? To the point of welcoming a Spanish invasion? Gray and Reeves heard gossip about money being raised and Mary's name was mentioned but it could have been nothing *but* gossip and perhaps the money, if any, was nothing to do with her at all. What's your feeling?'

Bartholomew roused from his silence. 'Sentimentality,' he said. 'People getting romantic, probably in their cups. You know the sort of thing. *Poor Mary Stuart, held a prisoner by Elizabeth, who pretends Mary is her guest but keeps her mewed up and forbidden visitors or correspondence. It must be terrible for her.* And then, if the company happens to be Catholic – we do have a Catholic community in this part of Devon, that's true – well, with them it's likely to be, *You must admit that Mary Stuart is brave. She has upheld the true faith throughout all these years.* But Protestant or Catholic, someone is likely to point out, *But she's never cleared herself of the charge of being party to her husband's murder. Married the principal suspect, didn't she?* Some wantwit then may sigh and say, *Oh dear, that's true, but that doesn't prove she knew he was guilty; perhaps she knew he wasn't, and just fell in love as any woman might, not heeding the suspicions of others – oh, how romantic, love conquers all.*

'And then they all sigh heavily and refill their glasses, and do nothing about it because they wouldn't dare – sentimental sighing over the dinner table is one thing but real conspiracies would be far too perilous and how would anyone go about it, anyway? I'd say that's all it amounts to for the most part. And yet,' said Bartholomew grimly, 'you recruited two agents to work here and now both have died in very strange accidents. So it looks as though a serious danger *is* lurking somewhere in our midst after all. Ursula, I am very fond of you, as Thomasina is, and George, but though I can't recommend the Marchers' Arms . . .'

'I could move to the Castle in Okehampton,' I said. 'I must visit Okehampton to talk to the Reeves family, and the Castle Inn is apparently where Peter Gray died. It's also the major hostelry there, I know.'

'Yes, it is, but you are supposed to be on a family visit to us. If you suddenly go off to stay in Okehampton – where both your agents died – anyone who is suspicious of you will be even more suspicious. You will have to visit the place, but you shouldn't stay there long. You had better remain in Zeal Aquatio and say that you were crowding us, because of the fire that destroyed four bedrooms. If only I could think of . . .' He frowned again, clearly searching his mind.

Then he said: 'I don't know where you could stay in our village but I can suggest someone who might. The vicar here, Lucius Parker. He knows every soul in this village and many outside it. And Dr Parker's sister Sabina helps a Plymouth charity for the aid of sailors' widows. She collects clothing for their children. Some of these widows are very poor and hard put it to clothe their little ones. Sabina has a wide acquaintance, too. Perhaps the Parkers can advise you.' For the first time, he smiled. 'But I am not throwing you out today. Today, please stay put and enjoy being with us.'

'Very well,' I said.

The danger was real. There was no escape. The sooner I left Ladymead, the better.

SIX
Indiscretion in High Places

That morning, Thomasina asked if she could borrow my carriage. 'I have a smart little painted cart of my own but it's having a new rim put on one of its rear wheels. I have calls to make and I can't walk far just now. I can use my own cob and let your Rusty doze in his stall. I expect he's tired after pulling the carriage all the way from Surrey.'

I was happy to agree and had no wish to join in the calls. Like Rusty, I was tired after the journey and felt glad of a rest. However, the morning wasn't as peaceful as I had hoped because Tom, the eldest Hillman son, and some of the grooms suddenly decided to have a rat hunt.

We had rat hunts at Hawkswood, of course, usually organized by Brockley, but tactfully planned to take place when I was out. Here at Ladymead, it seemed, no one worried about such things. Rat hunts just happened when the menfolk felt like it. This one involved Tom, the grooms, some of the menservants and Brockley, who had been invited to join in. Someone lent him a cudgel. It also involved three terriers, one belonging to Tom and two others kept by the grooms. Bartholomew apologized to me, but said that the hunt was really needed and then withdrew to his study.

Joyce equipped herself with an account of Hannibal's journey over the Alps; I took a favourite book of verse; Dale decided to embroider a cushion cover, and the three of us retreated to the big, untidy but comfortable parlour where we tried to pretend that the horrible cacophony outside among the outhouses and the fodder stores, the shouts and thuds and the hysterical barking and snarls from the terriers, and the terrified squeaking of the rats, wasn't happening.

It was a thoroughly noisy and disturbed morning and I was thankful when it was all over, and the uproar had given

way to the cheerful masculine sound of the participants saun-
tering to the rubbish pit with their sack of victims, loudly
discussing the morning's rat count as they went. Presently they
were in the kitchen, consuming ale and cider. A little later, the
cook shooed them out and Brockley came to the parlour grinning and wiping his mouth and anxious to give us an account
of the hunt, and how all the cats had hidden from it. We told
him we would rather not know.

There was peace after that, until dinner time was near, and
Thomasina came clip-clopping home behind her cob. She at
once came to find me.

'I hope the rat hunt wasn't too rackety,' she said. 'I didn't
know that my bloodthirsty son was planning it! I only found
out about it just now, as I came in. Ursula. I have done some
of your work for you. I have called on everyone – I am fairly
sure it's everyone – who you met socially with me last year.
None of them know anyone called Crispin Hanley. He clearly
doesn't live in this locality. And I did it all without mentioning
you. I think that for as long as possible, no one should associate
you with enquiries of any kind. Bart has been talking to me
– about Peter Gray and Gregory Reeves. Am I right?'

I thanked her heartily. One task at least had been completed
and in secrecy. Thomasina said: 'You have to go to Okehampton,
I imagine. Bart tells me that you must. You need to look into
those deaths – Gray's and Reeves', do you not? You may hear
news of Hanley there. It's a lively place. And you could ask
Lucius Parker on Monday. He really does know everyone for
miles. Tomorrow's Sunday. We'll introduce you to him after
the service.'

The rest of Saturday actually was peaceful, to my relief. Next
day, we duly attended the service at the nearby church, St
Ninian's. 'He was a Celtic saint,' Bartholomew told us as we
set off. 'There is much Celtic influence hereabouts – we are
not so far from the Cornish border, you know.'

I didn't know what to make of Lucius Parker when he got
into the pulpit. He was a tall man with round shoulders, a jutting
nose and short mousey hair, and he turned out to have a powerful
speaking voice and a kind of presence. However, I didn't like
the homily. His text was the story of the loaves and fishes but

in his hands it became a lecture on the sinfulness of vanity, especially when it took the form of spending money on oneself when others were in need. I was smartly dressed for church and felt that I was being accused of vanity myself.

The service included music, with three members of the congregation forming a small choir while a fourth played a little organ, but I detected more than a trace of Puritanism in the homily. I wondered if the new Puritan ethic, which at that time was gaining ground, had much support in the district. If so it would certainly hamper the activities of any Mary Stuart adherents. But the Puritans weren't likely to murder my agents.

I wasn't introduced to Parker after all, because just as the homily finished, Thomasina became unwell and whispered that she felt sick. We got her out of the church as fast and unobtrusively as possible. We had all walked the quarter of a mile from Ladymead and thought of sending Eddie off at a run for my carriage, but Bartholomew dashed back into the church and emerged with a friend who had brought his aged mother in a two-horse litter, which had been left out of sight behind the church. The friend brought three servants out of the church with him. They hitched up his horses; we put Thomasina in the litter and then Bartholomew led the horses to Ladymead at a careful walk.

Poor Thomasina was sick over the side of the litter, and later, when we were indoors and Bartholomew had taken her to their room, we heard that she was sick again. But she was better after a sleep and joined us in the hall for supper, though she did not eat much.

'Too much visiting yesterday,' said Bartholomew sternly. 'You shouldn't have lent her your carriage, Ursula.' His tone was tinged with the idea that I was a menace in his house. 'She is overtired.'

'I shall be all right tomorrow,' said Thomasina, but when tomorrow came, Bartholomew wouldn't hear of her walking to the vicarage with us and came himself to introduce us to the vicar.

The church of St Ninian's was built of grey stone and had the solid lines and the squat square tower of the days before the Conquest. It had an extensive churchyard, covered with winter grass, growing on and around the humps which marked the centuries of graves.

The rambling vicarage next door was probably of grey stone too, but most of it was covered in ivy. Dale remarked with a sniff that most of the rooms must be as dark as cellars, with all that ivy drooping over the windows.

The front garden was given over to vegetables. As we started up the path to the front door, a round-shouldered figure in shirtsleeves appeared from behind a redcurrant bush, saluted us with a hoe, and said: 'Master Hillman! You have brought me visitors?'

And then, before Bartholomew could speak, he said: 'I am Dr Lucius Parker, vicar of St Ninian's. My sister Sabina is indoors, entertaining Samuel Rossiter, our local constable. He's arrived with another list of seamen's widows in need of help and he and Sabina have taken the front parlour over completely. May I know who my new guests are?'

Bartholomew duly explained. 'Mistress Stannard has business in this district and in Okehampton and was hoping to stay with us, but the house is too crowded just now, what with my growing family and the loss of our guest wing. We are wondering if you knew of anywhere where Mistress Stannard and her companions could stay instead.'

'I will help if I can,' said Dr Parker and with that we found ourselves being cordially escorted inside, where we were invited to shed our cloaks before being shepherded into a dim parlour where a tall, lean woman and a middle-aged man, weather-beaten and heavily built, with a round, balding head, were sitting near the window and studying some papers which they had strewn over the only table and also over much of the seating. The man got to his feet when we came in, showering crumbs. The two of them had been sharing an apple tart as well as studying lists.

There were more introductions. The woman was Sabina and the man, as Lucius had already said, was the constable for Zeal Aquatio. He greeted us in a deep, gravelly voice with a strong local accent, smiled and seemed a little shy of me and Joyce. He had round blue eyes which seemed to stare, as though he rarely blinked, and his hands were powerful. He would be good at breaking up fights at the Marchers' Arms but I felt at once that the name of Sir Francis Walsingham would to him be as exotic as Cathay.

Sabina invited us to partake of refreshments while Lucius removed some papers from a straight-backed wooden settle and a couple of similar armchairs, none of them with cushions, while remarking: 'Sabina, I know you like to list the clothes you've collected in an orderly way – hose for big boys, jackets for six-year-old boys, gowns for tiny girls, and so on – but need the process create so much *disorder*?'

Sabina, apologizing, piled the papers on a stool, said she would fetch the refreshments and withdrew rather hastily, presumably to the kitchen. I thought how like her brother she was. And what a pity it was, too. Height and leanness, a long chin and that prominent nose suited Parker well enough but they did his sister no favours, and the grey eyes which were unremarkable in him, in her seemed cold.

Her hands were not beautiful either, but reddened and rough. We had seen no sign of a maid and it looked as though Sabina did the housework. But her brown hair, though bundled into a woollen net, was glossy and obviously cared for, and it was plain that she did look after her appearance though she probably couldn't spend much on it. Her apron protected a dress that was made of cheap woollen cloth, but was dyed a pleasant, warm brown. She had no farthingale, but women who do housework usually don't wear them; they're in the way. Her ruff was small but pristine and I caught just a hint of lavender scent, mingled, oddly, with the smell of horses. She brought in some more apple tart and a jug of cider. I tried a slice of tart and said how good it was and her face lit up with a smile.

'I enjoy cooking,' she explained. 'We still have apples in store and I made the tart this morning as soon as I had said good day to my pony.'

That explained the equine smell. Her brother, looking amused, said: 'You are foolish about that pony! Like a mother with a babe.'

'I am just as foolish about my gelding, Jaunty,' I said. 'I go to the stable every evening to say goodnight to him.'

'There!' said Sabina to her brother. She poured some cider

for each of us and then left us again, saying that she had washing to hang out. Lucius gazed after her with an air of regret.

'I think her pony really is her babe, in a way. My poor sister has never quite accepted that she is not good looking and therefore unlikely to marry – or not without a dowry bigger than any I could afford. She is clever with the housekeeping and I try to be generous with it. She saves what she can and I let her spend it as she pleases. She uses it for clothes and the like. I am not one to encourage vanity, and if you were in church yesterday, you must know that. But there it is, I am fond of her.'

I wondered what he thought of our clothes. Dale was in the discreet dark blue that she preferred but Joyce and I and Thomasina had all dressed smartly for this visit, just as we had for church. Our gowns were warm but all were of attractive colours and were made of fine wool with a glint of silk in the weave. I also wondered what he would think of the pouch that was sewn just inside the opening of my overdress, and held picklocks and a little dagger. I had worn such pouches for years, ever since I became one of the queen's agents. They had so often come in useful.

Constable Rossiter now remarked in his gravelly tones that he was sure that Sabina valued her brother's kindness. And then Joyce, who had been fidgeting a little on the wooden settle, asked Lucius, with a forthrightness that took me by surprise, if he was of the Puritan persuasion.

'Partially,' Lucius said, apparently not offended. 'I allow music. At heart I fear that I should not but I happen to have a liking for it. I enjoy hearing voices raised in melodious praise. Sabina is very fond of music too. She attends regular musical evenings in Tavistock – that's the little town halfway to Okehampton; no doubt you came through it on your way here. She plays the clavichord and the lute – our parents had her taught – so she can join in. She says that those evenings, and her charity work, give her something to care about, somewhere to *put* herself as she phrases it.' He shook his head sadly. 'She would be happier if she could accept that if she lacks beauty, well, these things are the will of God and no doubt serve some divine purpose.'

No one knew what to say to that, because I think we all felt embarrassed. Dr Parker, however, seemed unaware of our discomfort, and Bartholomew, firmly turning the conversation back to our original purpose here, said: 'Dr Parker, do you think you can help in finding Mistress Stannard and her companions somewhere to stay? You are so knowledgeable about your flock. You know many people that I don't.'

'I'll try.' Lucius frowned, thinking. Then he looked at me and said: 'Mistress Stannard, as it happens, I know who you are. I have known for a long time, years in fact. I have relatives among the senior clergy, among men who go to court and attend important functions. They have heard your name mentioned. You are related to the queen, I believe, and on occasion, you undertake private tasks for her. Are you undertaking such a task now and perhaps feel it better not to encumber your friends with it?'

We all remained silent, taken aback, by such perceptiveness. Rossiter seemed puzzled. Lucius said: 'I find it strange that a woman should be so employed but I want you to know that I will help you if I can.'

'Secret tasks?' Rossiter came to life. 'What kind of secret tasks can the good lady be about in these here quiet parts?'

I did not enlighten him. Instead, I said: 'If I were so employed at this moment, I would not be able to speak of it, to you or to anyone. Please don't ask me to do so.'

Parker smiled. 'Mistress Stannard, I regret to say that senior clergy are human and as prone to gossip as most. My cousins have not only heard your name mentioned by men in high office. They know much more than that and through them, do I. You were on her majesty's business when you visited this district last year.'

Concealment began to feel pointless. Besides, a vicar and a constable really might be useful allies. I wasn't actually bound to secrecy, for no one had sent me. I was sending myself. Very well.

'Last year,' I said, 'I was seeking young men willing to act as agents – as eyes and ears for the queen and her ministers – in Devon, and also elsewhere if I found suitable men. Now

I hear that two of the agents I found have met with very strange accidents. I need to find out why, and how.'

'One of my most gossipy cousins has perhaps put names to two of your finds,' said Parker. 'My cousin writes to me regularly and I write back. He is a secretary in the household of a Norwegian bishop and last October, his master visited England. There was a meeting between him and other bishops and also the queen's chief councillors, including Lord Burghley – Sir William Cecil, that is – and Sir Francis Walsingham. My cousin was there to take notes. Walsingham and Cecil were seated next to each other and sometimes spoke privately to one another. My cousin was near enough to hear a few words now and then, and he caught the names of Gray and Reeves and that made him pay attention for I had mentioned both those names in my letters to him. I had told him that I sometimes go to Okehampton and buy cloth from weavers called Reeves, and that I buy my bacon and hams from someone called Peter Gray. Oh, I often tell him about other tradesmen and friends, of course, but the coincidence of those two names, in such a different context, made my cousin's ears prick up. Walsingham seemed to be saying that they thought money was being collected, only they didn't know for whom. My cousin's letter astonished me, and my sister too, when I told her.'

Good God! I didn't say it aloud but I was reeling. It seemed that even Walsingham, usually as secretive as a tomb, was capable of talking when he shouldn't. True, he had been speaking to Burghley, from whom he wouldn't have many secrets, but he had let himself do it as an aside at an official meeting. He hadn't bargained for the long ears of Lucius Parker's clerical cousin. Indiscretion in high places, indeed!

Lucius was continuing. 'Still, at first it was just a coincidence. Until Gregory Reeves, the son of Andrew Reeves who owns the weaving business I patronize, and Peter Gray, who supplies, or supplied, my bacon and ham, both died in highly unlikely accidents, and only about two weeks apart. And now you are here, only a matter of weeks after.'

Before I could answer, Rossiter said: 'Oh, come. Accidents are accidents! What is all this talk of agents? What did they expect to find hereabouts?'

'Dealings with Spain, on behalf of Mary Stuart,' I said shortly. 'This coast is a likely landing place for an invasion.'

'What, here? Oh, my dear lady, that there's the stuff of tales and ballads. Round here, I've enough to do when the lads squabble over their girls, or a few sailors prefer Zeal Aquatio to Plymouth to get theirselves drunk in, and cause trouble, or someone's cows get into someone else's corn, or some gurt fool tries a bit of thieving. That's real life, but not all this talk of landings and secret goings on and agents slinking about. Them's things I just *can't* imagine.'

If at any time I needed help from someone in authority, I thought regretfully, Samuel Rossiter wouldn't be much use. He obviously did lack imagination. He couldn't conceive of his ordered world turning upside down, amid blood and fire and war cries in Spanish. Brockley and Dale were looking at each other and at me in obvious dismay though they didn't speak. Bartholomew did, however.

'I can imagine it,' he said sharply. 'And it would end with the Inquisition coming here, with all that that would mean. Surely, Master Rossiter, you recall the days of Queen Mary Tudor?'

'I've heard the tales. I was nobbut a child of ten when our good Queen Elizabeth came to the throne. But Mary wasn't a Spaniard.'

'Her husband was,' said Bartholomew.

'Oh, him, Philip. But he's gone back to Spain long since.'

I met Brockley's eyes across the room. He shook his head just a little and smiled and I knew we agreed about Constable Rossiter. Amiable, hard-working, honest, but with no imagination and little sense of logic. Joyce and Dale had probably come to the same conclusion: their faces were un-naturally expressionless. When Sabina came back in, it was a relief.

Lucius nodded to her and observed: 'We are talking of rumours that Mary Stuart is trying to get in touch with Spain and bring an invasion upon us. I don't see how, since rumour also says she is kept as close as a menagerie lion. Is that true? Do you know, Mistress Stannard?'

'She's in a place called Chartley now,' I said. 'I believe it's

a fortified manor house in Staffordshire. She is watched all
the time.'

'The rumours worry me, I don't mind admitting,' Lucius said.
'I don't like to think what would become of us Protestant clergy
if the Spaniards got here. Though I sometimes feel sorry for
Mary. She's been shut away for a long time.'

'She is dangerous,' Brockley broke into the conversation at
last, though not rudely; merely filling a space in it. 'She thinks
she is the rightful queen of England. But she couldn't even hold
her place as the queen of Scotland!'

'Brockley is right,' I said. 'And if she were restored to
the Scots throne, I think that five minutes later, she would be
collecting a pack of Scottish wolves and invading across
the border.'

'I'm not in the least sorry for her,' Sabina said roundly.
'In my opinion, from all I've heard, she's got winning ways
but no common sense. Our good Elizabeth has sense but Mary
Stuart . . . I think not. Those foolish marriages! Lord Darnley!
A wild boy who did nothing but drink and gamble, and that
man – what was his name? Bothwell, that's it – that everyone
says arranged the murder of Darnley. If she'd searched
the world over she couldn't have found a more unsuitable
alliance!'

There was a pause, and then Lucius said: 'Well, it isn't for
us to decide the fate of Mary Stuart, except, Mistress Stannard,
that if you are here on business concerned with protecting us
all from her – perhaps enquiring into two very odd accidents
– then you are among friends. We will support you if we can
and we will not blab to others. I think I can say that on behalf
of us all.' Everyone nodded, though Rossiter looked amused,
as though joining in with a childish game. 'Now,' said Lucius,
'about finding somewhere for you and your people to stay. We
don't recommend the inn.'

'Certainly not!' said Bartholomew.

'There are inns in Tavistock and of course in Plymouth,
and there's the Castle Inn in Okehampton . . .'

'I ought to stay in this village if I can,' I said. 'I shall have
to go to Okehampton briefly, but otherwise, I am on a family

visit in Zeal Aquatio. Or I wish to seem so. I need somewhere nearby.'

Lucius said: 'I am trying to think of somewhere in Zeal Aquatio but nothing comes to mind, I must admit.'

'What about the Greshams?' said Sabina. 'They don't make a show of it but they have rooms they don't need these days, so they sometimes let them out. They have had money troubles. Mildred told me – she is their daughter, Mistress Stannard, and she and I are friends, even though she's much younger than I am.'

'Do they have stabling?' Brockley asked.

'Yes, they do,' Lucius said. 'How many would you be?'

'Mistress Frost and me and the Brockleys,' I said. 'And our groom Eddie, of course.'

'Yes. The Greshams might do. Thank you, Sabina,' her brother said. 'They're not actually in the village,' he said to me, 'but they're only just outside it, a little way up the stream that feeds into the inlet. I expect you saw it on the way here. Their place is upstream far enough for the fresh water they need. They have a dyeing business. And it's true they've had money troubles, ever since that wild storm that burned your guest wing down, Mistress Hillman. When the rain came, it was as if a dam had broken in the sky. The river backed up and flooded the workshop. Their repairs cost them dear and they've struggled ever since.'

'And they're trying to assemble a reasonable dowry for Mildred,' said Sabina. 'She's a darling, but there's no denying that she's plain. She says that herself.'

Well, Sabina knew something about being a plain girl, I thought. Very likely she had wanted to marry and been forced to give up hope. I estimated that she was in her forties by now.

'I'll enquire for you,' said Parker. 'If the Greshams seem agreeable, perhaps Sabina could take you there tomorrow morning and introduce you. I shall have other duties tomorrow. Mistress Stannard, I hope you have now realized that I am to be trusted. If you need help, at any time, then call on me.'

'Thank you,' I said, and heard murmurs of agreement from the others. 'I will do so.'

We were halfway back to Ladymead before I realized that in the shock of finding out that Lucius Parker had guessed – virtually knew – that I intended to enquire into the deaths of Gray and Reeves, I had forgotten to ask him about Crispin Hanley.

SEVEN
Three Birds: One Stone

We made our way home for the midday meal and then I decided to rest. Joyce, however, did not, so I sent her off to give Patches some exercise, with Brockley as escort, on his Firefly. The horses had had one day's rest and for our spirited saddle horses, that was enough. Eddie was already giving my Jaunty an airing. I had asked Bartholomew to turn Rusty out to grass.

When she returned, Joyce found me reading, propped on my pillows. Taking off her hat, and shaking out her brown hair, she said: 'Mistress Stannard, you seem so very tired. You are not ill, are you?'

I shook my head and then, for the first time ever, I sought her sympathy. 'Guilt is a heavy burden.'

'Guilt?' Joyce asked. She sat down on the side of the bed.

'I recruited those two young men, Gray and Reeves. I told them not to take any action or any risk, just to be alert, to keep their ears and eyes open and report anything that seemed to suggest that there might be conspiracies afoot in favour of Mary Stuart – or in favour of a Spanish landing. I told them not to draw attention to themselves. It looks horribly as though they didn't heed that warning. Yet I still feel responsible. I threw them into the path of danger and it has swallowed them. And,' I added, 'I can hardly imagine how on earth I should go about finding out who . . . arranged their deaths. I am as sure as I can be that somebody did. If I find that somebody then I shall have a valuable report to make to Sir Francis Walsingham. I have to set about it and I have no idea how.'

'I suppose the first thing would be to find out all we can about what actually happened,' said Joyce reasonably. 'We only have sketchy details so far.'

'We!' I said. 'You said *we!*'

Joyce looked away from me. She hesitated and then, still not looking at me, said: 'I have, I know, been a difficult ward for you. Jane said I was mistaken, that our father himself wanted you to look after us, but I was so bitter about him, about his imprisonment. I blamed you. But just before we went to Withysham, I had a letter from him.'

'From Master Frost? I didn't know,' I said.

'A courier came when you were out. I met him as he was coming in through the gatehouse. He was in haste, with other deliveries to make, and he was glad enough to hand me my letter and turn his horse and go. I read the letter privately. My father said that since he was now free, he was preparing to resume his business journeys to the Mediterranean as captain of his own ship. My uncle has been keeping that side of things going by hiring captains.'

'Yes, I know,' I said.

Joyce swallowed and said: 'The letter told me that Father would be officially working for Walsingham now, passing false information to his Spanish contacts, who should have plenty of confidence in him, since he had had three years in the Tower as a treason suspect. Those years were now an asset and he hadn't been too uncomfortable. He commended me to you and hoped I was proving a pleasant and thoughtful ward. Which,' said Joyce unhappily, 'I have not been, I know. Only, I love my father and to think of him in that Tower . . . I know I must change towards you but it has been hard to begin.'

'Your father's imprisonment was not quite what it seemed,' I said. 'As you have just found out. Can we be friends now?'

'I would like that,' said Joyce.

I put my book of poems aside and sat up straighter, she leant towards me, and we hugged.

Parker had said that he would speak to the Greshams at once and he kept his word. Sabina came next morning to take us there, arriving in the hall just as breakfast was finishing.

'The idea is to see if you and the Greshams will suit each other,' she said as we set off, all of us, including Eddie. 'This way, they can meet you all, and you can see if the accommodation pleases you. Father is sorry that he can't come as well, but he has a wedding to conduct this morning and a christening this afternoon, and tomorrow he's bound for Plymouth – something to do with a reception for the Bishop of Exeter.'

Bartholomew then suddenly demonstrated his disconcerting sense of humour by saying that he hoped the wedding and the christening didn't concern the same couple. Thomasina nudged him with an elbow, but Sabina laughed.

'Fortunately, no,' she said. 'Shall we go? It's within walking distance.'

It was a cold and windy morning and Sabina set a brisk pace. As she led us out of the village and on to the track beside the stream, she said: 'I don't think I've told you exactly what the rooms are like. They're in a small wing that was built on to the house about twenty years ago when Mr Gresham's parents were old and were ailing. By the way, he and his wife like to be called Mr and Mrs, in the modern way. Anyway, they built the new wing for the parents. It has four rooms, two down and two up. The old couple died after a few years, but then the rooms were used for a time by the son of the house – he works alongside his father. He is married. He and his wife lived there until they had two children and then they decided that they needed more space so they live in the village now and the rooms are spare. The Greshams let them sometimes but just now they're empty. I think you'll be comfortable. I hope so, since I have recommended them!'

'They sound very suitable,' said Joyce comfortingly.

When we reached the place, I remembered it, for we had passed it when we first rode in. It was a thatched house with attic windows poking out of the thatch. Counting those, there were three storeys in the main house. The extension, which we could see on the northern side, was one storey lower. In the distance, perhaps a furlong further upstream, Sabina pointed out a slate-roofed building at the water's edge, with two cottages beside it.

'That's their dyeworks,' she said. 'And those are the supervisors' cottages. However, here's the Greshams' house.'

We were expected and a very young and serious maidservant ushered us into an entrance vestibule where she took our cloaks and hung them on a row of hooks. Another row held keys and there was a shelf of lanterns. From there, she showed us into a parlour which was polished and tidy but cold. Despite the weather, the hearth was empty. The Greshams were waiting for us, side by side in the middle of the room, and I at once realized why no fuel had been wasted on a day which didn't absolutely want a fire, and why the little maid was so solemn.

They were smiling as we entered, but they were both dressed in black, well cut but relieved only by their white ruffs and little matching cuffs, and Mrs Gresham's hair was completely hidden by a white headdress. She had no jewellery beyond a small amethyst pendant, strung on a silver chain. They were Puritans, more thorough ones than Dr Parker.

I instantly felt that although I was actually a quietly dressed and dignified lady arriving in the company of her equally modest and dignified ward, her buff-clad manservant and a respectful tirewoman in a dark-blue gown (Eddie had slipped off to look at the stables), we were all clad in scarlet and gold, surrounded by raucous musicians and accompanied by Bacchus in person with a cartload of wine kegs.

However, the Greshams themselves seemed not to have noticed this and appeared pleased to see us.

They introduced themselves as Mr Henry and Mrs Catherine Gresham, and Henry said: 'You are fortunate to find me at home. I am usually at my dyeworks on weekdays. My wife persuaded me to go later today because you were to come. However, our son can take charge meanwhile.'

They asked us to be seated, saying that their daughter Mildred would bring in some refreshments, and at that moment, Mildred appeared with the tray. The contents consisted of cider and some slices of cheesecake, all well presented in tankards and dishes of pewter. The same could not be said of Mildred. She was in fact a shapely young girl but her dove-grey dress and her concealing white cap made her look like a wraith. Also, she wore no jewellery, not even a simple pendant such as her mother wore.

I had never cared for Puritan ideas, and regretted that they were becoming so widespread. Now, talking to Mildred Gresham and seeing her alongside Sabina, who struck me as another victim of those ideas, I felt quite indignant. I had taken great care over seeing that Meg not only studied Latin and Greek and housewifery, but also knew how to choose dresses to suit her, how to care for her beautiful dark hair and make goose-grease ointments to keep her hands smooth, and how to play the lute and the spinet and how to perform, with grace, the steps of all the fashionable dances.

Sabina was genuinely plain, but Mildred was not. It was just that her unremarkable features needed enhancement which they weren't getting. Her eyes were somewhere indeterminate between blue and green but they were bright enough and the few mousey strands of hair that did escape from her cap were trying to curl. As an unmarried girl, she should wear pretty colours and have her hair loose. Her parents very likely called that worldly show and insisted on extinguishing her in a grey gown and an unbecoming cap.

I longed to release the hair and put Mildred in more colourful clothes – light green or light blue would have suited her – and give her just a little jewellery, perhaps small gold earrings and a pretty pendant. She was no more than twenty, probably less. Sabina had implied that her parents were anxious to get her married but they weren't giving her any help. Why couldn't they see?

'I hope the rooms will be satisfactory,' Mrs Catherine Gresham was saying. 'The two above stairs are somewhat cramped, we must admit, since they're under the slope of the thatch. And when the wind is in the north, there is always some smell from our dyeing works.'

'My dear Catherine,' said Henry Gresham, 'you are not gifted at selling!'

'One must be honest,' said his wife gravely. She turned to me. 'We have adopted Puritan beliefs, as no doubt you realize. We have only the one maid; my daughter and I do much of the work of the house. Idle hands are the devil's instruments. We try to adhere to the truth at all times, which is why, as my husband says, I am not gifted at selling.' She looked at the empty dishes on the table and remarked: 'We seem to have finished the refreshments but perhaps you would care for another mug of cider each. Mildred, fetch a fresh jug, and then take these platters away and help Tilly to wash up.'

Over the second mug of cider, Henry Gresham said: 'We are sorry that we have to charge, but we have not yet recovered from the damage the great storm did. You will have heard of that, no doubt.'

'It's the reason why we are here,' I said. 'The storm caused the guest wing at Ladymead, where I intended to stay, as the Hillmans are relatives of mine, to burn down. I am supposed to be making a family visit but we are crowding them and as Mistress Hillman is soon to give birth, well, we thought it best to stay somewhere else and visit often.'

'It was a terrible storm,' said Sabina. 'I feared that one of our chimneys would come down!'

'We must not complain too much, however,' said Henry Gresham. 'God has been gracious, bringing us new work of late. The Reeves weavers in Okehampton have granted us a contract.'

'The Reeves family!' said Sabina. 'But surely there are dyeworks in Okehampton or Tavistock?'

'I believe Andrew Reeves had some kind of quarrel with the one in Okehampton,' said Henry. 'I don't know the details but I think it was something to do with a mistake about colours. As for the one in Tavistock, they're overburdened and can't take on any new work. So the Reeves have come to us instead. They don't mind; I understand that they sell to customers further away from Okehampton than we are – even in Plymouth.'

'We shall have to visit Okehampton ourselves soon,' I observed. 'We may have some business to conduct there. As it happens, we want to see the Reeves family. I met them when I visited the Hillmans last year. I believe they have just lost their son. I met him, too. I would like to give them my condolences. By the way, have you ever heard of anyone called Hanley, living hereabouts? He is the uncle of my steward at my Sussex house and my Robert Hanley is anxious to find him.'

'Hanley? Now there's a coincidence!' Catherine exclaimed.

'A coincidence!' I was instantly alert.

'Yes! My husband sometimes takes finished work to the Reeves instead of leaving it to them to collect it. Do you not, Henry?'

'It's an attention that pleases customers,' said Henry. 'If you undertake work you should do it as best you can and better if possible. But go on, Catherine. What is the coincidence?'

'Last time you went to see them,' said Catherine, 'you came back saying that Andrew Reeves had grumbled because a tiresome old man who lives near them had been going about asking people to contribute to some charity or other – something to do with founding a home for orphan children. His name was Hanley, apparently.'

'I think I've met him!' said Sabina. 'More coincidence!' She turned to me. 'I had no idea you wanted to find him. He sometimes comes to the musical evenings I attend. He does collect for orphans, or says he does.'

'Says he does?' I queried. I exchanged glances with Joyce.

'Well, I did once give him something,' said Sabina, 'though not much, and Lucius said I should have asked more questions about this charity of his. Only I don't like to, so we don't know anything more.'

'Was his first name Crispin?' I asked.

'That I don't know,' said Sabina. 'I've only ever heard him called Hanley,' and Catherine, agreeing, said: 'Mr Reeves just called him Hanley. I've no idea what his Christian name might be. Well, I see your glasses are empty. Shall we go and look at the rooms?'

She led us out into the vestibule. Opposite to the parlour, we saw a heavy oaken door with a brass-ringed keyhole, into which Mrs Gresham thrust a big iron key, taken from the row on the wall.

The key made an unpleasant grating noise, and refused to turn. Mrs Gresham struggled with it, going pink with embarrassment as she apologized, explaining that the lock hadn't been used for months.

Mr Gresham said exasperatedly that it needed oil and he'd better find some, and hurried away. Sabina went to help Catherine and together they struggled with the key. While it went on grating and Sabina was saying did it turn the other way and Catherine Gresham was saying no, no, it didn't, I whispered to the others: 'We will go to Okehampton tomorrow. I must see this Hanley and he's the perfect excuse for going

there at all. I shall start enquiries about Gray as well as
Reeves. Three birds with one stone!'

'Here we are,' said Henry, reappearing with a small bottle
and a rag. He applied oil to the key and presently, the lock
surrendered. Henry took the oil away and his wife led us inside.

'The key and the lock will be thoroughly oiled before we
leave them to you,' she promised. 'Now, this is the first downstairs room, quite big, as you see, and furnished as a parlour
but we can turn it into a bedchamber if you wish. The second
room is furnished as a bedchamber and is through this door.'

She showed us in. Both rooms smelt musty from disuse
and badly needed a duster, and the furnishings were sparse.
However, the bed was curtained and wide and there was a good
washstand. Catherine Gresham brought us back into the first
room and pointed out some spiral stairs in the corner. 'Those
stairs lead to the upper rooms. I'm sorry they're so steep and
twisty but we had to make the best use we could of the space
that we could afford . . .'

The spiral stairs to the upper floor were precipitous to the
point of being perilous and the two upstairs rooms under the
thatch had poor headroom on three sides. Brockley said heroic-
ally: 'Fran and I could take these. We can put the baggage in
one, and sleep in the other. Then you, madam, and Mistress
Frost can have a room each downstairs, or share a bedroom and
have a parlour of your own.'

'If Mistress Stannard and I share a bedchamber,' said Joyce,
'surely you and Dale can be comfortable in the other downstairs
room. We can still use either as places to sit. Can't we, Mistress
Stannard? The baggage can go upstairs, of course, and be out
of the way.'

'If we can *get* it upstairs,' said Dale pointedly, looking at the
spiral staircase. Mrs Gresham and Sabina stood looking at us,
I think feeling somewhat confused. I had introduced us all very
carefully, emphasising that Joyce was my ward and that the
Brockleys were not mere servants but friends and that I wished
them to dine at the same table as myself. Though Brockley
would of course help our groom Eddie to look after our horses
and Eddie would share the quarters of the Greshams' own groom
or grooms.

However, now that our unusual arrangements were being demonstrated, both Sabina and Catherine obviously found them surprising.

Well, they would get used to it. 'I like your idea, Joyce,' I said. I looked at the Brockleys, who both nodded. 'I think we are all happy with that,' I said to Catherine.

'You wish to stay, then?' Catherine said.

I didn't really like the rooms; none of us did. But they were our best alternative to crowding and perhaps endangering Ladymead. 'The rooms will do very well,' I said cheerfully. 'What about terms?'

Sabina went home. I paid the Greshams a month's rent in advance, whether or not we were in the rooms all the time, and then we returned to Ladymead to collect our baggage, our carriage and our horses. When we got there, we found that Bartholomew had a surprise for us. He had learned of Dale's dislike of riding and now offered to lend her Thomasina's mare, Brown Betsy.

'Thomasina can't use her just now,' he said, 'and Betsy is an ambler. It's that rough trot that bothers Mistress Brockley, no doubt. Off fore and near hind, and then off hind and near fore, and all that rising to the trot or just miserably bouncing. With an ambler, the offside pair of legs move together and then the nearside ones and it's all much smoother. If Mistress Brockley tries an ambler, she may be surprised. And Brown Betsy is as quiet as any lamb. She's a safe ride if ever there was one.'

I wasn't sure about this as Dale could be very awkward on occasion, but she did try Betsy and was agreeably surprised.

'All I need do is sit there, or that's how it feels, ma'am. And she doesn't make me nervous. Most horses do.'

I was pleased as this would simplify many journeys, including the one to Okehampton. When we returned to the Greshams, I reminded them that I had mentioned a journey to Okehampton, to see the Reeves family and search for news of Crispin Hanley. It did seem possible that we would find him there. We would in fact be leaving the next day. We would be back in a few days – we couldn't be exact – and would leave most of our baggage behind.

If the Greshams thought we were a little odd, setting off for somewhere else, for an unknown length of time, almost as soon as we had moved in, they didn't say so. Henry had gone to his dyeworks when we returned but he came home at suppertime, bringing with him a curious smell. Dale wrinkled her nose and he smiled and told her that some of the dyes had odours and that he would need to change all his clothes and wash before it would vanish.

'And then it will come back the next day,' he said, though not with amusement but as though he were just stating a fact. Dale, full of embarrassment, apologized for noticing and Mr Gresham said gravely that it was of no importance. This was not a household where people laughed easily.

Over supper, far from behaving as though he thought us odd, Henry Gresham offered us some help, in the shape of Mildred.

'Do you know where the Reeves family have their workshop?' Mr Gresham asked. 'If not, our daughter does. She has been to Okehampton with me several times when I visit them on business. She can take you to an inn, too. The biggest is the Castle.'

'I have heard that the Castle is recommended,' I said. I had every intention of staying there anyway. It had been the scene of Peter Gray's demise.

The supper was well cooked but not exhilarating, since it consisted only of toasted cheese served on slices of toasted bread, along with some fried beans and cider.

'We eat plainly,' said Catherine Gresham. 'But with sufficiency, we hope.'

'This is very tasty,' I said gravely.

The food was at least served hot, but the dining-chamber hearth was as cold as the one in the parlour. The Greshams apparently took this for granted for Catherine, in the most matter of fact way, had met us as we crossed the vestibule on the way to supper and recommended that I and Joyce and Dale should all go back for shawls. Eddie, who ate in the kitchen with Tilly and the Greshams' groom, told us afterward that they were very snug beside the kitchen fire. We felt envious.

Conversation was casual but after Mildred had once more

been sent to help Tilly wash up, Catherine said to me: 'I am glad that our daughter is going with you to Okehampton and I hope she will be useful to you, as she knows the town well. It could be a good thing for her, too.'

'Oh?' I said, surprised.

'We are having some trouble with Mildred,' said Catherine in rueful tones, and Henry said: 'Yes. We are. Diversion may help.'

'The problem is,' said Catherine, 'that we have found her a husband, not an ideal match, but it hasn't been easy to get her settled and this is good enough. He's older than she is but he's healthy and he's a sheep farmer, knows the world of wool. He can put business our way. He's a widower and he needs an heir. We think it's a suitable arrangement.'

'He had two sons but they died while they were just boys – one of a fever, one in an accident,' Mr Gresham put in. 'And then his wife died – of sheer sorrow, or so he says. She couldn't have any more children after the birth of the second son. She died four years ago. Mr Baines has been lonely. He says he does want children but I think it's more than needing an heir. I fancy he hopes for company in his old age. I think it's a fine opportunity for our daughter.'

'But Mildred is being difficult,' said Catherine. 'She says she doesn't like Miles Baines and would you believe it, when we took her to his home to show her what a good house she would have as Mrs Baines and what a good position she would have in the world, well, while we were there, she met his bailiff and afterwards she told us she'd rather marry him and please would we approach him on her behalf! A bailiff!'

'He has no property,' said Henry Gresham. 'He lives in a tied cottage and depends on his salary. There's no advantage to us in such a marriage. In any case, we met him in Miles' company and he hardly glanced at Mildred. It's all on her side. We think she has managed to meet him since then, accidentally on purpose, but he hasn't come knocking on the door and asking for permission to court her, and we wouldn't say yes, if he did.'

'Mildred needs things to do,' said Catherine, 'occupation to take her mind off all this nonsense. An expedition to Okehampton in the company of new friends, who need her help, may give her space for thinking. We have spent so much time on finding a husband for her and she shows us no gratitude.' Her face, which had formerly seemed pleasant enough, seemed suddenly hardened, and sharp. 'We are going to insist that she behaves.'

The bailiff might have taken notice of Mildred if she had been anything like visible. 'She may certainly accompany us to Okehampton and act as our guide,' I said coolly and without any comment on their matrimonial plans for her. 'Does she have a horse?'

'Mildred has a little grey cob of her own. Grey Cob, that's what we call him. We don't believe in fancy names for animals,' said Mr Gresham. The owners of horses called Jaunty, Firefly and Patches listened respectfully and didn't comment. 'Mildred knows where to find the Reeves' workshop,' Mr Gresham said, 'and she is known at the Castle Inn. While she is with you, you would greatly please us if you would talk sense to her.'

It was an order but I didn't intend to obey it. If I did, Mildred would probably want to lead us to the worst inn she could find or else direct us on to a lonely moor or into a morass.

Inside my head, there was a jolt. Had someone done precisely that to Gregory Reeves?

EIGHT

Okehampton

We left for Okehampton after breakfast the very next morning. 'The sooner this is all over, the better,' I said.

Breakfast was ample but austere. The Greshams did not believe in food as a pleasure. Tilly and Mildred served us small ale, bread with only dripping to spread on it, and porridge with milk but no honey or raisins to sweeten it. Afterwards, as we were carrying our saddlebags out to the horses, Joyce said she was going to buy some honey for our future breakfasts, whether or not the Greshams approved.

'I'll help. I'll get some raisins,' I told her, and made her laugh. She had rarely laughed since she came to live with me, and she had a pretty laugh. I hoped to hear it more often in future.

Eddie, who was coming with us on Rusty, because Brockley would need help with all our horses, had done better than we had. Tilly and the groom, Will, were given the same breakfast as we were, but according to Eddie, had secret supplies of honey and plum preserves.

The day was overcast and the track ran along the edge of moorland which in that grey light looked forbidding. The little town of Tavistock lay on our route and we reached it too soon for dinner in the normal way but the landlord of the hostelry we called at was evidently used to people from Plymouth and its surroundings arriving in mid-morning and wanting food. His ducks in a sharp sauce, with fresh bread, butter and honey, were a great improvement on the Greshams' breakfast and we set out in good heart to cover the remaining seventeen miles to Okehampton.

We got there in the afternoon. As we entered the town we saw Okehampton Castle away to our right, high on a grassy mound, exposed to the weather and abandoned now, Mildred told us. The track took us straight into the main thoroughfare, Fore Street, which cut like a knife through a tangle of smaller streets. Everywhere was busy with carts, riders and pack animals, as well as people on foot, and Fore Street was lined with tradesmen's shops, many displaying their wares outside as well as inside: wooden furniture, trays of trinkets, gloves, footwear, hats, bronze dishes, earthenware, fire-irons, cooking pots.

I suggested that we made straight for Reeves' workshop but Mildred recommended arranging our rooms and stabling first. We could walk to the workshop, she said; it wasn't far from the Castle Inn, and the horses had come a long way; best get them stalled and fed. We agreed and she led us at once to the inn. The Castle was nearly full. However, the landlord, whose name was Barratt and who, like the Greshams, preferred to be addressed as Mr, was ponderous in build but quick on his feet and willing to be helpful. He said he had one room which the ladies could share, while Brockley and Eddie could have beds in the grooms' quarters over the stables.

'My wife is with me,' said Brockley, at which the landlord laughed. 'That'll be all right. None of my grooms are married but customers' grooms sometimes are. There's a few little rooms over the visitors' stable block. Not very spacious but you can have your wife with you and be private.'

It would do. We stabled the horses, put Eddie in charge of them, deposited our baggage in the rooms and prepared to set off.

'Are we all going?' Mildred asked.

'I usually have Brockley as a male escort and Dale as an attendant,' I pointed out, 'and I can't leave my ward alone in a strange hostelry. We shall be quite a crowd but I don't suppose it matters. Four ladies and just one man – that won't frighten anyone.'

The only frightened person was myself. I had no idea what to say to Andrew Reeves. I was virtually a stranger to him and it might seem odd that I had come to offer condolences, and so long after the event, at that. I had better say I was speaking on behalf of the Hillmans. He knew them better. They had probably given him their condolences already but I must start somewhere. I supposed I could ask him if he knew a Crispin Hanley but I didn't want to say that I had recruited his son as an agent and that Gregory had probably been murdered as a result. Yet, if I didn't say so, how could I ask for details of what had happened to Gregory? I would sound like a ghoul!

The Reeves establishment was no more than five minutes away from the inn, a rambling slate-roofed house alongside a big shed. The shed doors were open and I could hear shuttles slamming back and forth. As we approached, I smelt the distinctive odour of wool in bulk. 'We'll probably find Master Reeves here,' Mildred said. 'He may even be working at a loom himself. He often does.'

She was right. Andrew Reeves, a big, brown-bearded man, was working a loom faster than anyone else in the shed. Mildred presented us and he stopped work, bowed politely to us all and asked, in a pleasant West Country burr, if he could be of service.

'In a very simple way,' Mildred told him, taking the initiative and speaking loudly because there were two other looms in the shed with shuttles slamming back and forth. 'My father says you have mentioned the name of someone called Hanley to him. This is Mrs Stannard, a visitor from Surrey. I believe she met you once, last year, in the company of the Hillmans of Zeal Aquatio. I think you know them. Mrs Stannard is on a family visit to their home at Ladymead though this time she is staying with us because Ladymead is too crowded. She is trying to find a man called Crispin Hanley. Can you help?'

Mildred, bless her, had saved me some tedious explanations. Briefly, I added: 'A man called Crispin Hanley is the uncle of Robert Hanley, a steward in my employment. Robert wishes to trace his uncle. I am acting on his behalf.'

I too spoke loudly but the noise didn't seem to worry Master Reeves, who was presumably used to it. At the name of Crispin, he showed obvious recognition and now snorted with obvious dislike.

'Him! A nuisance on feet, that's what Crispin is. He lives in the street backing on this.' He jerked a thumb towards the rear of the shed. 'It's a scruffy back street. Robbs Lane. Hanley's got rooms in a lodging house squeezed in between a pottery and a place selling elderberry wines and the like. Lately, he's got an idea in his noddle about gathering funds for some sort of home for orphans. No details about where it is or anything solid like that. I wouldn't give the old pest a bad penny.'

'I won't either,' I said. 'But I must see him. If the man you know is called Crispin, then he must be the person I'm looking for.' I then drew a deep breath and tried to approach the business of Gregory. In what I hoped was a winning tone, I said: 'Before I go, I believe I should offer my condolences to you, on behalf of the Hillmans and of course, on my own behalf too. Have you not had a recent bereavement? Your son, Gregory.'

Reeves stared at me. 'Indeed I have. The Hillmans told you about it? Well, half the world's been marvelling at it. January, it were, an accident, and the weirdest one you could dream of!'

I explained (again briefly and loudly) that the Hillmans had said that Gregory had got lost on the moors. 'And they said he had been brought up beside them and how could such a thing befall him?'

It was a blatant question about something that was not my business but it worked. Andrew Reeves sighed and leant against the loom as if for support. 'That's what no one knows,' he said. 'Gregory had no call to be out on the moors at all. I last saw him when I thought he was leaving for home at the end of his day's work. I thought he'd taken his horse and gone and so he should have done. He took his horse right enough. Next day, it come wandering into my stable yard at the back here. We all thought it had thrown him. But he should have known better than to go up there, on foot or on horseback, in January at dusk *and* every warning of a bitter night to come. It were a daft thing to do, and him only a couple of months married.

'Not afore time,' he added and then, with a surprising burst of candour: 'Young men will be young men but I didn't like him going with a married woman ten years older than him and that's what he'd been doing. And when folk started saying he'd still been hot for her after he was wed . . . that's a nasty idea to my mind and it won't leave me be.'

'Oh dear,' I said inadequately.

'You'm thinking I shouldn't say such things about my son?

Maybe not, but till he were wed, I didn't think the worse of him except that it shouldn't have been with a woman like Jane Leigh. That seemed all wrong. I were wild enough in my youth.' There was a flicker of a grin, apparently at some long-gone memory, but he was quickly grave again. 'Folk have been saying he went out there thinking to meet Jane Leigh. Except that she didn't ask him to meet her; we know that 'cause that came out at the inquest.'

'Of course,' I said. 'There would have been an inquest. It must have been an ordeal for you.'

'But someone might have used her name. Crowner said as much. Maybe someone played a trick and he fell for it. He might of gone thinking to meet Jane, even though he'd got a sweet wife of his own at home, looking out of the door for him. If he did, well, I'm not pleased, and him being dead makes no difference. And we thought he was so happy!'

'In his marriage?' Mildred asked.

'Aye. We reckoned, me and Joan, that he ought to wed and we saw to it that he met a likely girl or two, and when he and pretty Sally Baker took to each other, I was that glad and so was Joan. We got him safely wed to her last November and he seemed happy as could be and already it looked like there was a little one on the way.'

'I am so sorry,' I said. 'What a dreadful shock for his wife!'

'Just a young thing, she is,' Andrew Reeves said compassionately. 'Gone home to mother now. She didn't lose the child; Joan and I will be grandparents afore Michaelmas, please God. She and Gregory had a cottage out at Hatherleigh, little place north of here. She was expecting him home that evening. Oh, you don't want me telling you all this. I'm sorry. It's just that it's so on my mind that . . .'

'The Hillmans have been puzzling over it,' I said quickly, before this useful flow dried up. 'There's been quite a lot of talk.'

'Aye, I know. Even away down at Zeal Aquatio.' But Andrew seemed glad to talk, as though relieving himself of a burden.

'Poor Sally come to us late that evening, walked all the way, she did, over six miles, in the dark and the cold, carrying a lantern and sobbing, worried sick because he hadn't come home.

She were heartbroken when he was found. We had search parties out everywhere from dawn next morning. They found him in two hours. Sally's broken her heart twice over, once on account of him dying and then again, thinking about Jane Leigh. It was Sally as told my wife Joan that she was afeard he'd still been meeting the woman.'

He leant heavily against the loom, as though speaking of his loss had somehow weakened his body. 'I said to Sally that my boy was in love with *her* and wouldn't be agreeing to meet Jane Leigh anywhere. I wanted to comfort her, see, and I went cold inside at the inquest when they actually called Mistress Leigh! Word had got around, about the pair of them. But she said that though she sometimes walked on the moor, she wouldn't go up there on a bitter cold January evening and she'd never been more than casually friendly with Gregory anyway. No one believed that, but then a neighbour of hers got up and asked to speak, and said that late on the afternoon of the day in question – about the time when Gregory left this workshop it must have been – he'd noticed Mistress Leigh in her garden, playing with a lapdog, and then another neighbour stood up and said she'd seen Jane later that same evening; yes, she knew which evening it was because next morning, men had been coming house to house to collect a search party to look for Gregory Reeves. That evening, she'd called to return half a dozen eggs she'd borrowed from Mistress Leigh and seen her and talked to her. So Jane Leigh can't have had anything to do with it. But that don't mean her name weren't used, and crowner asked if anyone could think of a reason why my son should have such a trick played on him. He got no answers. I can't think of a reason and that's the truth. But the question's still there. Misadventure, that was the verdict, but it were just for want of anything better.'

He turned away, and there was a silence, until I said: 'I am sorry. I have upset you after all. I only meant to express condolences! Let me make amends.' I had noticed that the right-hand wall was covered with shelving laden with rolls of cloth. 'Are those cloths over there finished and for sale?'

'Yes, as a matter of fact they are.'

'May I see that roll of pale green? It's such a pretty colour.'

'Certainly.' He looked round and then shouted to somebody I couldn't see: 'Alf, on your feet! Bring that light green roll of wool cloth over here! Sure you want wool cloth?' he added to me. 'It's fine wool, fit for summer wear, if summer ever comes, but I do have silk as well, on that top shelf.'

I had already seen it but wool was better suited to my nefarious purpose. The fabric I had chosen was brought.

I meant it for Mildred, who might be intimidated by silk. Joyce and I could make a dress of it and when we left the Greshams, we would present it to her as a farewell gift. It would be up to her whether or not she wore it. I would buy her a pretty cap to go with it too – a small one, which would give her hair a chance to be seen. One never knew. As long as her parents didn't forbid her to wear it, the oblivious bailiff might suddenly notice she was there. What happened next would be up to them.

Mildred knew where Robbs Lane was and led us to it. It was certainly scruffy but it was as busy with shoppers as Fore Street. We saw the pottery first, since it was obvious, with a table outside, on which various products were displayed. As we approached, a thin man in rough homespun wandered across the road and began to paw through a tray of pottery earrings.

'Surely that man hasn't got a sweetheart,' Joyce said to me. 'He's so unattractive!'

'Perhaps he wants earrings for himself,' said Brockley. 'There are men like that.'

Dale at once looked prim and Joyce said innocently: 'I thought only sailors wore earrings – but only one, and they're always gold. Some of the crew of my father's ship *The Dainty Lady* wear them.'

'There's the lodging house,' I said hurriedly. 'I'll knock.'

I could see why Master Reeves had said that the house was squeezed between its neighbours. It was narrow for its height and looked as though it had been hastily built to fill up the space between pottery and wine-shop. I knocked on the door and it was opened by a tired-looking woman with a brush in one hand and a dustpan in the other. She gazed at us in dismay.

'I've no more rooms to let. I'm Mistress Amory, the landlady here, and if anyone told you I let rooms, well, that's true, but I'm full up and have been for months, God be praised, and anyone who knows anything about me ought to know that. I'm sorry, but . . .'

Joyce cut her short by saying bluntly: 'We don't want to hire rooms. We're looking for a Master Hanley. Does he live here?'

'Oh, yes.' She looked relieved, as though just coping with an enquiry for rooms was almost too exhausting to be borne. 'Yes. He's in. He rents my second floor. Just go straight up the stairs and tap on the door facing you.'

She stood back to let us pass and thanking her, we set off up the stairs, which were narrow like the house and very steep. There was only one door on the second floor. I rapped on it. No one opened it but a man's voice shouted to us to wait, and then, after a pause, called to us to come in. Brockley lifted the latch and we all filed through.

My steward's uncle, if this were he, was hastily fastening the ties of a creased shirt; we must have caught him in a state of undress. The room had an uneven floor and it was an untidy cross between a parlour and an office, with a writing set on a pewter tray occupying the window seat and papers of some kind strewn all over a table and mixed up with the cushions on a settle. A door on the left stood open and through it we could see a bed, with covers carelessly thrown back. Our host had presumably been having an afternoon snooze.

Brockley didn't waste time on these idle speculations. 'Are you Crispin Hanley?' he enquired. He spoke brusquely, and our host immediately bristled.

'Yes, I am. Who are you? You sound as though you're here with a warrant to arrest me, though if you are, why are you surrounded by ladies?' Like Andrew Reeves, he had a West Countryman's burr, though Hanley was more rough-spoken.

'All right, Brockley,' I said. 'Master Hanley, do you have a nephew called Robert Hanley, at the moment employed as a steward at Withysham House in Sussex?'

'Yes. I have. What is it to do with you?' Master Hanley was tall and gaunt, with deep hollows under his prominent cheekbones, and big hands with jutting knuckles. He had now dragged a doublet out from among the settle cushions and was pulling it on. It was a thin affair, scuffed round the wrists. If Crispin Hanley was making a career of extortion, he wasn't being all that successful.

'I am Mistress Stannard,' I said, 'the owner of Withysham. Robert Hanley is a good steward and he has asked my help. You have been pressing him for money. Money that he doesn't have.'

'He's well paid, b'ain't he?' Crispin showed no sign of embarrassment. 'And I want it for a good cause. Getting funds is no easy business; folk keep their purses tight shut, mostly.'

'You have also,' I said, 'threatened to tell me, his employer, about a past misdeed of his, unless he makes these . . . contributions to your cause, whatever it is. I am here to tell you that I know about this misdeed. He has told me himself. I must also tell you that the way you have extorted money from him is unlawful and that you could be arrested for it. Neither of us wishes to go to those lengths. But I must insist that you leave Robert Hanley alone from now on, and I must warn you never to behave like this towards anyone else.'

Crispin Hanley grinned, unimpressed, revealing a mouth full of large yellow teeth. 'He'll have told you just his version of what he did. Maybe he b'ain't quite the injured innocent he pretends to be.'

'That is possible,' I said. It had already occurred to me. 'But if so, it lies in the past. I have no complaint of him, and his contrition seems real enough. Nor does it matter. Extortion is extortion and you now know what will happen if you repeat the offence.'

'A pity,' remarked Crispin. 'Every little donation is useful. What I got from Robert covered the cost of the couriers to and fro, with a good sum to spare. And, madam, it goes to house and feed orphaned children, who otherwise might have nowhere to live.'

'Does it? Do they really exist?'

'Aye, madam, they do and I support them. The charity is my creation and my charge. Why do you think I live here in these cheap lodgings? I've a nice small farm and a farmhouse if I chose to live there and work the land. As it is, the rent I get for it feeds me and puts a few cheap clothes on my back and pays the rent of these two ramshackle rooms and the orphans get the rest.'

'We haven't thought about it. Why should we?' said Mildred.

'I let my farm,' said Crispin, 'at the best rent I can get, and live cheap. You talk about extortion. I extort from myself! Madam Amory cleans the place all right but God's teeth, her cooking! Her bread's a lead weight in the belly and her stews are pale and thin, like victims of starvation. All her tenants have indigestion.'

'Just where is your orphans' home?' I enquired.

'I've leased a house in Glastonbury town, just below a hill called the Tor, with the ruined church of St Michael on its peak. Legend says that in his youth, Our Lord came there for a while. Do you know it? It's maybe seventy miles from here but it has a holy air; comforting for bereft children,' said Crispin piously.

Dale had been staring through the door to the dishevelled bedroom. Now she turned and caught my eye and in it, I read disapproval. 'I've said what I came to say,' I informed Master Crispin Hanley. 'What I promised Robert I would say. I meant every word of it. God help you if you ever attempt to get money from my steward again. Good day. Come,' I added to the others, and with that, we filed out, leaving him to gaze after us, still with a grin on his face.

When we were out in the street, Dale said: 'I had a good look at the inside of that bedchamber. There's a crucifix on the wall and he has a cross round his neck as well; I saw it when he was doing up his shirt. I think he's a papist.'

'In which case,' said Mildred slowly, 'his charity may well not be orphans at all.'

'No,' I agreed. 'It could well be the cause of Mary Stuart. We can't be sure. Better say nothing to anyone. But I do wonder.'

I wondered very much. Had we for the first time found a trace of the fundraising that Walsingham suspected was going on in this district?

NINE
A Tankard Six Feet High

Well, we had found Crispin Hanley. I had promised his nephew that I would deal with him and I hoped I had done so. One part of my business here was accomplished. But I was still concerned with my two mysteriously deceased agents. I didn't wish Mildred or her parents to know about them and I hoped that Mildred's friend Sabina Parker wouldn't tell them. My hidden world – my dark world – was nothing to do with them. I wanted to protect them from it.

I considered going to Glastonbury and seeing if Hanley's orphans actually existed, but every instinct said that my first duty lay here, where my agents had died.

I now had some sort of picture in my mind of what might have happened to Gregory Reeves. Probably, someone, somehow, had inveigled him into going out onto the moor near nightfall on a night of savage cold. Had he supposed himself to be going to a tryst with this woman Jane Leigh? It did seem likely. Her neighbour had testified that she was at home that evening but someone could have used her name. The coroner had said as much. If so, whoever it was had met him – where? Surely not at a tryst on the high moor! Anyway, wherever he went and why, someone had seen to it that he didn't return. But if they didn't meet on the moor, how had he got there? Had he had any injuries, such as a bump on the head?

I could do no more about Gregory today. I might however make a start on Peter Gray, who had staggered drunkenly out of the Castle Inn into the path of a cart with runaway horses. I needed to talk to the landlord.

When we were back at the inn and had done the unpacking we hadn't taken time to do before setting out for the workshop, I said: 'Dale, you'll want to join Brockley in his quarters, I take it? I'll walk over to the stable block with you. I want to make sure that you and Eddie have been properly looked after.'

At the stables, we found Eddie happily playing a dice game with the Greshams' groom Will. His quarters suited him, he told us cheerfully. Satisfied on that point, Dale and I went to the Brockleys' room, which turned out to be a cupboard-sized place above the stalls where our horses were champing at their hay. There were no stools, so I sat down on the bed. 'Peter Gray,' I said tersely. 'I think I must consider him next.'

'I've already spoken to the landlord about Gray,' said Brockley, looking pleased with himself. 'I didn't come straight here. I bought a tankard of ale from the landlord and sympathized with him over the tragedy that overtook Gray. "Glad to see your inn so busy. A disaster like that can upset people and make them stay away. Just what happened?" The landlord looked at me very sharply and said, "You mean it can give an inn a bad name. The Castle's been here too long for that."

'That wasn't a hopeful start, so I took a long drink of ale and kept quiet for a while but after he'd scurried around for a few minutes, supplying other customers, he came back to me.

'"You want to know what happened to that fellow Gray?" he said. So I said: "Well, it's as strange a tale as I ever heard," and then he said rather curtly that he hardly knew how or what had happened.

'He told me that Gray was known at the inn and came in for a drink or two whenever there was a fair or a market. He'd talk to people, maybe join in a game of darts. The night he died, he'd been playing darts and winning his games; he was drinking cider but he wasn't drunk as far as the landlord could see. "But all of a sudden he said he didn't feel well. He clutched at his head and started saying everything looked queer and what in God's name was in that cider, and another fellow who was nearby said to him, 'You need fresh air,' and steered him to the door and just then, some fool of a carter lost control of his horses and came crashing past, and that was the end of Peter Gray. I don't ever again want to see what he looked like after the hooves and the wheels had been over him. Turned me sick to the stomach, it did." The landlord's own words.'

I shuddered. The picture he had made in my mind was all

too graphic. But I said: 'Thank you, Brockley! You've saved me the trouble of talking to the landlord myself. And you've done it as if you were just casually gossiping, one man to another. It wouldn't have been so easy for me.'

'So what next?' said Brockley pertinently.

'I don't know. I've got some idea now of *how* Gregory Reeves was lured to some meeting place or other but where was it and who lured him and how did they get him out on to the moors? All that is a mystery. It seems fairly clear how Gray was killed. Two must have worked together; one to put something in his drink and then encourage him out of the door, and the other to run him down with a wagon. Who was driving that wagon? And what did he have to say for himself at the inquest?'

'The landlord mentioned that,' said Brockley. 'I haven't yet told you everything he said. The carter said he'd loaded his cart and then sat in it for a while, taking a rest. When he was ready, he started his team. A pigeon shot up from under the horses' feet, and one of them took fright and bolted, dragging its partner and the wagon along with it. Peter Gray tottered out of the inn straight into its path. There were witnesses at the inquest, who confirmed that.'

'Who confirmed that they saw Gray walk into an ambush,' I said grimly.

'It's growing late,' said Dale, folding a shift more neatly and for want of adequate storage space, stowing it in the saddlebag in which it had travelled. 'Surely it's near supper time, ma'am?'

'Yes, it is,' I said. 'Come. We'll all go back into the inn. I could do with a meal.'

The working day was over and the downstairs room of the inn, where people gathered to drink, was crowded. We edged our way through as best we could. I caught sight of the thin, homespun-clad individual we had seen inspecting pottery earrings. Tankard in hand, he was talking to a couple of men who, to judge from their weather-beaten faces and the earth on their boots, were probably farmers. 'Look who's here,' I muttered. 'He isn't wearing earrings. I wonder if he bought any?'

Dale chuckled. We pressed on towards the stairs and met Mildred and Joyce coming down them.

'We're growing hungry,' Joyce said, 'and we thought we could smell supper cooking.'

The ponderous landlord was just emerging from what was presumably the kitchen. He was red in the face and wiping his hands on a stained apron. Brockley accosted him and came back to say that supper was indeed being served and we had best find places in the dining room before it filled up, and the landlord regretted that he couldn't offer us a private parlour but they were all occupied.

Like the big drinking room, the dining room had timber pillars. We threaded our way through and found places at a bench along one side of the several lengthy trestle tables. As yet, the room wasn't full. A plump maidservant came to ask what we wanted to eat. It was Lenten fare now, but we were pleased to be offered pike fresh out of the river that morning, cut into fillets, browned and simmered with spices, or we could have mackerel with a choice of sauces, or bread and cheese, toasted or not, and diners could choose between black barley bread or white manchet. Onions and fried beans were to be had with anything. To drink, there was ale, cider or a choice of wines.

'Or well water cold as ice from they polar regions, if 'ee'd like that better,' said the maidservant. We made our choices, and Mildred asked what was on offer for the sweet course.

'Almond fritters or bread pudding. Lots of raisins in the pudding an' sugar too an' it's browned on top; real toothsome it be . . .'

'That wench is wasted here,' Brockley said when we had ordered our sweet dishes and the maidservant had gone. 'Mildred, your parents should employ her if they want to bring in business. That bonny lass could sell eyeglasses to eagles.' Joyce giggled and I was happy to hear it.

Our drinks arrived, delivered by a dignified manservant in black. The maidservant followed him with our food and we set to, glad that we had come in good time, for the benches were filling up.

Though we weren't entirely comfortable because people searching for spaces kept bumping into us, causing Joyce to spill her wine just as she was attempting to drink it, and making Dale splutter because a mouthful of spiced pike had gone down the wrong way. I patted her on the back until the coughing stopped. Joyce mopped her sleeve and grumbled that she had lost half her wine, but another black-clad manservant appeared just then to top up the wine that Joyce and Mildred were both drinking, and refill my tankard of cider.

Dusk was falling. The landlord had already been round with a taper, lighting the candles in the holders mounted on the walls and pillars. They gave a fair amount of light, though in that big room, it was uneven. Joyce said she could hardly see her own platter. We talked while we ate and, bent on being more discreet than Walsingham, I kept the conversation to safe things like the Hillmans, the disaster to their guest wing and the excitement over the prospect of another baby.

However, Thomasina's baby turned out not to be the safe topic that I thought it was, for suddenly, Mildred, who by now had drunk two and a half glasses of wine, to which I don't think she was accustomed, put down the piece of bread she had been using to mop up her pike juices and announced bitterly that she would like to have children but she would have to marry their prospective father first and her parents had chosen a fat widower called Miles Baines and she loathed him, and with that burst into tears.

I gave her a handkerchief and Joyce said consoling things such as *You may get to like him* and then, because that only made Mildred cry harder, *Surely your parents won't force you* and *Does Mr Baines realize that you aren't happy about marrying him?* Brockley and Dale talked of something else in low tones and pretended not to hear.

The arrival of the sweet course was a welcome interruption. I was sorry for Mildred, but I didn't like the exhibition she was making of herself. People were peering at us. I felt restless and irritable and my mouth was dry. I reached for my tankard of cider and then stopped, wondering why the tankard suddenly seemed to have become enormous. Really enormous. How could a thing like a tankard grow? Well, mine had. It was still growing. It towered above my head. It was surely six feet high. My mouth was more than dry. It was shrivelled. So was my tongue. I had never been so thirsty in my life. My stomach hurt . . .

At this point, with what remained of my sanity, I realized that I was ill. Or poisoned.

TEN
Fleeing the Field

Brockley and Dale between them half carried me out of the dining room and with the others at our heels, exclaiming in alarm, got me upstairs to the bedchamber. Mr Barratt the landlord and his wife, a woman as large and bustling as he was, saw us and came after us, wanting to know what was amiss. I remember the staring faces of the other diners as I was borne out of the room. I was laid on the bed that Mildred and I and Joyce had all meant to share and the landlord, much alarmed, despatched his wife for a physician. It does an inn no good to have its patrons collapsing halfway through a meal.

Meanwhile, somebody fetched salt water and an empty basin and Brockley made me drink the water. Dale held the beaker for me, and then held the basin while I threw up, itself a frightening business because like the tankard, the basin had grown to enormous proportions and I feared I might fall in.

After that, I lay back exhausted. I was vaguely aware of confusion around me. Joyce was saying that she would use the truckle bed that was part of the room's furnishings and requesting another for Mildred so that I could have the bed to myself. Then Joyce and Dale were undressing me and putting a nightgown over my head. A maid had been called to light a fire. When Joyce hung my gown and kirtle in the clothes press, the gown swung against the wall with a bang because it was one of the gowns with a hidden pouch in it, containing picklocks, dagger and a little purse of money. The maid, who was kneeling by the hearth while she coaxed the fire, looked at it, startled. So did Mildred, who stopped folding my stockings and stared.

'Just a belt pouch with some keys in it,' said Dale resourcefully and even in my misery, I managed to smile, and then stifled a scream as the fire appeared to blaze into a great conflagration.

At that point, Mrs Barratt reappeared with the physician. He proved to be a sensible man in middle years. Unlike most physicians, he didn't insist that I should be bled. I managed, though with difficulty, to pull myself together enough to tell him about the visions.

'If I didn't think it was impossible, I would say you've eaten henbane,' he said. 'I've seen it before though not in England. I sailed to the eastern Mediterranean when I was young, wanting to see the world and learn about medicine in other countries, and I saw a case of it in Turkey. I was ashore, living among the local people for a while and talking to the local doctors. One of them used henbane to ease pain and one of his patients took too much. He kept saying that the walls of his room were closing in on him, and why was there a tree growing through the floor?

'But he survived,' the physician said comfortingly. He turned to the others, who were standing anxiously round. 'Rest, water or milk to drink, and plenty of it – if it really is henbane, she'll be thirsty – and someone should stay with her through the night.'

'There are three of us,' said Dale. 'I shall spend the night here too.' I heard Mrs Barratt saying she would fetch water and milk and then I became drowsy and when I tried to look at my companions, I couldn't see them clearly. My eyes were blurred. After a while, I slept.

But some time in the small hours, when somebody had woken up and was replenishing the fire, I too awoke, to see such visions that I thought I was going completely mad, an idea that terrified me as much as the visions themselves. It seemed to me that the fire was once more a wall of flame and that armed men were advancing on my bed, their faces full of menace, and their hands grasping drawn swords. I shrank away in fear and cried out as they reached me.

'Dear Ursula, it's us,' said one of them. 'It's just Joyce and Dale. Don't be afraid of us,' whereupon, they vanished and so did the fire and I was alone in a bleak wilderness except that no, I was not quite alone, for above me a giant bird of prey, a monstrous eagle, was hovering. I saw its hooked beak, its mighty talons, curved and tipped with steel. I screamed and tried to roll away as it swooped, and nearly fell off the bed.

All three of them were suddenly there; soothing me, lifting me back into safety. I heard Dale say: 'We need Gladys,' and the sound of her voice briefly brought me back to reality, though it was an unpleasant reality, for I was burning with fever, my head splitting and my throat so dry that I couldn't ask for water. I could only croak but Joyce understood and held a beaker to my lips and with relief, I felt water run coldly down my gullet.

Then I was lost again, losing touch with where I was or even who I was. Far away, I heard Dale's voice, which I did dimly recognize, saying: 'She's going, oh dear God, she's going,' and I knew that Dale was crying and I wanted to help her but could not. I was sinking into darkness. But the darkness didn't take me for I was suddenly overwhelmed with nausea, and there were hands beneath my shoulders, lifting me up and leaning me forward and I was once more violently sick, into a basin that someone was holding for me. It looked like an ordinary basin this time. But I heaved and heaved until I wondered if I would ever stop, and the muscles of my abdomen began to ache. Then it was over, and I fell back on to the bed once again, drowning in exhaustion and suddenly, I fell asleep.

I woke again before dawn, opened my eyes and saw that the room was expanding. It reached the size of a cathedral and then began to dwindle until I feared I would be crushed between floor and ceiling, or between its walls, like the patient the physician had seen in Turkey. I cried out in panic. But Dale was there, offering a beaker, saying it was newly drawn well water. My head felt ready to burst but the water cooled my throat. Once more, I lapsed into sleep. When at daybreak, I woke yet again, my fever had gone and my head was clear. I sat up and saw the tired faces of Dale and Joyce and Mildred suddenly burst into smiles. Dale began to cry as well, this time with thankfulness.

What had woken me was Mr Barratt, who had come to see how I did. I said a hoarse good morning to him and his relief was plain but when Mildred described the night's vigil to him, she had him wringing his hands.

'That such a thing should happen to a guest of mine, in this hostelry! To have someone poisoned in my very dining room!'

Dale, drying her eyes, said primly that she was sure he was not to blame. Barratt, after promising that he would not charge for our visit and saying I was welcome to stay as long as I needed for a full recovery, went away, still distraught. I sat up a little more and knew that I was much too weak to stand, but also realized that I needed to relieve myself. Dale helped me to use the utensil the inn provided but the effort made me dizzy. Joyce and Mildred, now dressed for the day, came to ask if I could eat any breakfast.

I wondered. My skin was cool and I was no longer hallucinating but I wasn't sure whether I could manage food. It wasn't so long since I had been very sick and my abdomen still ached. Cautiously, I said I was willing to try. Dale suggested bread and milk with honey and I agreed, but couldn't bear the idea of small ale. I would drink some more well water instead, I said.

It was brought to my room, along with bread and honey and small ale for the others. I swallowed a few mouthfuls but that was all and I still had no strength. 'I want to get out of this inn!' I said. 'Only, I can't.'

The landlord, meanwhile, had been asking questions and after breakfast came to tell us the answers. It seemed that he had had two menservants and one maidservant serving at yesterday's supper and none of them, apparently, had topped up any drinks at my table before I was taken ill. He brought one of the menservants, a dignified middle-aged individual called John Carey, along to confirm it.

'Your table was my responsibility and I didn't refill any tankards or glasses until after you were taken out, madam,' he said. 'Neither of my colleagues attended your table at all; they were busy with their own.'

But someone had. Someone unauthorized; someone dressed in black like the inn servants. In the tremulous light of the candles, with the pools of shadow between the pillars, someone had passed himself off as another waiter. But whoever he was, he had come and gone like a ghost.

'There's people moving about all the time, in and out of the candlelight,' Carey said. 'You see someone and then you don't see him and then all you see is his back. You're busy and you don't think about it, or notice that the figure you can see doesn't look like your fellow servant. It must have been done that way.' He drew himself up. 'But it certainly wasn't done by me!'

There was no reason to disbelieve him. He could have no conceivable motive, after all. Two guests who were staying in the inn and had dined at our long table were brought in as well and said that they had certainly not been offered any refills before my collapse, though Mr Carey had done so later on.

That was all that could be discovered. 'You've had a lucky escape,' Brockley said, coming to see me, his eyes anxious. 'Whoever did it must have got the dosage wrong.'

'Not very wrong,' I said. 'I only took a little of that cider. I think that's what saved me.' I thought of the night and knew, with a quiver of fear, how near to death I had slipped. I had heard Dale's tearful cry that I was going; I could feel the shocked weakness in my body. I had been so grateful to see the dawn. I very nearly hadn't.

But in the evening I asked for bread and oatmeal porridge, found I could eat it, and then told Dale to pack my belongings. 'Tomorrow,' I said, 'even if my knees are giving way, even if the heavens fall on my head, we're leaving. I wish I didn't have to face another night here.'

'We will fetch all your food and drink from the kitchen ourselves,' Joyce said. 'No one will interfere with it, and there will always be someone here with you. You surely need another day here.'

'No!' I said, and dragged myself up against my pillows the better to explain. 'Don't any of you understand what has happened? Someone has tried to get rid of me and what reason could anyone have except that I am trying to track down the killers of Peter Gray and Gregory Reeves? That someone knows who I am, what I am about and where I am. That someone got at my drink last night. As long as I stay here, I feel vulnerable.'

I wanted to be back in Zeal Aquatio. Or better still, in Hawkswood. I was terrified. I knew it was my duty to go on but how would I ever summon up the courage to do it?

'But, madam,' Brockley was saying, 'you are not fit for the saddle!'

'Can't you borrow or hire a carriage of some sort, or even a cart? You can tie Jaunty behind.'

We reached the Greshams' house in mid-afternoon, and our arrival caused a stir, especially the spectacle of Brockley tenderly helping Mistress Stannard out of a cart and then seeing her guided indoors by Mildred and Joyce, one on each side of me. It brought Mrs Gresham running down the front steps, followed by Tilly, both of them exclaiming and wanting to know what the matter was.

'I'm all right!' I said, untruthfully. It had been a long journey, in the jolting cart. There were carriages for hire in Okehampton but only two as far as Brockley could discover, and they were all out. It was a cart or nothing. I had been wrapped in a blanket, with a cushion for my head, and I had slept part of the way, but I still felt ill and exhausted.

'I have had a . . . a stomach upset,' I said. 'I will need to go to bed for a little while. I shall be quite well before long,' I added, as convincingly as possible.

Much distressed, Mrs Gresham joined in with helping me to our quarters in the extra wing, where Dale and Joyce put me to bed. Mildred fetched a hot posset from the kitchen and said that she had left her mother and Tilly discussing invalid diets. 'We will take great care of you, Mistress Stannard,' she said anxiously. I thanked her, and then, while I sipped the posset, I asked where Brockley was.

'He and Eddie are seeing to the horses,' said Dale. 'Shall I call him, ma'am?'

'No, no, it's just that I ought to send a message to the Hillmans. They will be expecting us to visit them, to spend time with them. After all, I am part of a family gathering! I want Brockley to ride to Ladymead and tell them that I am indisposed but will come to see them quite soon. He must say it's nothing serious, which is true.'

'It isn't serious now,' said Dale. 'But it might have been. Ma'am, does it really mean . . .?'

'Yes, it does. Whoever topped up my cider put something

into it that nearly killed me, and as I told you yesterday, the only reason I can think of is that I have begun to ask questions about Gray and Reeves. But my message to Thomasina and the rest of the family mustn't mention that. As far as they are concerned, I have simply been ill.'

'I'll find Roger now,' said Dale.

Brockley set off with the message within the hour and I relaxed in bed, thankful to be out of the cart. He returned that evening, with surprising news. Dale brought him to my bedside to tell it to me. The Hillmans sent their love and concern, hoped to see me soon, and all was well with them, but there had been some trouble at the vicarage.

'Mistress Thomasina had come back just before I got there,' Brockley said. 'She had gone to the church to help clean it, as she sometimes does – at the moment, she just does dusting, I gather – and she heard it there. Mistress Sabina rode home from one of her musical evenings in Tavistock early one morning, on her own. They haven't a groom; they look after their horses themselves. As usual, she'd stayed somewhere overnight; her brother won't let her ride home in the dark. On the way home in the morning, her horse threw her. She kept hold of the reins but she banged her head and bruised her shoulder badly in the fall and she says she just doesn't know how she got back into the saddle. She rode on, slowly, and reached home safely, anyway. Dr Parker had gone off to Plymouth on Church business and wasn't yet back. He's back now and he's saying that troubles never come one at a time because he caught a chill, riding in the cold, and he's had to go to bed, though he fetched a physician for Sabina first. A neighbour is helping out with meals. The physician has told Sabina not to do too much because of the bang on her head. It's Sunday the day after tomorrow but Lucius won't be well enough to take the services and there's a panic over finding someone else. Someone's gone into Plymouth to try and find a replacement.'

'What a tale of calamity!' I said weakly. 'I ought to go and see them as soon as I can. He and Sabina have been so kind to us.'

'You shouldn't go just yet, madam,' said Brockley. 'The

physician apparently said that Mistress Sabina should be very quiet for a few days.'

'Well, we must send our good wishes tomorrow and visit them when we can,' I said. I noticed that for the first time I had begun to feel genuinely hungry and asked Dale what they had had for dinner.

'Braised trout with a prawn sauce,' said Dale. 'It was very good.'

'If there's any left,' I said, 'I would like some, just a small portion, heated up . . .'

'Of course, ma'am!' said Dale, clearly and touchingly over-joyed to see these signs of a real recovery.

Recovery. That meant, once more, being able to think and my thoughts were unhappy. Who was, or who were, the shadowy foes who had fed poison to me? That they caused the deaths of Gray and Reeves, I was certain. There were two, at least, I thought; two had surely worked together in Gray's case.

And they had so nearly disposed of me. My stomach shivered. I tried to think how to pursue my enquiries. What should my next step be? What plans had I been revolving before I collapsed? I must find and talk to the carter whose horses had got away with him. Had he been bribed, or was he himself one of the two killers? Either way, he would probably lie but I must try. He might contradict himself, give his guilt away somehow. He had evidently convinced the inquest of his innocence but I was dismissing the thought of his innocence and assuming the worst.

I must do it. Did I dare? Was I brave enough, after this deadly warning? Would there be another attempt on my life? And would Brockley and perhaps Dale and Joyce too, also be in danger?

I slept badly that night, and not on account of the henbane, if that's what it was.

In the morning, I was well enough to get up. Dale dressed me in a loose gown with no confining ruff or farthingale and though I was shaky, I joined the breakfast table. I ate little, however, and Joyce, who had been watching me, asked me what our next plans were – were we visiting Okehampton again or preparing to go home? Brockley looked at us both sharply. I said I had made no plans as yet. After the meal, Brockley said quietly that he would like to talk to me privately and we repaired to his and Dale's room.

There was little danger of interruption. Mildred was helping Tilly to wash up while Dale and Joyce were for some reason deep in talk with Catherine and were still in the dining room. I closed the door to the vestibule. And then realized that this was the moment to say what, in the night, I had decided that I must say, and wondered how I would get the words out. Would Brockley, would Joyce and Dale, be relieved or sorry? Would they despise me? And what was Brockley about to say now?

He began to speak but immediately, a feeling of illness overwhelmed me. I stopped him with a shake of the head and turned away to lean my forehead on the sill of the window. Outside, was a view of grass and a track and a stream. In this grey, still weather, the water looked as though it was made of lead. I felt as though the very blood in my veins had turned to liquid lead as well.

'Madam?' Brockley spoke from behind me. 'What is it?'

'I'm tired,' I said, blurting it out suddenly. 'Tired of danger, tired of being expected to find answers to impossible riddles. I don't want to go on. I *can't* go on. It's too dangerous. I'm giving up. We're not going back to Okehampton. We're not staying here either. We're going home!'

'Come, madam. You are not properly better yet. You should wait until you are before you make decisions,' said Brockley.

I turned to face him and met his eyes. There was compassion in that steady blue-grey gaze of his, but there was also something else. Something implacable.

'I feared something like this,' he said. 'I saw your face when Joyce spoke to you at breakfast. That's why I asked to speak with you now. Madam, someone thought it necessary to dispose of the two agents you recruited to work in this part of Devon. To me that suggests that those two agents knew something. Whatever it is, probably lies in this part of Devon. Very likely, they both came upon evidence of the *same* plot or conspiracy, unless there is more than one hatching out somewhere between Okehampton and Plymouth.'

'I know,' I said, pettishly.

'An invading fleet might well make for this part of the south coast,' said Brockley. 'Imagine it: Spanish vessels arriving after dark, soldiers swooping on Plymouth, landing craft full of more soldiers, slipping through the waterways like claws planted into this patch of Devon, while the rest of the fleet sails on up the English Channel to land as near to London as they can get. Didn't Walsingham put it to you that way? I am sure you told me so. And what do you think would happen next?'

'I know, Brockley, I know.'

'It's possible. It could mean that the conspiracy your agents found is highly dangerous.'

'Brockley!' I had rarely known him so fluent.

'When you visit the court, madam, Fran and I go with you and I keep my ears well open. I hear things. The fear of invasion from Spain is very real.'

'*Yes, I know!* It's why Walsingham asked me to find agents for this area. And I recruited Gray and Reeves, and now they are dead. My fault. And now I have invited the same danger too and perhaps called it down on all of you. I would like to avenge Gray and Reeves but I can't.'

'Vengeance is an empty affair. But if we can finish their work for them, madam, that's worth doing. Otherwise, they died for nothing. We need to know not only who attacked them, but why. Because they got wind of a plot that could endanger us all, could endanger England? Would you like to see a Spanish army on English soil, here to kill Queen Elizabeth and put Mary Stuart on our throne in her stead?'

'*Brockley!* The Inquisition would come with them, the lashing tail of the Spanish tiger. I *know*. But I can't pursue this, not now. I'll report to Walsingham. Others can take over. I can't go on. I'm too afraid.'

'Others? When agents die mysteriously or disappear, is the matter usually pursued at an official level?'

I was silent. It had never actually been said to me or even in my hearing but I knew it all the same. In almost all cases,

agents were on their own. Walsingham didn't want their existence to be made public. Very likely, if I didn't take up the hunt,
no one would.

'You'll feel different when you're properly well,' said
Brockley firmly.

'You're as bad as Hugh,' I said with resentment. My late
husband, Hugh, had once insisted that I undertook a task for
the queen against my will. Most husbands would have wanted
to protect their wives from such things but Hugh had insisted
that it was my duty.

'Rest a day or two more,' said Brockley firmly. 'You *will*
feel different then. I know you.'

It was true. Trembling inside, frightened as never before, I
knew that for all my talk of going home, to desert Gray and
Reeves would be like a warrior fleeing from a battlefield. I
mustn't. I must *not*. I was coming to this unhappy conclusion
when Joyce walked into the room. She was smiling cheerfully.
We looked at her in confusion.

'There's to be a formal dinner on Monday, for a guest,' she
announced, obviously quite unconscious of the tension in
the air. 'Mr Gresham is staying at home for it and Mrs Gresham
asks us to dress well for it. The guest is Mr Miles Baines, the
man they want Mildred to marry.'

'And Mildred doesn't like him,' I said, wrenching my mind
with difficulty away from conspiracies and violent deaths, to
concentrate on a social problem instead. It was like receiving
a message from the moon. 'What a jolly occasion it will be.
But are we invited? We're not family. Surely we'll be served
dinner in our quarters.'

'No,' said Joyce. 'The Greshams want us there. Dale and
Brockley as well. I think her parents feel that guests will
discourage Mildred from being difficult. Do you feel strong
enough?'

I said yes. I wouldn't have to leave the house and could
withdraw at any time if I felt unwell.

'By the way,' Joyce said, 'Eddie has taken the hired cart
back to Okehampton. I lent him Patches for the return ride.'

I tried to imagine riding a horse, and couldn't. 'I'm glad
this dinner we've got to go to is being held here,' I said.

'I'm not strong enough to mount a horse. I wonder if I ever will be.'

'Of course you will,' said Joyce, and went away, presumably to re-join Dale and Catherine. Brockley said: 'Well?'

I said: 'We go on.'

ELEVEN
The Art of Selling

When abroad, or in an unfamiliar house, one feels a natural urge to fit in with one's surroundings, with the attitudes of one's hosts, or the customs of the country. I thought hard about my choice of gown for the Greshams' formal dinner. My best blue and silver brocade gown was a court dress and would be out of place in this Puritan house. Or would it? If the Greshams had especially wished us to dress well . . .

Brockley was right to say that I was still unwell. Sunday was the next day but I didn't feel like making the journey to church. The others went and Joyce, on returning said, that the homily, given by a curate hastily borrowed from Plymouth, had been sadly dull.

'Never mind the homily,' I said. 'I want to talk about clothes. Very reprehensible on a Sunday, I know, but there it is. What should I wear for this dinner tomorrow?'

'I thought about clothes all through that tedious homily,' said Joyce, straight-faced, but with a merry gleam in her greenish-hazel eyes which I rejoiced to see. 'Mistress Stannard, I think you should wear your cream and tawny gown and kirtle. You like those colours and you look well in them, but they aren't . . . I mean . . .'

'Showy,' I said. 'I think you're right. Now, about you. You have a pale green gown with you. It's nearly the same colour as the material we've bought for Mildred. Wear that, and give her ideas! Luckily, neither of us like big ruffs. You have your peridot earrings and pendant. I shall wear my topaz necklace and earrings.'

I added thoughtfully: 'If anyone is somehow keeping watch over us, perhaps if they see that we're staying quietly here and joining our hosts' social events, they'll think we've given up making nosy enquiries, or were never really making them in the first place.'

'I doubt it,' said Joyce candidly. 'Aren't we hoping to talk to that carter? That surely won't go unnoticed. But you do still need a little more time to recover. You had a bad turn. I shall never forget that moment when Dale and I thought we'd lost you. We were terrified!'

The Brockleys were circumspect about dress. Dale put on the dark-blue gown which she always wore when she felt herself to be on duty while Brockley always wore buff on such occasions, which made him look like a military man. On Monday, therefore, we all went to the Greshams' dining chamber, feeling that we were suitably arrayed, though when we got there we at once felt that despite our efforts, we were still overdressed, because the Greshams were a positively funereal trio, Mr and Mrs Gresham in black, though with freshly starched white ruffs, while Mildred was wraithlike in pale grey.

We were at least warm. The weather had continued extremely cold but for once, there was a fire in the hearth, the first we had ever seen there. There was no need for shawls this time. At first, we all stood about in an awkward fashion, because the guest hadn't yet arrived. However, at last, we heard hooves, and then the voice of a groom taking charge of a horse. We heard Tilly asking someone to come this way and in walked the man that Mildred's parents wanted her to marry. Mr Miles Baines in person.

I looked at him with curiosity. Mildred, who had been standing as stiffly as a basalt pillar, softened enough to bob a curtsey to him but didn't smile. Her father, however, stepped forward with an outstretched hand and Mrs Gresham gave him a deep curtsey. There were introductions all round and then we all sat down to eat.

Catherine had placed Mildred next to Baines and I could see him pouring wine for her and trying to make conversation. For the first time ever, I saw wine on the Greshams' dining table, and this was a good one, a warm red from the Mediterranean. No doubt the Greshams wanted to be hospitable to Baines. He might be here to woo Mildred but her parents were wooing *him*.

The nature of the meal proved that. The first course was a saffron soup with cheese and egg yolks beaten into it and it was followed by a dish of trout with wine and verjuice and ginger, accompanied by onions. They were elaborate dishes, far more so than trout with a prawn sauce, or side dishes of fried beans, and I saw in them another indication of how much the Greshams wanted Baines in their family. I studied him covertly.

Since no one was trying to marry me to him, I probably saw him more clearly than Mildred did. He was well into middle age, possibly around fifty, and he was bulky, with heavy jowls and a paunch and thick forearms filling the sleeves of his brown velvet doublet. His hair was scanty and what there was of it was dust-coloured. But his small pale eyes were shrewd. He wasn't a fool, I thought. He must know that he was no one's idea of a desirable bridegroom and he probably knew that Mildred didn't like him. He could hardly expect her to like him! But he was persisting. He had a use for her. Few women of childbearing age would find him attractive and few parents would want him for their daughters. Here, he had willing parents and a girl who had few other chances. Poor Mildred.

At that moment, he became aware of my scrutiny and looked straight at me. 'I believe you are related to the Hillmans of Ladymead House, are you not, Mistress Stannard?'

'You know the Hillmans, sir?' I said. 'My companions and I are staying here because there's not enough room at Ladymead. It may not look like it but we are really having a family get-together.'

'I have a wide acquaintance,' said Baines. His voice was deep and chesty, as though he had lung trouble. If Mildred did marry him, she might not be a wife for long. Though meanwhile . . . I was no innocent maiden but the thought of being squashed under Baines' massive body and invaded by it, made me shudder. Again, I thought, *Poor Mildred.*

Baines was enlarging on his wide acquaintance. He was only lightly acquainted with the Hillmans, but yes, he had met them. He had cousins in Plymouth and his sheep farm was on the edge of the moor, out towards Tavistock; he often had business there and also in Okehampton; so he knew most of the foremost people in all those communities, including the Reeves family.

'Mr Reeves has lately lost his son, in a most extraordinary accident. Have you heard about it?'

I said that we had, and that *extraordinary* was surely the right description. 'How could such a thing happen?' I asked, marvelling, and probing for any new information that Baines might supply.

'No one can account for it. Dreadful shock for that pretty little wife of his. Expecting her first child, too. I know her people as well. The Bakers – big family; Sally's one of ten. Number seven, I think. Her parents were glad to see her well married. Andrew Reeves has a prosperous business and Gregory was his heir. Now Sally's back on her parents' hands again. The Reeves family ought to be looking after her but I think she just ran home to her mother.'

He turned to Mildred and said jovially: 'If aught happens to me, my bird, you needn't run home to mother. I'd see you were looked after. I have plenty of servants, outdoors and in. You'd have a good home and security. You must come and see my house again. You've been once but it was back in January and it was even colder and darker than it is now. You didn't see the place properly, and you saw hardly anything of the property outdoors.'

Beaming, he looked round the table. 'Let me see – come on Saturday next. The eighth of March. That will give me time to arrange a good dinner for you all – perhaps as good as this!'

His shrewd gaze embraced everyone. 'Yes, Mistress Stannard, you and your people too. You have been unwell, so Mrs Catherine has told me. I hope you're now recovered?'

'I think so,' I said, and realized that it was true. All of a sudden, I felt that I could mount a horse after all. 'This splendid dinner is helping,' I said. 'I must congratulate you on it, Mrs Gresham.'

There were murmurs of agreement. Catherine said: 'Mildred and I and Tilly worked together to create it. We live more plainly as a rule,' but she was pink with pleasure at the compliments.

'There is a right and wrong time for everything,' said her husband. 'Does Holy Writ not tell us that there is a time and a season for every purpose under heaven? Ah, here is dear Tilly with the sweet course. Mildred prepared this. She is a wonder with preserved fruit, and we are fortunate enough to have a little orchard. We have preserved plums to hand all the year round, and apples stored so carefully that we rarely run out before midsummer, and then the redcurrants have begun.'

He had said that Catherine was poor at selling, but Henry Gresham, I thought, was clearly good at it and what he was selling now, was Mildred. While Baines, who although not attractive was certainly not stupid, was attempting to sell himself *to* Mildred. The situation had a certain piquancy.

'I shall not expect my wife to spend all her days in the kitchen, unless she wishes so to do,' Miles was saying in jovial tones. 'My ample supply of servants includes a cook and two kitchen maids.'

Catherine gave Mildred a *There, what did I tell you?* look. Miles enquired whether the groom who had come with him was also being given some dinner. 'I should have asked before. I consider such things to be important.'

'Certainly,' said Mr Gresham. 'And your horses will have been cared for and fed. We take care of our horses and our servants. The grooms and Tilly will partake of this dinner as well, in the kitchen.'

'I approve. That is how things should be,' said Miles. He smiled at Mildred. 'And I am sure that when we are married, my good wife will see that such rules are observed.'

'She will. She has had a good moral upbringing,' said Catherine primly.

I began to wish that this embarrassing meal would end.

When at last we were back in our rooms, Dale came to help me out of my gown and its farthingale into something looser, and remarked: 'Ma'am, that was like being in a market. They were treating Mistress Mildred like fruit on a stall.'

'I know. I hardly knew where to look,' I said. 'I wonder what Baines thought. Tomorrow, I suggest we do something more agreeable. It's time I visited Ladymead. I feel capable of riding a horse now and Jaunty must be wondering where I am. I haven't been to say goodnight to him for days!'

TWELVE
Gathering Strength

I was glad to be at Ladymead again, and the Hillmans were glad to see me. Everyone crowded round us as Joyce, Dale and I came into the hall. 'Family gathering, indeed!' said Bartholomew. 'You hardly arrive before you are off to the Greshams' and then away to Okehampton and then you fall dramatically ill in the Castle Inn. Brockley told us all about that. We have been very worried. And,' he added reprovingly, 'worry isn't good for Thomasina now.'

I agreed with that, for Thomasina was now very bulky indeed and she looked tired. I had sent Eddie off on Monday evening with a note to ask if I might visit Ladymead on the following day and the note he had brought back said a hearty yes but I hoped it hadn't put Thomasina to any trouble. Contritely, I said: 'There was no need to worry. It was just a brief stomach upset.' And then caught Dale's eye just in time, I reckoned, to stop her from telling everyone that I'd nearly died.

The hall was scattered with stools and settles and evidently dinner was not to be served yet for the dining table had been pushed back against one wall. Thomasina came to sit beside me. 'We are going to have some music before dinner. Some other guests are coming – we're making an occasion of this. Ursula, what really happened in Okehampton? Brockley . . .' She glanced round but Brockley was presumably still seeing to the horses and was not present. 'Brockley was awkward somehow, when he told us of your illness. What was really wrong with you?'

This was difficult. I didn't want Thomasina or any of her family to realize that my life had been attempted and that the attempt had come within a hairsbreadth of succeeding. Bartholomew knew that I was about possibly dangerous business and no doubt Thomasina knew as well but I didn't want them to realize just how dangerous.

'I ate something that disagreed with me,' I said firmly. 'You never know when you're eating in inns, even in the best ones. Such things do happen.'

'Well, I noticed that you rode here on that fine bay gelding of yours,' Thomasina said. 'You can manage the saddle, it seems.'

'Thank you, yes. Jaunty is a well-mannered horse. We all rode. Dale is very pleased with Brown Betsy.'

I led the conversation on into a discussion of horses, which lasted until the other guests arrived, who turned out to be Lucius Parker with Sabina and also with Rossiter. Brother and sister had apparently been invited to dine but Rossiter was one extra. 'Samuel called just as we were getting ready,' Sabina said brightly, 'to see how we were after Lucius' illness and my accident. We thought you wouldn't mind if we brought him too.'

'No, of course we don't mind,' said Thomasina, though I could see from her eyes that she was mentally making sure that the food would go round and wondering where she could fit in another place at the table. Meanwhile, Lucius and Sabina, answering an enquiry from Joyce, were explaining that the physician Lucius had called to Sabina had not thought the bump on her head to be dangerous, but she was having headaches and he had bidden them to call on him again if these persisted. Happily, they had not, she told us, while her shoulder had only been bruised and didn't hurt now, and Lucius had recovered from his chill.

'Yesterday I was able to get to Plymouth to a meeting of my charity members,' Sabina said. She turned towards me and Joyce. 'Do you know about us?' We obviously looked as though we didn't, for she went straight on. 'There are quite a lot of us. We all collect clothes, and also money if we can, and pass everything to the two vicars who are in charge of us. They use the money to buy children's clothes when asked – by sailors' widows who've been left hard up. The charity doesn't give money to the widows; being a sailor's widow doesn't mean you're bound to be a saint – there are one or two who would drink it in the nearest tavern. A list is kept of women who may be in need and every time a Plymouth man is lost at sea, one of the vicars calls upon the widow if there is one, and if she is in want, he adds her to the list. Any of the women on the list can ask for new shoes or tunics or cloaks for their young ones.'

'You are always ready to describe your charity to strangers,' said Lucius. 'I suppose it's one way of seeking out new contributors.'

Sabina bit her lip and didn't reply. Thomasina said: 'I've seen your piles of used clothes, at the vicarage. A worthwhile charity, I would say.'

'Indeed I hope so,' said Sabina.

I set about changing the conversation by asking her how she had managed to get back into the saddle after her fall. It's never easy to get into a side saddle without a mounting block or a helpful groom.

'Oh, I ride astride when I'm on my own. It's safer. I keep a pair of breeches handy,' said Sabina. 'It's only good sense. I once recommended Mildred Gresham to do the same, but she rarely rides alone and her parents wouldn't approve anyway. How is Mildred now? We are friends, you know, and I think her parents are too strict. She has often said that she would like to come with me to the musical evenings I enjoy so much but music is another thing that her parents don't like. Perhaps when she is married, her husband will be more open-hearted. Is the wedding date settled yet?'

'She's your friend but she clearly doesn't tell you everything,' said Lucius, unexpectedly breaking off a conversation with Bartholomew and turning to us. 'She is objecting to the match, which is very wrong. Her parents have done their very best to settle her in life. They have found her a man of substance and all she has to do in return is to look after his home and, God willing, give him children. Just before I went to Plymouth, I met Mr Gresham in the street and we stopped to talk. He is most upset by his daughter's intransigence. She should obey her parents and adapt herself. Obedience is her duty.'

I said mildly: 'Her dislike may be a kind of fear. Because of . . . er . . . physical distaste. He is much older than she is and not very attractive. I can understand her feelings.'

'She should trust her parents and put her feelings aside. She will get over them once she has been married for a while and got used to her husband. It is not a woman's business to seek lustful gratification. She accepts her husband to please him and in the hope of children. And a daughter owes obedience to her parents!' Lucius was positively vehement.

I wanted to recommend marriage for love, but my own marital history was too complicated. I kept silent. However, Joyce said: 'My sister Jane has married for love and she is very happy.'

I took heart. 'My daughter Meg also married for love,' I said. 'And it has prospered.'

'No doubt the love match is best,' Lucius said stiffly. 'But who is going to fall in love with Mildred? She's a plain girl, you must admit. I know the family quite well. They are Puritans but they attend my church. They know I am really of their persuasion.'

I found myself growing annoyed with the Reverend Lucius Parker, who seemed to have no understanding at all of the feelings that a middle-aged hulk like Miles Baines was likely to arouse in a young girl who was about to be pushed into bed with him. I wondered if he had ever seriously tried to find a husband for Sabina. Admittedly, it might have been a difficult search, and wouldn't have produced a handsome hero. Such men have a wide choice and wouldn't be likely to choose Sabina, who had never learned to temper her height with gracefulness and whose long bony face and beaky nose were, not actually ugly, but very near it. She obviously didn't agree with her brother's sentiments and her eyes were shooting sparks at him.

She took care of her appearance, though and I approved of that. Her blue woollen gown had sleeves slashed to show glimpses of cream silk and her brown hair was arranged in glossy waves in front of a blue hood. Her ruff, sensibly moderate in size, was spruce and fresh and when I greeted her, I had once more caught the scent of lavender. Sabina, whatever the disadvantages that nature had thrown at her, had kept her self-respect.

To escape from the topic of Mildred, I asked Sabina how often she went to the musical evenings.

'They're held weekly,' she told me, 'on Wednesdays, at a private house in Tavistock. I don't always go but I enjoy it when I do.'

'And you do a little collecting for charity while you're there,' said Lucius jovially. 'You've even made a special embroidered purse for that, haven't you?'

'I go for the music most of all,' said Sabina, a little defensively.

Joyce, interested by the mention of an embroidered purse, asked Sabina if she enjoyed embroidery, whereupon Lucius took it upon himself to answer for her and said: 'Yes, she does, but she's not very skilful, are you, Sabina?' His sister reddened and fell silent.

'Well, we're about to have some music here.' Thomasina, firm and tactful, interrupted. 'Dinner isn't ready yet, so . . . here are some minstrels!'

Into the hall came Thomasina's two eldest children, fifteen-year-old Tom and thirteen-year-old Ann. Tom was carrying a lute, and Ann was with a manservant who was trundling a wheeled clavichord. They had been wise, I thought, not to try squeezing the clavichord into the minuscule minstrels' gallery. I realized now why the dining table had been pushed back. It was to give the two young musicians room to perform.

It was a charming performance. Ann had a pretty singing voice, not loud but tuneful. With Tom's lute to accompany her, she gave us several songs, which we applauded with pleasure, and then played a piece on the clavichord. After that, Tom played a piece for us on his lute. 'He used to sing but his voice is breaking just now,' Thomasina whispered to me.

The entertainment finished just before dinner. The clavichord was wheeled away and the dining table was pulled forward. A pair of maids, assisted by two more of Thomasina's daughters, Alice and Kat, twin girls aged eleven, came to put a cloth on the table and set out dishes and spoons. Sabina complimented Ann on her singing and her skill on the keyboard.

'I play the clavichord myself,' she said. 'I am not just part of the audience at the musical gatherings. I join in.'

'I like music very much,' I said, before Lucius could say something else to put his sister down. 'I play the lute and the spinet. My son is showing some musical gifts, too.'

It was pleasant to talk about Harry. Indeed, in spite of Lucius, it was pleasant to be in a normal household, and not have to think about my frightening mission. But then I was pulled back to reality by Samuel Rossiter, who suddenly leant forward and said: 'Have you found your mare's nest yet, mistress? Do mares lay eggs?'

I turned to look at him. 'I don't think it's a mare's nest, sir. I may need you.'

'I'm ready and willing once you've got your claws into someone, mistress. But I still can't believe there's anyone to find. Not as I'll hinder you.'

'I trust you for that,' I said. The mention of eggs had reminded me of Peter Gray and I wished it hadn't. I turned back to Lucius, who was asking his sister if she meant to go to Tavistock the next day, as it was a Wednesday. 'You should take Mistress Stannard with you, Sabina.'

'Not tomorrow,' I said. 'I don't think I'm up to the ride to Tavistock just yet.'

'The meetings are very informal,' said Sabina. 'If you really want to go, of course . . .'

'If Ursula does want to go, could I go too?' asked Joyce wistfully. 'I would like it very much, I'm sure.'

I was becoming very fond of Joyce and if a musical evening in Tavistock would appeal to her, then she should have one. 'May we come?' I asked Sabina. 'Next week, not tomorrow. Would we be welcome, as strangers?'

'Of course they would. Especially if Mistress Stannard can play the spinet and the lute,' said Lucius.

'I can play the lute,' said Joyce. 'I should love to go to a musical gathering and I would be glad to join in if they let me.'

'Well, Sabina,' said Lucius, 'it looks as if you have accidentally sold our friends the idea of an evening in Tavistock.'

'Oh, well . . .' said Sabina.

She didn't seem particularly anxious to take us, but the arrangement had somehow got itself made. Joyce and I were going to a musical evening in Tavistock and that was that. Meanwhile, the reminder of Peter Gray was nagging at me and an idea had occurred to me. I turned to Thomasina and said in low tones: 'You used to buy eggs from Peter Gray. That's how

I met him. I need to know more about him. Do you know where his smallholding was?'

'Yes. It's called Larkhurst. It's up on a rise, about three miles north of here. You'll have passed within sight of it on the way to Okehampton. So you do intend to probe into his death and that of Gregory Reeves? Bart has talked to me, you see.'

'Who has the smallholding now?'

'I don't know. Whoever it is, isn't selling eggs,' said Thomasina ruefully. 'I've had to find someone else. I think it's time we had some chickens of our own. What do you hope to find there?'

'I have been thinking and it has suddenly struck me that Gray might have left some notes behind. I mean, what if he had suspicions of anyone and noted his reasons and named names! If we can find his papers, we may find the answer to all our questions! If only his papers are still at Larkhurst. Did he have any family? Did anyone come to collect such things?'

'I haven't the slightest idea,' said Thomasina. Her brown eyes were anxious. 'Ursula, do try not to run into danger!'

'All right,' I said gently. 'I have the name of Larkhurst, anyway. That will make a start.'

At that moment, Lucius suddenly cleared his throat and asked loudly if anyone had any commissions in Exeter. 'I'm going there on Church business tomorrow. I must make an early start in the morning. I intend to do some shopping for Sabina while I'm there. There are excellent merchants in Exeter, even better than the Plymouth ones, and some of the prices are lower. So – can I do a little shopping for anyone else? Sabina, remind me, what do you want me to buy for you?'

'Some linen to make shifts,' Sabina said. 'Oh, and perfume! I am getting tired of lavender water.'

'I can't approve of perfume, though I suppose the lavender water that you make yourself is harmless enough. Can't you make rosewater if you must wear scent and want a change?'

'Where's the harm in a little perfume?' asked Thomasina. 'There are some nice Eastern fragrances for sale sometimes in Plymouth – and Exeter too, I dare say. I found a lovely sandal-wood scent last time I went to Plymouth. I bought three bottles in case it wasn't easy to find again. I haven't used any yet, not until I'm back to my normal shape. I'll give you one! Ann!'

she turned to her daughter. 'Run to my bedchamber and look in the little cupboard beside my dressing table. You should find my phials of sandalwood scent there. Bring one here.'

'No, really . . .' Lucius began but Rossiter was laughing at him. 'All women like scent! It's natural.'

Lucius shrugged his shoulders and gave up the battle. From Thomasina and Joyce he collected a couple of small commissions, respectively for white linen and silk thread in several colours, and then Ann came back with the sandalwood fragrance. Everyone, of course, even Lucius, wanted a sniff and the phial was passed round amid happy exclamations. *Lovely! Exciting! The very scent of the distant east!* It was new to me and I found it oddly disturbing, full of secret promises, to be kept in the darkness of a tropical night. Lucius gave the phial only a perfunctory sniff and then shook his head. 'The strange things that women like to waste their substance on. It's made my mouth dry,' he said dampingly. Lucius was good at creating embarrassment.

'You'll have full saddlebags, coming home,' Bartholomew remarked, probably to change the atmosphere.

'I'm taking Sock with me,' said Lucius. 'I want to buy a new bedcover as well and I can't squeeze that into a saddlebag.'

'You're taking a sock?' said Joyce wonderingly.

'It's the name of Sabina's pony,' Lucius explained. 'She lets me borrow him if I need to. He has one white sock, on the off fore.'

'Just like my pony,' Tom said. 'I even call him White Fore.'

With a completely straight face, Bartholomew said: 'That pony has a strange fancy for limewash. We use it sometimes, to refresh the stable walls, and whenever he sees a pail of it, he goes and stands with one hoof in it. Time and again, Tom, I've told you not to let him.'

There was a bewildered silence, until those of us who were familiar with Bartholomew's peculiar brand of humour all laughed, and those who were not – in this case Rossiter and the Parkers – just looked puzzled.

I didn't give Lucius any commissions. I couldn't like him. He had no need to be so hard on Sabina. I was as sorry for Sabina as I was for Mildred.

We were now being asked to take our seats at the dining table and I found Lucius beside me. Rossiter was some distance away and Lucius chose to lean towards me and say: 'I wish Rossiter hadn't made that remark about all women liking perfumes. I try to make Sabina content but . . . well, we've always known Rossiter, and there was a time when she and he were younger, she made such a set at him, it was embarrassing. Then he got wed and Sabina quietened down, to be fair to her. I always see she has plenty to do; our home to run and there's her charity for the children of men lost at sea. But with Rossiter, well, it's still there, in a way. When he talks of women and perfume like that, it encourages what's worst in her.'

'Or what's natural,' I said, repeating Rossiter's words, which made Lucius look at me sharply. Then the first course was arriving and Brockley hurried in, just in time, and was given a seat on the other side of me. I began asking him questions about the horses. I didn't want to go on talking to Lucius.

The guests left after dinner and by the time we were back at the Greshams', I was tired, although once it was evening, I went to see Jaunty in his stall as I so often did. 'I like to talk to him,' I said to the others, 'and I like to see him turn his head when I come in and prick his ears towards me.' They all laughed at me but I went anyway.

The stable was peaceful. The only light came from the lantern I was carrying and the only company was that of the horses, rustling their hooves in their straw as they turned to look at me, catching the lantern light in their big dark eyes.

I found a brush and gave Jaunty's mane some extra attention and while I worked, my mind ranged at large and in the warmth and quiet, I seemed to gather new strength. What must I do next? How could I pursue this terrifying hunt? I had told Thomasina that I wanted to see if Gray had left any notes. Why ever hadn't I thought of that before?

It applied to Gregory Reeves, as well! And what about the carter with the runaway horses? That must be set in hand immediately. There was work to do, work I had been shirking, I had been *paid* to recruit those two. I thought of my new property, Evergreens, with distaste.

I leant against Jaunty's strong bay shoulder and made up my mind. I must and *would* find out who had killed my two agents and had presumably tried to poison me, as well.

Preferably before they tried again.

THIRTEEN
Following the Scent

'I have been convalescent long enough,' I said bracingly, next morning. It was an effort to sound determined but I made myself do it. 'I think the first step is to interview the carter with the unruly horses.'

'Not you, madam,' said Brockley. 'Leave the carter to me. He may be rough-spoken, or aggressive. And Okehampton is too long a ride for you yet. So you can stay in the shadows for a little longer.'

He was gone all the next day. He returned before supper, tired but visibly pleased with himself. As he sat on a stool in my room, his hat on his knee, while Dale dragged his riding boots off, he said: 'It wasn't too difficult. Not at all difficult, in fact.'

I put my book aside and Joyce put down her embroidery. We waited.

'I went into the Castle Inn,' he said. 'I got into conversation with a group of local men, bought them some drinks, gossiped, said what a grim experience it must have been for that poor fellow who was driving the horses that ran away and killed Peter Gray. After a little while, I got the name of the carter. Ned Hethercott, that was it.

'One of the men I was talking to said he'd been at the inquest on Gray and poor old Ned had cut a sorry figure, obviously frightened half out of his wits, saying that that flea-bitten mare of his was allus skittish; a pigeon goes up under her great big hooves and her'll carry on like someone's thrown a cannonball at her . . .'

Brockley's imitation of the Devon accent was so good that it made us all laugh. I recalled that when I first knew him, Brockley had had a country accent. It had faded over time but evidently came back on demand when required.

When our hilarity had subsided, he said: 'It had half the men in the Castle laughing too and then someone said wasn't Ned that fellow with the great big family that lives at the far end of Robbs Lane . . .'

'Robbs Lane again!' I said.

'Not significant, I think. A lot of people live in Robbs Lane,' said Brockley. 'Anyway, I left the inn and went to find Hethercott. His home is an untidy hovel of a place, right at the end of the lane, and there's a horde of children and a big, buxom Mistress Hethercott. The eldest child still at home is a girl of fourteen and they're looking for somewhere where she can go into service. There are two older girls already out in service. One of the boys will eventually work with his father; the others will be packed off to be grooms somewhere as soon as they're old enough. It's the only way families like that can survive. It was midday and Hethercott himself was home for his dinner. Looking down in the mouth, too. I gathered that business is bad, on account of the accident. Folk don't trust him the way they did. He's a short, thin fellow, the opposite of his wife.' He caught my eye and from the wicked glint in his, I concluded that he was visualizing the Hethercotts' love-life. So was I. We didn't comment, however. Brockley said: 'It seems he isn't employed by one man; he carts loads for anyone that needs things shifted. The day Gray was killed, he'd collected building materials, planks or something, he couldn't rightly recall, to be delivered to somewhere outside Okehampton. He can't now remember just where, either. But he said he was just starting off with them when, as the man in the Castle Inn said, a pigeon shot up from under the hooves of his flea-bitten mare, and she panicked and charged off, dragging her team mate and the laden cart with her.

'I told him,' said Brockley, 'that Peter Gray had relatives who were anxious to know more about his accident. His story seemed odd to me. Pigeons are getting in amongst traffic all the time, and getting out of the way with a flapping of wings often enough and it's a funny sort of horse that's out on the roads every day and isn't used to them. And if a man found he'd got a horse that just won't get used to them, well, he's a funny sort of driver that wouldn't get rid of a liability like that and buy something with more sense. He had plenty to say about the pigeon but he was muddleheaded about the load he was carrying and where he was taking it. Or even where he'd picked it up. So, madam, I'm sorry to say, I got him to walk with me outside the hovel and – I bullied him.'

'Dear, dear,' I said.

'Gray is dead,' said Joyce quietly.

'I know,' I said. 'All right, Brockley, what did you succeed in bullying out of him?'

'I was brutal,' said Brockley. 'I said that Master Gray's relatives – I gave the impression that they were people of standing – were not satisfied with his testimony at the inquest and believed he'd been paid to be on hand, waiting for Peter to be first made drunk and then pushed out of the inn, so that he could run him down. But if he would confess and say who paid him, they would be merciful. They would be willing to make a deal – the names of those who purchased Gray's death in exchange for not hounding Hethercott.

'I said that no doubt the people who wanted Gray dead had ways of forcing a poor man like Ned Hethercott into agreeing to their plot. They were the ones who should be brought to justice. But anyone who shielded them would probably go to the gallows with them. We were in his vegetable patch with a double line of bean poles between us and the house. No one could see us so his wife wouldn't rush out to his defence. I reckon she was capable of it! I was free to bully and threaten and I did, until Ned burst into tears and went down on his knees to me. Then I got the truth.'

He had been right to insist that I left the carter to him. I could not have done as he had. 'And?' I said.

'He wasn't driving the cart at all that day,' said Brockley. 'He was paid, but not to run Peter Gray over. Just to let someone else do his job for a day. A man he didn't know approached him and said it was a bet. The man was well dressed, he said, and well spoken. The sort that Ned Hethercott might be nervous of, I think. He told Ned that someone had bet him that he couldn't do an honest day's work. So Hethercott let him hire the cart for one day. He charged for the hire and the fellow paid without any argument. Ned warned him about the mare being skittish. He was horrified to hear that his cart had run someone down but he thought it was an accident.'

'It must have been a most unpleasant piece of news,' I said.

'He got frightened at the inquest, it seems,' Brockley said. 'He thought perhaps it was against the law to hire out a cart as he had done, without making sure whoever it was could drive it properly. I don't think it's really against the law though if he'd admitted it at the inquest, I expect the coroner would have said some sharp things. I fancy Ned was paid well. With all those hungry mouths at home, he was probably glad of it. I took a look at his horses on my way out, by the way. Said I'd been a groom, which is true, and was interested. They're big, strong animals, built for pulling loads. I wouldn't like to be in the way if they bolted. Or were thrown at me, as it were.'

'It was murder, all right,' I said.

Dale sat back on her heels, holding Brockley's boots, and said: 'But did the man who paid Hethercott give no name?'

'No,' said Brockley. 'And Hethercott is ignorant; he didn't think to ask. Are we any further on? Not much, I fear. We know how the so-called accident was arranged, and that's all. Apart from saying the fellow was well dressed and spoke pretty, Nethercott couldn't describe him.'

He stood up, shedding his cloak. Dale promptly whisked hat, cloak and boots away to their quarters. As she came back, Brockley remarked: 'There's something else I wanted to mention, madam. Are you not in need of more help in the house, since we lost Netta?'

'Even before,' I said. 'She was only able to come in for a few hours each day. She used to leave the children with the wives of the two married grooms at the trotters' stud, but with a third one expected . . . well, that was going to cause difficulties.'

'I mentioned the eldest Hethercott child just now,' said Brockley. 'The girl aged fourteen. Strong-looking like her mother, and bright as polished silver. Her name is Bess. Whatever her father's been up to, she's not responsible. Suppose we take her on?'

'She's very young,' I said. 'Our little maid Lucy was as young as that – remember her? But she was so homesick that we had

to send her back to her parents. It can be a mistake to take them
at that age.'

'This one isn't likely to be homesick,' Brockley said. 'She's
been reared to know that she'll have to leave home as soon
as she's anything like old enough and I doubt if she'd pine for
that grimy, overcrowded place anyway! And as I said, she's
bright. Lucy wasn't.'

'I will consider it,' I said. 'But not now. We have our next
task to tackle. We need to know if either Gray or Reeves left
any notes behind. They could hold the answer to everything.
Today is nearly gone. We start on that tomorrow.'

I knew now where Gray had lived, but didn't know who was
there instead. I wondered if they would really let me go through
any notebooks or letters that he had left behind. However, there
was no point in being defeated before I began.

All the others wanted to come, of course, and at first, I
objected.

'This is a matter of business. I can very properly have a
male escort but why would I want two female companions? I
think Dale and Joyce should stay behind.'

'But we want to come,' said Joyce, and Dale pointed out that
she could do the ride now that she had Brown Betsy. They both
gazed at me beseechingly, and I gave in.

Larkhurst stood on a low hill that resembled a piece of
Dartmoor that had been displaced and put down on the other
side of the Okehampton track. We rode up a slanting path
through heather and grass, under a wide sky, and I remarked
that it was well named for it was a likely place for larks. In
summer, that sky would be full of their music. Brockley
wondered aloud where the smallholding was that Gray was
supposed to possess. The house was obvious enough, he said,
pointing, but where was the rest of it?

The house was a grey stone building with a massive air,
as though it had once been part of a Norman castle. The front
door, at the top of a flight of steps, had surely been designed
to withstand a siege. It had an iron latch and a brass knocker
shaped like a lion's head.

'What now?' enquired Joyce. 'Do we just knock on the door?'

'I can't think of anything else to do,' I said. 'Brockley . . .'

Brockley was already out of his saddle and passing his reins to Joyce. He walked up the steps, seized the lion's head and knocked, twice and loudly.

We waited. After a while, Brockley tried again. Again there was no reply. Brockley lifted the latch and pushed. The door opened.

'That's a surprise,' I said, and slipped out of my saddle.

Brockley had stepped inside and was shouting, 'Anyone home?' Only silence answered. He returned down the steps and said: 'There's no one here. If there was, they must have heard me.'

He looked at me and from the gleam in his eyes, I knew that Brockley's latent adventurousness had once more awoken. 'Madam, we would of course be trespassing, but if you feel that this search is urgent enough, I think we can take a chance and just go in.'

'I do think it's urgent,' I said. 'Now, Dale and Joyce, I didn't leave you behind when we started out but I really think I had better do so now. That way, if we are found searching the house, well, all you will have done is stand outside and hold the horses.'

'I wouldn't want to come in, ma'am,' said Dale with feeling. 'But I wouldn't like to wait alone either. If Mistress Joyce doesn't mind . . .'

'I don't mind at all. I don't like the idea of tiptoeing through someone else's house and reading old notebooks without permission,' said Joyce, also with feeling. 'Somehow I took it for granted that someone would be here!'

As Brockley and I started up the steps, I heard her say: 'You've known them for years, Dale. Is this a kind of madness that overtakes them now and then?'

I turned round. 'At night,' I said, 'I like to sleep with the bedcurtains looped back and I love to sleep in the light of the full moon and everyone knows what that can do!'

'Come, madam,' Brockley said, stifling amusement. 'We have business to deal with.'

The place *felt* unoccupied. A stone staircase faced the front door and somehow seemed to lead only into shadows and emptiness. We decided to start with the ground floor. First, we found ourselves in a parlour of sorts. This at once convinced us that this house really had been part of a castle. The windows were glazed but they were tall and narrow and pierced through what was evidently a very thick wall. Adapted arrow slits, in fact.

The parlour was poorly furnished and dusty with disuse. The settle had no cushions, the walls were bare stone, without panelling, without even the small homemade wall-hangings that the wives of poor men usually make to brighten their surroundings. There was a hearth, not large, and empty.

The next room was a badly kept dining chamber. There was another cold hearth and on the sideboard there were piles of earthenware dishes and cups, mostly chipped, and someone had scratched a chequerboard pattern on the dining table. Hot dishes had apparently been put down on it, too, and scorched what should have been the polished surface.

In both rooms we looked in such cupboards and drawers as we found, but they were all empty. 'Someone's done some clearing out,' I said. 'Someone has been here even if they don't live here.'

'Where's the kitchen?' said Brockley.

The kitchen had a trivet and a cauldron and a small spit; enough for one chicken or one joint. There was a shelf with pots and pans on it, some knives and skewers in a drawer beneath the shelf, spoons of various sizes in another. It had a fair-sized hearth, but this too was empty. We found a larder with a small loaf of rye bread and some cold, cooked sausages in it.

'This is *someone*'s midday snack,' said Brockley.

'Well, whoever it is, isn't here,' I said. 'We had better face that shadowy staircase and see what's upstairs.'

On the next floor, we found three bedchambers. Each contained a single bed with straw mattresses but no hangings or canopies. On each mattress was a pile of folded bedlinen and a coverlet. In each room too there was a clothes press and a chest. They were all empty.

'If anyone is here they're living a bleak kind of life,' I said. I stood still, listening. 'What's that? Brockley! I'm sure I heard something.'`

'It's only Joyce and Dale talking down below. Let's see what's at the top.'

At the top we found some small attic rooms. Most were completely empty except for dust and cobwebs but one held a small table which like the dining table downstairs was scratched and scorch-marked. There was also a stool which should have had three legs but actually had only two and a half, and an old chest with iron hoops and a rounded top. It wasn't fastened in any way and I threw back the top without difficulty. Inside, there were documents tied into bundles. 'Ah!' I said.

I said it too soon. We took everything out and put it on the table. There were three bundles. I pulled off the twine round the biggest one and it only took me a few minutes to find that it consisted of invoices and receipts, all older than five years ago, and referring to sales of produce and the purchase of agricultural tools.

'Disappointing,' I said. I looked round to find that Brockley was peering out of the window, another adapted arrow slit. 'I've found the smallholding,' he said.

I joined him and looked out on to an expanse of vegetables, in orderly rows, stretching well away from the rear of the building. Beyond was what looked like an orchard.

'There's no livestock here,' I said. 'But by the look of those vegetables, someone is weeding them.'

Brockley left the window and opened the second bundle of documents. 'This one is letters, all old, I think. Some of them seem to be rough drafts of letters that Gray presumably sent as fair copies. *To Master Henry Atbridge, greetings from Master Peter Gray. I agree to your terms for the young boar. I will bring the payment and collect the boar on the tenth of this month.* Oh, and here's a thrilling item. Dated two years back. *To Mistress Mary Alton, greeting from Master Peter Gray, I regret that three of the dozen eggs you bought from me last week were addled but I cannot see through eggshells. It is a case of Caveat Emptor.* Gray clearly had some education. I wonder if Mary Alton, whoever she is, knows any Latin or if he was just using it to quell her . . . oh, yes, here's the letter she sent, complaining about the addled eggs and there's another complaining that there was a rotten onion in the basket of onions that he delivered two days ago – just one onion in a basketful; really! The date is four years back – and here's another – oh, this is a good one – saying that she can't understand why when he delivered the cabbages and eggs to her yesterday, he came in the afternoon instead of the morning as usual. She was not present when he arrived and he will therefore not receive payment until his next delivery, when she hopes he will come at the proper time. She sounds as if writing letters of complaint was her favourite occupation. Still is, perhaps.'

He paused briefly while he flicked through the rest of the bundle and then put it down, shaking his head. 'Everything here is letters from customers and a few drafts of letters too, madam, and they're all some years old.'

I came back to the table and pulled the twine off the third bundle, which fell apart in my hands. It consisted of a mixture of letters and invoices and these were all so old that the paper had become brittle. Some of the pages broke when I touched them.

'If Gray made any notes about his other work,' I said, 'then I don't think they're here. Yes, disappointing.'

'If I knew what kind of notes you were looking for,' said a very polite voice from the doorway, 'maybe I could help.'

We turned round. A young man was standing just inside the door. He was a handsome fellow, with curly brown hair and amiable light-brown eyes, and strong, square features, bronzed by an outdoor life. He was neatly dressed in a brown doublet and hose, though with an open-necked shirt and without a ruff. He might be a farmer, I thought, but he was no hired labourer.

'I won't insult you by assuming you'm criminals,' he said. He had a Devon accent but not a strong one. 'The women I found holding horses outside look like a well-bred young lady and her maid,' he said, 'and they horses are something, too.'

He paused, smiling and taking us in: me in my good blue-wool riding dress, neat ruff and blue hat with a feather in it; Brockley in his military-looking buff doublet and hose and his matching hat and polished boots.

'We have legitimate business here,' I said. 'And we only entered as we did because no one answered when Brockley knocked. I am Mistress Ursula Stannard and this is Roger Brockley, my manservant. May we know who you are?'

'My name's Pascal Bryers. I'm a bailiff for Master Miles Baines, who's taken this place over. I've been keeping it in order for him until he finds a tenant.'

'Pascal?' I asked.

'I were born on Easter Sunday.' He sounded as though he had to answer that question rather too often. 'Now, your business here? You spoke of Gray's other work. What might that be?'

So this was Mildred's indifferent bailiff. Her mother had said she had fallen in love with him when they were visiting Baines. No wonder she preferred him to Baines. If I were a young girl, so would I.

'I am sorry,' I said, 'but my business is confidential. It arose when I was in this district last year. I am seeking certain documents that Master Gray may have left. I asked him to do something for me. But I am not at liberty to say what that something was.'

'You'm taking orders from Sir Francis Walsingham, I take it,' said Bryers, surprisingly. 'All the world's heard of him, and a good few have heard of you, Mistress Stannard. Master Baines recognized your name when he met you a day or two ago.'

He grinned, a very attractive grin, I thought, and I could understand the effect it had probably had on Mildred. 'If Master Gray's other work was mixed up with what's called affairs of state, I wouldn't care to know about those,' Bryers informed us. 'I'd be afeard of running into trouble. However . . .'

He paused, while still surveying us with interest and then said: 'You'm a strange party to be concerning yourselves with state affairs. A group of ladies, I mean. I was here, weeding and that, and just taking a last look round when I came face to face with those two downstairs. I can't imagine either of them as interested in state papers. I envy you those horses. I wish my roan mare was as good. Hairy heels and straight shoulders, that's her. But she does my work well enough. Well, little as I would want to hear about affairs of state, I suppose I must ask if I can help you any further?'

I said: 'Did Master Gray leave any other documents besides

these?' I tied the twine round the bundle of old letters and put it back in the chest. 'More recent ones? Perhaps notes, lists—'

'He left a few recent papers,' Bryers said. 'Left 'em down-stairs in his parlour. They weren't notes or lists, though. Nothing that could be of interest to you – or Sir Francis Walsingham. I've given everything to Master Baines. There was an accounts ledger; otherwise it was all bills and receipts and half a dozen letters. I looked through 'em – there was one axin' was there a chance of a sucking pig for someone's birthday dinner, and a letter from someone called Mary Alton, complaining that the basket of radishes he'd delivered didn't amount to the weight she'd ordered . . . what are you laughing at?'

'We've found several letters of complaint from her,' said Brockley. 'We think it's a way she has of amusing herself.'

'Ah. There are people like that,' said Pascal. 'All the rest was orders for things, and one, two years old, from Master Gray's sister, saying that she had just had a son. The sister's a widow now, lives in Dorset and doesn't want Larkhurst. She couldn't sell to Master Baines fast enough. There was no hindrance, seemingly. She was his only living relative and his will left everything to her. No one stopped her from having it cried for sale, and Master Baines snapped it up.

'I see,' I said. Whatever Gray had been doing that had fright-ened someone into killing him, he had left no record of it here.

'I think we should start for home now,' I said.

'I ought to offer you some refreshment,' said Pascal. 'But there's next to no food in the house barring my noon snack.'

We thanked him and took our leave. As we rode away, Brockley remarked: 'We have only his word for it that the papers he gave to Miles Baines would be no use to us.'

'We shall see Baines soon,' I said. 'We'll ask him.'

FOURTEEN
Unanswered Questions

I was beginning to doubt if we would really find any notes, left by either Gray or Reeves. A distant memory had now surfaced, that I had warned both of them against writing down any suspicions they might have.

Reeves had certainly taken that advice. The day after our visit to Larkhurst, Brockley and I rode off on Jaunty and Firefly, who were fast and stayers, to make it there and back in a one day visit to Okehampton to enquire. Dale dithered over letting me undertake such a ride so soon but my strength had returned and I wanted to do what I must and get on with it. It was Dale and Joyce who had to stay behind. Neither Patches nor Brown Betsy could have managed the journey at the speed we intended, and Dale couldn't have ridden so far anyway, even on an ambler. She hated it when I rode off anywhere alone with Brockley, and Joyce would have enjoyed the expedition but there was no help for it.

We found Andrew Reeves once more beside a loom, but not working it. Instead, he was ranting at the young man who should have been, but was now listening contritely to Andrew. Well, fairly contritely. He was finding it hard to suppress an impudent grin. He was a strapping young fellow and would have been strikingly handsome if so much of his face hadn't been hidden by wildly unkempt black hair. Master Reeves seemed to hold a similar opinion for as we came up to him, I heard him remarking acidly that *one of these days, Hal Gurney, you'll get that hair of yours caught in the loom and woven into the cloth and then where will you be?*

The young man apologized, in a tone which didn't sound at all apologetic and then Andrew Reeves noticed me and Brockley.

'You're back again? What are you after this time? Gurney, get on with your work!' He led us away from Gurney's loom towards the back of the workshop, where the noise of the looms was a little less, and then said: 'Pardon my bad temper. Gurney is a brilliant weaver but he is so damned impertinent that at times I could kick him. I only keep him on because his work is so good. Better than mine and I've been at it since I was seven years old. What can I do for you?'

This time, honesty seemed best. I told Master Reeves frankly that Gregory had been employed to seek for traces of plots to assist Mary Stuart, and that I was empowered to find out if he had left any notes about his work.

'Ah,' said Reeves. 'It's no surprise. You're the queen's kin, ain't you, Mistress Stannard? These things get known.'

'I didn't think this was so widely known,' I said, taken aback.

'No? You're the subject of tales that mothers tell to their children. The Adventures of Mistress Stannard – oh, yes, though I think they discourage their daughters from taking you as an example! I recognized your name right away but reckoned you might not want me mentioning it. Now it seems you're saying you're here on the queen's business. Got that right, haven't I? So I can take it that it's honest business. Yes?'

'I don't know how to prove it,' I said, 'but it is honest, yes.'

Andrew hesitated and then took what was plainly a plunge, like a dive into cold water. 'You think, don't you, that he was murdered. Tricked into going on to the moor and then . . . well, don't you?'

'I'm afraid so, Master Reeves.'

'I feared it. At the inquest, crowner suspected it. There weren't no proof of that and in the end, the inquest said accident, getting lost on the moor, but Gregory wasn't that sort of a fool. You going to try and find out about that too?'

'I mean to try, yes. And if his papers contain any notes about his secret work, that could point a finger at his killer or killers.'

'I never thought about his papers; I'm not a man for documents. His wife has them but no doubt she'll let you see them. Say I sent you. Can I help in any other way?'

'May I ask some questions?'

'Aye. Hope I know some answers.'

'Just when did Gregory leave his work on that day? I would like to be clear about what *exactly* happened.'

'It was January and getting dark early and we don't work after dark. Flambeaux and candles are too dangerous for a place like this here, with bales of wool everywhere, and they don't give light enough anyhow nor lamps or lanterns neither. So we stopped mid-afternoon, like, and that's when he said goodbye and I reckoned he'd gone to saddle up to go home to Sally. That was the last time I saw him, till he was brought home, dead.'

I was silent, hearing the grief in his voice. But Brockley said: 'This will be painful to answer but it could be worthwhile. You knew your son. If he *had* had a message from the woman Jane Leigh, or one that seemed to come from her, would he really be likely to respond to it?'

We were interrupted briefly as Hal Gurney, who had left his loom while we were talking, came past us with a basket full of hanks of orange yarn, tripped on something and spilt his basket. Orange hanks tumbled everywhere.

'Pick those up!' Andrew thundered at him. 'And if you'd cut that there hair of yourn, Gurney, maybe you could see where you're going!'

Gurney began to crawl about under our feet. Andrew drew us away and said: 'I fear that he might. For old times' sake yes, perhaps. But a message saying to meet that Jane Leigh up on the moor? In bitter weather? That's the part that don't make sense. But afterwards, I did find out that afore Gregory were wed, he sometimes met that woman Jane in an empty cottage on the edge of the moor. Gregory liked a drink in the Castle and so do I and one of his cronies there did some gossiping to me, that's how I know. I recognized the place from what he said about it. It used to be a shepherd's cottage, but the shepherd died and the new man had somewhere of his own and didn't need it. It's no great distance from here; Okehampton itself is on the edge of the moor. Gregory might have gone there, thinking to meet Jane. Young fool!' said Andrew, misery visible.

He swallowed and then went on. 'Well, if he did, and someone else was waiting for him, not Jane, but someone . . . *Gurney!* Leave whatever's still under there and go away! What's still on the floor is too dirty to use until it's washed. I'm sorry,' he added, turning back to us. 'If I'm here in the workshop, I can never take my mind off the work, not for one moment.'

'Someone,' said Brockley, 'could have been waiting for him, someone who felt he was dangerous to them, because he supported Mary Stuart and Gregory had come near to sniffing him out. Or them.'

Andrew nodded. 'Quite. I've been to the cottage. Just to see if there were any traces but there weren't. Well, there might be something useful in, his papers, as you say.' He frowned. 'If someone was waiting for him in that cottage, they'd have had to overpower him. There'd be marks if he'd been bound. He did have a bump and a cut on his head but at first, everyone, me, crowner, everyone, reckoned he'd got that when he was thrown from his horse. It was only afterwards that I started thinking and wondering. It was the cold as killed him, anyhow; no one ever thought different. About his papers. You'll find his wife with her parents. Should be here with me and Joan, and we're going to insist on that afore the little one's born. It'll be our grandchild. If it's a boy, he'll inherit this place and if it's a girl, I hope she'll marry a fellow who'll keep it going. If Sally wants to wed again, we'll help her, but we hope she'll leave the child with us. Likely it'll be better that way; men don't all want to be stepfathers.'

'It's rather soon to be thinking about her next marriage!' said Brockley, mildly protesting.

'Aye, I suppose so.' The sounds of some other hitch in the work reached him from a distance and he showed signs of wishing to attend to it. 'Anyhow,' he said, 'for the moment, she's in the home of her girlhood. I hope she's still got all his papers; don't know what she'll make of them; girl can hardly read or write. We were going to teach her. We still will, if she'll come back to us. She ought to be here.'

The conversation seemed to end, but although Andrew was hovering, with one ear bent towards whatever the trouble was on the other side of the workshop, still I sensed that he had something on his mind. I looked at him enquiringly.

'There's one queer thing about all this,' he said. 'Least, it seems right queer to me.'

'Yes?' Brockley and I said it together.

'I go to the Castle for a drink now and again, like I said. I know Barratt, the landlord. I heard about that fellow Peter Gray, killed in an accident just outside the inn. I also heard that you, Master Brockley, had asked questions about Gray's death, and that you, Mistress Stannard, were nearly poisoned there.' He smiled at our surprise. 'Everyone who goes to the Castle Inn as a habit knows all that by now! The accident to Gray, whoever he was, sounded as unlikely as my son's death, and you fall sick straight after asking questions about it.'

'I asked the questions really,' said Brockley. 'I talked to Barratt.'

'Same thing. You're Mistress Stannard's manservant. It's weird.' He seemed to be following a train of thought. 'It's haphazard, like. How do you arrange for a team of horses to bolt at just the right moment – and Gray might have dodged, however drunk he was. My boy might have ignored a message. And you . . . well, with you, if what happened to you was an attempt to kill you, it didn't work, did it, because here you are, still alive and well. That's all. You'd best go and see Sally now.'

'Where do Sally and her family live?' I asked, wondering if once again we would be directed to Robbs Lane.

We weren't. The parents of the younger Mistress Reeves had a house at one end of Fore Street. Reeves directed us and then dismissed us, turning back to business. We set off.

Sally's parents didn't mind when we asked to speak to her, once we had explained that we had permission from Andrew Reeves.

'Time she went back there,' said her mother. She was plump and cosy but sounded grumpy. Probably she didn't want a gravid widowed daughter returning home like a tennis ball in a volley, needing attention and being another mouth to feed. 'Reeves are her family now and so I keep telling her. Come in.'

We did so, and were shown into a parlour where Gregory's widow, a small figure dressed in black, was stitching what looked like baby garments.

It was a short interview. Little Sally Reeves had some papers left by Gregory and her father had examined them, told her what was in them and said they were of no importance. She'd kept them because they were his and her father had also said to her, never destroy papers; she could fetch them for us if we liked . . .

We did like, but Sally's father was right; they were of no importance. There was a rough draft of a letter about buying a copy of Geoffrey Chaucer's *Canterbury Tales* and there were the usual bills for personal things: the purchase of a new hat, a bridle for his horse, the repair of a boot and so forth. Bills to do with the weaving business were presumably Andrew's province. There was one letter from Sally, who evidently could read and write up to a point, but was no great hand at it. She expressed affection and eagerness for their wedding. Her mother came into the room just then and saw what I was looking at.

'There, Sal, that's the letter you sent him just afore the wedding and you cried over it when we found it, because he'd kept it and that's proof he really cared about you, and not about *her*, that other one . . .'

And then she stopped, flustered. 'It's all right,' I said, 'I've heard about Gregory's earlier affair. But most young men have someone like that in their pasts. They don't marry them. It's different when they find the right girl for marriage.'

'Jane Leigh is married right enough but I doubt she's much of a wife from all I've heard,' said Sally's mother with a sniff. 'Her husband's at sea most of the time and when he do come home, no one's going to tell him aught; folk don't make trouble for each other around here.'

There was nothing else. We thanked Sally and her mother and they asked us to stay a little, and take some cider and honeycakes. It was clear when we did so that Sally just wanted to talk about Gregory, how much she missed him, and what a dear he had been. Now and then she patted her stomach, where his child was growing. She was no more than sixteen, I thought, and pale, as though she rarely went outdoors. Her hair was fair, judging by the few strands that had escaped her black, concealing hood.

'You should not prolong your mourning too much,' I said to her gently. 'You would be better at home in your own cottage, or with Joan Reeves. You don't dislike her, do you?'

'No, I don't; we get on well,' said Sally wanly. 'But when it happened – I was frightened. I wanted my home . . . this home. I mean . . .'

'Your home is with the Reeves family now,' her mother said, in a persistent tone, as though she had said it many times before, which was probably so. 'The cottage is only rented; you should give it up and move in with the Reeves like they've asked you to.'

'You'll be happier there,' said Brockley. 'Believe me.'

We left it at that, said thank you for the refreshments and made for home, planning to take a meal in Tavistock on the way. 'Poor little thing,' I said to Brockley as we mounted our horses.

'Poor us!' said Brockley. 'What do we do next?'

'I think,' I said, 'that we look at an empty cottage on the edge of the moor. Andrew Reeves said there was nothing there but I would still like to see it. He said it was no great distance from his workshop. I expect we can find it without worrying him again.'

We found it easily. It really was right on the edge of the moor, for the first heathery slope of Dartmoor began only a few feet away from it, and swept up to a distant skyline, crowned by naked rocks, as if by a battlement. The cottage itself was a sorry sort of place with tufted thatch and a front door hanging crookedly on its hinges. The door opened straight into the first of the two rooms. The second one was behind it, and there was only a leather curtain to fill the doorway between.

The place had never had glazed windows. There were shutters, and inner windows made of semi-transparent animal skin. The untidy thatch was leaking; in one corner of the front room, damp was streaming down the wall and – ugh! – a patch of mushrooms was growing on the plank floor. Some of the planks were rotting. But there were some pieces of old furniture and in the back room there was a bed with a straw mattress on it and a sheepskin cover, in reasonably good condition.

'It's quite possibly the place where they met,' I said. 'Though it's a squalid love-nest by my standards. But it doesn't tell us whether Gregory came here in January or not.'

'It's all questions and no answers, it seems to me,' said Brockley.

FIFTEEN
The Wrong Romance

Our invitation to dine at Baines' home was for the next day and I would have thought it a waste of time and tried to get out of it, except that Baines had the rest of Peter Gray's papers and although I didn't expect much if anything to come of it, I still wanted to see them if I could.

As soon as Brockley and I had returned from our exhausting double journey, we found that Joyce and Dale had asked for a cold supper to be served in our quarters. While we ate, we talked.

'Going to see Miles Baines may be useful,' I said. 'But after that, I'd like to find out more about Crispin Hanley's charity for orphans. I'd like to know where the money he raises is really going. We should have tackled that before.'

'We have been following other scents,' said Brockley reasonably. 'At speed and over considerable distances, if I may say so, madam. Even Firefly is tired.'

'I know,' I said. 'Eddie's smouldering with disapproval. We brought them in sweating.'

'And I heard you, madam, coaxing Jaunty to eat up his bran mash like a good boy,' Brockley said.

'I *like* saying goodnight to him. There are worse habits! I don't really suspect Crispin. If he was the manservant who doctored my cider, I think I would have recognized him. Those teeth!'

'But we know there must be two of them,' said Joyce. 'The other one probably played the serving man.'

While I was at Okehampton, Joyce and Dale had made a start on our new gown for Mildred but it wasn't finished and in any case, beguiling Miles was not our intention. The next day, Mildred, therefore, was once again arrayed in dove grey.

Her parents were both in black, as usual, though as this was supposed to be a happy occasion, Henry Gresham's doublet had silver buttons and silvery slashings for sleeves and hose, while Catherine's sleeves had some discreet white slashings.

We set off in good time, for we couldn't ride fast. I was more wearied by our one-day visit to Okehampton than I wanted to admit and the horses were still tired too. Also, the day was wet, with fine drizzling rain that blurred the moorland out of sight and turned the track to mud. We all had stout cloaks and were glad of them. It passed, however, just as we neared Baines' House. The moors reappeared and a gleam of sunlight surprised us by displaying the house as unexpectedly beautiful, half-timbered, with patterned red-brick chimneys and a thatched roof which must have been lately renewed, for the thatch was still golden.

But it stood all alone on a heathery hillside. A few fields stretched up the slope behind it but they were dwarfed by the bleak expanses beyond and around them. Where the breaking clouds still cast their shadows, the heather was sombre, and the grey rock outcrops were like the teeth of some underground monster. The house resembled a piece of jewellery that had been accidentally dropped in the street. Henry Gresham had told us that it had no name beyond being known as Baines' House.

'We approve,' Catherine Gresham said. 'So unpretentious. Our house has no name either – everyone just calls it the Greshams' place.'

Miles Baines had seen us approach and was standing in the front doorway to greet us, jowly as a mastiff, tree-trunk legs stoutly apart, his torso encased in a mustard-coloured doublet with pale green embroidery and pearl buttons straining over his paunch. Grooms came running to take our horses. We dismounted and Baines came to meet us. He kissed Mildred's reluctant hand and led us inside.

Baines' House had a real great hall – quite unlike the Hillmans' miniature one. This too was beautiful, panelled in a pale wood, with a wide hearth and two big tapestries on its walls, depicting festively dressed men and women riding through a wood, and a lively hunting scene. A broad staircase, lit by a

high stained-glass window, led up from one corner; fresh rushes
were strewn on the floor, mingled, my nose informed me, with
lavender and rosemary, and the ornate silver salt on the dining
table was reflected in a tabletop which had been polished like
a mirror.

Two maidservants now came forward to divest us of our
cloaks and hats, and a masterful steward with a drooping
grey moustache was commanding a third to hide the gleaming
table top beneath a white damask cloth. This maidservant was
younger than the others and very pretty and when she had her
back to the steward she glared openly at Mildred.

'I don't think Baines has been living like a monk since
he was widowed,' muttered Brockley, taking care that the
Greshams couldn't hear him.

'How will Mistress Mildred deal with that?' Dale whispered
back.

'I could deal with it,' Joyce muttered. 'But I doubt if Mildred
could, unless he does it for her.'

We were now being led on towards a panelled door at the
other end of the hall. Here we found a parlour where cider and
wine awaited us. 'To get you warm after the cold ride you've
had,' said Baines jovially. The steward came in with a tray of
snacks. And then, surprisingly, Baines turned to me.

'Mistress Stannard, my bailiff says he met you by chance
the other day and that you are interested in seeing any
papers that were left by a man called Peter Gray. I knew him
slightly. He died recently and I have bought his smallholding,
Larkhurst, as I understand you know. I took his latest papers
away in a box and I have put the box out on a table in the
next room. In there.' He pointed to a low door opposite
the door from the hall. 'I haven't looked at the papers myself.
I am always busy and I haven't had time. I haven't removed
any, either.' He let out a chesty laugh. 'Let me know if you
find anything of interest.'

Much taken aback, I thanked him. He smiled. 'Mistress
Stannard, I realize that I have had the pleasure of entertaining
the half-sister of the queen and I know you sometimes, well,
carry out tasks for her.'

'Oh? Indeed?' I said, wondering how many more people were

going to say that to me and whether there was anyone left in the world who didn't know who I was and all about the duties I tried to keep so secret.

'Yes. Indeed. I take it that you need to see Master Gray's papers as part of some official business. So do please examine them.'

I could do nothing but curtsey, while the Greshams stared, much astonished. I then took Brockley and Joyce with me into the next room to look at the box, as suggested.

It was as I expected. Gray's latest papers consisted of invoices, receipts, a letter from an ironmonger saying that the new spades and hoes he had ordered were ready, some other letters from his regular customers concerning their contracts with him, and, naturally, a letter of complaint from Mary Alton, about a late delivery of capons.

'Dead end,' I said regretfully, and led the way back to the parlour, where we thanked Master Baines again for his helpfulness, partook of the snacks the steward had brought and I admitted to the Greshams that yes, I was related to the queen and sometimes undertook privy tasks for her. Then the steward reappeared to say that dinner was ready and the subject, thank goodness, was dropped.

The dinner was good, and deftly served. Over the main course, Baines enlarged to Mildred on the kind of life she would have in the Baines' place, indoors and out.

It then became plain to me – and probably to everyone else except Baines himself – that Mildred found the prospect of being in charge of Baines' House quite as alarming as she found Baines himself. He was obviously cultivated enough to appreciate a beautiful home (though I suspected that his late wife had created it and that he merely maintained it) and it also sounded as though he knew all that could be known about sheep. But in other ways he was obtuse. He didn't seem to realize that with almost every sentence that he uttered, he was terrifying his intended bride more.

Mildred need not work with her hands, he said. She need not cook meals or polish the furniture. She would only have to instruct the servants in whatever she wished them to do. His steward, Stacey, would be happy to have a mistress for the house. The steward, who was at the sideboard, carving a beef joint, bowed.

'I like my home to be polished and sweetly scented and I like my food to be good,' Miles said. 'I hope you will enjoy the rice dish that is to be offered as well as the beef. My cook invented it himself; chicken, cooked on a spit, cut up, served with a spicy sauce poured over it and surrounded by rice with saffron in it. Planning my meals will be your task, though other hands will carry out your orders. I hope to enjoy new dishes that you know about, and I have not met before.'

'Our daughter has been reared on plain, simple food,' Catherine Gresham said at this point, but Baines merely laughed and said that perhaps he would give her a chance to spread her wings. Mildred looked horrified. I wondered whether, plain and simple food apart, she had ever given an order in her life. She was accustomed to help Tilly rather than command her. Baines didn't notice. He had now gone on to talk about his accounts. He would be glad of her help with those. They would mostly concern sales of wool, but he bought and sold sheep as well. Considerable sums were involved; it would be interesting work. Mildred's expression had by now become blank with fright. No doubt, Mr Gresham looked after his family's finances. Mildred had probably never set eyes on a ledger.

And of course, said Miles, he sometimes needed help with the lambing. He had noticed that Mildred had slender hands with long slim fingers. Once in a while a ewe had trouble because a lamb had a forefoot bent back or something like that, and a slender hand was ideal for straightening out bent legs without hurting the ewe too much . . .

I had read Joyce's book with its account of Hannibal taking elephants over the Alps. I knew what kind of animals they were. Miles Baines, I thought, had all the tact of an elephant trampling through a cornfield. At the mention of lambing, Mildred had turned so pale that I feared she might actually faint. I almost wondered if Miles were trying to discourage her on purpose; perhaps he had changed his mind about the marriage but didn't want to say so. But then I looked at him again and knew that he hadn't; he really thought that he was describing a busy and useful life that he thought Mildred would like. And now he had got on to the subject of children.

'Of course, when we have a family, you will want to attend to them. I think that when we know a child is coming, you should find a competent housekeeper. I will leave that to you. I hope to make you happy and also make you the mother of many fine sons and pretty daughters.'

The attractive maidservant, who was just then offering sauces, glanced at the back of Mildred's head as though she would like to hit it with the sauce boat. Mildred, cringing in her chair, seemed to sense the hostility behind her. She waved the sauce nervously away and then was obliged to eat her roast beef without it. Her hands were trembling.

When the meal was over, Baines said he would show Mildred everything she needed to know. He would take her on a quick ride round his farm – thank goodness the sun was now out – and he would show her the lambing pens. Lambing had begun; if they were lucky they might see one come into the world. Then they would come indoors and he would show her the kitchen and introduce her to his cook, and then they would visit the office where he kept his ledgers. He hadn't had time to do so much during her earlier visit.

'And, my dear, I must show you the recipe book my late wife left me. Since she went, I have just chosen things from it, or else given the cook his head, but as I said, I'm sure that for all your mother's modest comments, you will have your own ideas.

'And of course, she must also see the rest of the house in more detail than last time, and the rooms that might make a nursery . . .'

As he made that last remark, he looked Mildred up and down as though imagining her enceinte with his child. Mildred didn't answer. Presently, he took her away and one of the older maids came to tell us where the necessary house was, for anyone in need of it. After that, we foregathered briefly in the little parlour, until Stacey came in to say that upstairs, in what he called the large parlour, arrangements for our entertainment had been made. If we would like to follow him . . .

As we followed him back into the hall and up the broad

staircase, Catherine said quietly: 'I think Mildred is feeling a
little overwhelmed. I shall talk to her and assure her that she
need not worry. She has been taught all the household arts. She
has only to learn some new recipes and pick up the trick of
instructing others.' I think I then heard Brockley whisper something about whistling in the dark but I couldn't be sure.

The upstairs parlour was comfortable and very warm with a
lively fire in its hearth. There were several small tables where
packs of cards and chess and backgammon sets were arranged,
and there was ample light from some stands bearing branched
candlesticks. In one corner there was a spinet, with a lute hanging
on the wall above it.

We were not, however, invited to make music with them.
Instead, Stacey bade us make use of the games, and waved a
hand at a shelf of books, in case anyone preferred to read.

He left us briefly but came back with one of the maids (not
the young one) bearing trays of flagons, glasses and astonishingly, as if we hadn't just had a hearty dinner, pippin pies, nuts
and raisins and cold sausages. 'There's wine and cider here,'
the steward said. 'Is anything else required?'

Bemusedly, we said no. 'Call my name if you need anything,'
said Stacey austerely and the two of them departed. Mr Gresham
said: 'We don't approve of games. They waste time that could
be better spent and cards especially lead to gambling. Many
lives have been wrecked by gaming debts.'

No one said anything. Mr Gresham realized that his remarks
were out of tune with the rest of us and added: 'But we must
not interfere with others. Catherine and I will read.'

And for the next two hours, they did so, while Brockley
played chess with Joyce, and I played card games with
Dale. And we all wondered silently what was happening to
Mildred.

Eventually, the steward came to fetch us down to the great
hall, as the master and Mistress Mildred were waiting there for
us. There, we found wine and cider and yet another cold repast
– which none of us wanted – awaiting us too. But Baines was
not the expansive host we had first met. He was pacing rest-
lessly about, hands clasped behind his back, and emitting little
puffs of breath between pursed lips, as if annoyed. Mildred,

hands in her lap, was perched on the very edge of a settle and watching him. Her eyes were frightened.

Probably Master Baines had not only terrified her with account books and recipe books and lambs with bent legs; I suspected that he had tried to make love to her as well. Even as the thought crossed my mind, I saw her surreptitiously rub her hand across her mouth, as though to wipe something away. He had probably kissed her. If so, she hadn't enjoyed it. And it looked as though she had angered him.

'Well,' Mr Gresham was saying heartily, 'I am sure Mildred has had a most instructive afternoon, but now, my dear, we must tear you away from your future home and take you back to ours for the time being. You must long for the day when you are the mistress of this beautiful house.'

Mildred drooped but her father ploughed relentlessly on. 'And I am sure that you are now beginning to know your future husband and that you are impatient for your wedding. All in good time. We won't keep you apart for long. I hope . . .'

His voice faded slightly. Even this kind of determined enthusiasm couldn't survive the lack of it in the faces of the betrothed couple. A merciful interruption intervened. The hall door opened and Stacey appeared. 'I am sorry to disturb you, sir, but the bailiff is here with an urgent message. I have told him to wait in your study.'

'Oh, bring him in here,' said Miles impatiently. 'This is a fine opportunity for Mistress Mildred to witness something of daily life here. Yes, yes, bring him in.'

A moment later, Pascal Bryers was walking into the hall, curly head politely bared, cap held in one brown hand, bowing courteously but briefly to the company. At the sight of him, Mildred's face was flooded with crimson, but as he made his bow, his glance slid indifferently over her. He began to explain that the new flock of sheep recently bought by their neighbour Mr Hart had escaped from the pen where he had put them, wandered on to the moor, got onto Mr Baines' land, and mixed themselves up with Mr Baines' flock of yearlings. Mr Hart's shepherd wanted permission to collect all the sheep into a pen belonging to his master, because it was the nearest, where he would sort them out and drive the Baines animals back on to the moor. But the Baines shepherd thought that his master's permission was needed.

'Of course, of course,' said Baines. He turned to Mildred. 'Hales, my shepherd, is a proper old woman. Always wanting me to decide things he could well decide for himself. You will have to do the deciding at times when I am away.'

Mildred avoided his eyes and looked at Pascal instead.

Pascal, however, was attending to his master, who now turned to him. 'Of course I agree, and no, I won't accuse Mr Hart of trying to steal my sheep if I see them being herded into his pen. I know the one you mean; and yes, I know it's handy. All my flock have earmarks. There should be no difficulty in sorting them out.'

'Thank you, sir.' With that, Pascal took his leave. Once again he bowed briefly to the company and once again he paid no heed to Mildred.

Miles glanced after his departing bailiff and remarked: 'Bryers is a good fellow, in his way.'

He added, after noticing that this qualified praise had puzzled us all: 'He needs a wife. In fact, he's looking for one. I rent him a cottage and a patch of ground and he grows wheat and barley enough for his own bread. He'll suit the right young woman.'

Mildred sat still, staring at her hands. Stacey came and hovered, and pressed the refreshments on us. None of us was even remotely hungry, but for politeness' sake, we nibbled a pippin tart or two, washing them down with red Bordeaux wine or the sour, cloudy cider that refreshed the palate but went to one's head with surprising force. At the same time, we made conversation as best we could. I noticed Joyce talking earnestly to Catherine Gresham, and then both of them spoke to Mildred. Mr Gresham sat stiffly alone. I talked to the Brockleys and wished the visit would end.

At last it did. There came a moment when Miles looked out at the sky and said: 'I can see that it is time for me to say goodbye to my guests. But no doubt we will all meet again soon. Stacey!' The steward appeared as if by magic. 'Are the horses ready?' Miles asked.

'Yes, sir.'

'Excellent,' said Miles. 'It will be a cold journey back for you all. Still, you will have a warm house to thaw you and dry you at the end of it. I pity all who have not. Even prisoners, whatever they have done.'

The maidservants had appeared with cloaks, hats and gloves, and in the case of the youngest one, with another scowl for Mildred. We began to array ourselves for the journey but Baines continued to talk.

'I even pity that woman Mary Stuart. A prisoner for so long; it has been hard for her, whatever folk may say. All those years – not far short of twenty, surely – spent in stone castles. I wonder if she is warm in winter. If she is forever plotting to escape, as everyone says she is, one can hardly blame her.'

'I can blame her for wanting to murder my sister and put herself on England's throne,' I said, coldly and boldly and probably encouraged by the cider.

'But is all that true, or is it just tattle? Who is to know?'

My tone hadn't disturbed him at all. I doubt if he noticed it. He was helping Mildred on with her cloak. Dale came to help me with mine. It was high time to leave.

On the way home, Joyce said to me: 'Isn't it strange, that Master Baines actually met Peter Gray and has bought Larkhurst. Everyone we meet seems to know everyone else. The vicar knows the Greshams, the Greshams know Master Baines, Master Baines knew Peter Gray . . .'

'And he sells wool to Andrew Reeves,' I said. 'And,' I added thoughtfully, 'he is sorry for Mary Stuart.'

'Do you mean you . . . suspect him?' said Joyce.

'Yes,' I said, feeling that it was as well that the Greshams were now riding ahead of us and couldn't hear this. 'I think he's a possible. No more than that.'

'Poor Mildred, if so!'

'Poor Mildred anyway,' I said. 'She's terrified of him – and his house and his lambing pen. I think we must finish that dress though I doubt if we can help her dreams about Pascal Bryers. He isn't likely to make eyes at his master's bride. But *someone* might look at her twice, and step in. That's been the trouble. No one has really seen her, so far. How can we somehow arrange for Mildred to come on visits with us, without her parents? Thomasina has many friends and if only Mildred's parents would let her attend those musical evenings that Sabina likes so much . . .'

We discussed ways and means for all the rest of the journey.

The next day was Sunday. We rode to St Ninian's for the morning service. There were benches to sit on so that the congregation could listen in reasonable comfort to long homilies. Lucius Parker celebrated his return to health by presenting us with one and we found ourselves listening – much to our indignation – to a prolonged dissertation on the virtue of obedience, noticeably aimed at Mildred.

Mildred, who was sitting rigidly and had turned fiery red, was being obliquely accused of ingratitude, self-will and insubordination to those who deserved her respect, and was courting danger, for God knew all and His wrath always in the end descended on such transgressors. I wondered if her parents had arranged this horridly official attack. They were exuding satisfaction. I saw them nod once or twice and exchange glances. I was thankful when we left the church. Dr Parker, as ever, stood at the church door to bid good-day to his congregation but I hurried past him with just a quick nod. I couldn't bring myself to speak to him.

SIXTEEN
Money and Music

'I have something to tell you,' said Joyce, looking pleased. 'Something very satisfactory. Mildred told me just after breakfast.'

It was the following Tuesday, the day before Sabina was to take us to Tavistock to hear music. We had exercised our horses and returned quite exhilarated from galloping in the cold. Brockley had stayed in the stable with Eddie to look after the horses, but Joyce and Dale and I were settling down to read or sew in the Brockleys' quarters.

'Go on,' I said, threading a needle and wishing the light were better.

'At the end of our visit to Mr Baines, while we were all in the hall eating nibbles and trying to look as though we were enjoying ourselves,' said Joyce, 'I had quite a long talk with Mrs Gresham.'

'Yes, I noticed.'

'I mentioned the musical evening you and I are going to in Tavistock tomorrow. I asked if Mildred could come too. Mrs Gresham at once said no and I asked why. Mrs Gresham began saying that music is worldly and inspires unregulated emotions especially in young girls such as Mildred. She said that sacred music was acceptable but as far as she knew, the Tavistock event wouldn't be an evening of psalms. She went on for some time – how Mildred has never as much as touched a musical instrument. Mrs Gresham said that she herself, as a girl at home, had been taught the lute but her husband had shown her better ways and she now understood that Christians should give up such worldly excitements.'

'Oh dear,' I said.

'And Mildred overheard us,' Joyce said. 'I saw her biting her lip and not daring to speak and I just felt sorry for her. Hemmed in – Miles Baines on one side and all that piety on the other! So I said that I had seen the musical instruments in the upstairs parlour, and when Mildred was married, what if Baines wanted her to learn how to play them? I told her about our visit to Ladymead, and how the children played the lute and clavichord for us. I said that you can play the lute and the spinet and so can I, and you are having your son taught music and surely we don't all seem to be the victims of unregulated emotions!'

'What did Mrs Gresham say?' I asked.

'She seemed surprised. Then she leant over to Mildred and asked if she really wanted to go to this musical gathering and Mildred said yes, she did. She said it,' Joyce told me, 'as though she were confessing a crime that would send her to the gallows.'

'And?'

'Mrs Gresham said she would have to ask her husband. Well. She has done so. He has agreed to Mildred going to Tavistock, because he too had noticed the musical instruments upstairs. He'd realized that even if Baines didn't ask his wife to learn an instrument, he would assuredly take her to houses where she would hear music. Her parents would have no say in that and they wouldn't want her to quarrel with her husband. She will after all have to promise to obey him. It would be point- less therefore to forbid her to listen to music now, on the eve of her marriage. In fact, she might as well get used to it. And so,' finished Joyce triumphantly, 'Mildred can come with us to Tavistock.'

'Joyce,' I said. 'You are a marvel. Where is that half-finished dress? Where is Dale? We must have it ready by tomorrow!'

'It won't act like a magic spell and summon a lover to her,' Joyce said. 'And even if it did, her parents have betrothed her to Miles Baines and she can't escape. She daren't really refuse him. I am free to refuse offers if I choose, but she is not.'

Brockley joined us shortly after that, and was also pleased to hear the news. However, we had other things to talk about, mainly the progress of my – or rather, our – enquiries into the deaths of Peter Gray and Gregory Reeves, and what steps should we take in the future. 'So far, what have we discovered?' I asked.

'We have found,' said Brockley, 'that neither of them left any notes about anyone they suspected. As far as my understanding goes, madam, they had reported people being sentimental about poor Mary Stuart, and had learned of money being raised but didn't know by whom or for what. Maybe the money being raised is innocent, intended for genuine charities, and the rest of it is just a few sighs over an imprisoned queen with a romantic history. We've heard both Mr Parker and Mr Baines do just that. If you can call it romantic to marry a spoilt young wastrel with a pretty face and then, when someone obligingly murders him, marry the principal suspect.'

There were times when Brockley could match Walsingham himself for sheer cynicism.

'But someone tried to dispose of me,' I said. 'Somewhere there's a viper in the grass.'

'Ursula, do you really suspect Mr Baines because he spoke of her with pity?' Joyce asked.

'Only because he knew both of them,' I said. 'He has bought Gray's smallholding and he sells wool to Andrew Reeves. It's a link that holds all three. And he is sentimental about Mary. If only,' I said impatiently, 'Gregory or Peter had left us one name to pursue!'

'We have that man Crispin,' said Dale, with some vigour. 'Him with the popish symbols that I saw in his room.'

Dale had her own reasons for detesting popish symbols. Once, when in France with me, she had nearly been condemned as a heretic.

'I haven't forgotten him,' I said. 'And Sabina Parker says he sometimes goes to the musical evenings. I shall look out for him. He's possible,' I said thoughtfully. 'I do wonder about those orphans of his. Maybe there's only one of them and her name's Mary!'

'So we do have some names, in a way,' Joyce said. 'Two of them. But they're not very promising. It would be a coincidence if either Crispin or Baines is the man we want. I mean, why should we expect to find him, or them, so easily? It seems too convenient.'

'Hethercott hired his cart out to someone else the day that Peter Gray was run down,' I said. 'Brockley, he described him

to you as well dressed and well spoken, didn't he? It doesn't
tell us much. How about Gregory? Let me think it out. He could
have been lured to that empty cottage on the edge of the moor
and then knocked out, trussed up – I think he must have been
trussed because he'd probably come round from that blow
on the head and start struggling. He was heaved onto his own
horse, most likely, and carried up to the moor . . .'

'And left there long enough to kill him?' said Joyce, frowning.
'But if he was bound . . .'

'I suppose,' I said after a moment, 'that once he was dead,
or nearly, his assailants might come back and untie him so that
it would look as if he just got lost. If they were clever about
his bonds, they might not have left much in the way of marks.
Or perhaps he was drugged in some way. Then his horse was
turned loose and came home by itself.'

'Well,' said Brockley. 'What next?'

'A musical evening in Tavistock,' I said. 'We just *might* catch
Crispin Hanley in the act of raising money. Maybe we'll learn
something.'

Tavistock was a lengthy ride away and the sky was overcast,
too. Riding home in the dark wouldn't be pleasant. Anyway,
Sabina always spent the night in Tavistock with friends,
and we decided to stay at the inn which we had already
found. We could all ride there. Dale was getting on very well
with Brown Betsy. When we went back to Hawkswood, I would
buy her an ambler of her own. 'I should have done it before,'
I said to her.

Sabina called for us, cloaked against the cold, and beneath
the cloak, clad in doublet, shirt and breeches. She had a bulging
saddlebag, however, which no doubt contained a change of
clothes and when she greeted me with a hug, I inhaled a waft
of something that certainly wasn't lavender water. Sandalwood,
I thought. Joyce, Dale and I simply rode in the dresses we
would wear for the evening. 'We're not going to a ball, after
all,' I said as we prepared to start out. 'Joyce, we'd better take
our lutes. We can hang them from our saddles.'

In Tavistock, Sabina went first to the friends who were giving
her a bed for the night, so as to change into her gown. The rest

of us made our arrangements at the inn and waited for her to join us and lead us to the venue.

At the house she took us to every window was bright with candlelight. Sabina knocked, and when the door was opened, a melodious mingling of spinet, harp and sackbut rolled out to meet us.

We were admitted by a dignified lady with white hair piled up in high and elaborate swirls, a crimson velvet gown with a wide farthingale and an open ruff. Her feet were in high-heeled white-leather slippers. Her grey eyes, and her voice, were incisive. 'Ah, Mistress Parker. And these are your friends? You sent word that you were bringing guests.'

'Yes.' Sabina introduced us. 'May I bring them through, Mistress Brewster?'

'Of course. I am Laetitia Brewster.' She stood back to let us in. 'Ah, here is our maid. Deborah, take the guests' hats and cloaks. I see you have lutes with you. Excellent!'

We divested ourselves of our outdoor garments and, looking at Mistress Brewster and Sabina, I was glad that we had all dressed with care for this occasion, although on horseback, we couldn't very well have farthingales. Mildred had put on the green gown Joyce and I had made for her, and in it looked astonishingly pretty. We had presented it with some formality and her parents had not objected. Catherine had said that Mr Baines would surely like it, but fortunately Mildred at that moment was pointing out some feature of the embroidery to her father and didn't hear.

Another lady emerged from the shadows and Mistress Brewster brought her forward. 'Here is my sister Katherine. She and I live together and arrange these evenings for the pleasure of musical friends. And ourselves. We are both very fond of music.'

The second Mistress Brewster was also pleasingly arrayed, in her case in turquoise, and, like her sister, she had white freshwater pearls for her jewellery. She was clearly the younger of the two, less stately and merrier, with a smile in her eyes. 'Do come this way,' she said.

Since they both had the surname Brewster, they had presumably never been married. I glanced at their hands. Both wore rings but neither wore a wedding ring. They probably gave meaning to their lives with music. Well, better than making life exciting with conspiracies. I hoped that no plots were being hatched or financed under their roof.

We followed the sisters through a doorway and found ourselves in a large panelled parlour, where more than a dozen people were gathered, some standing but mostly seated on the ample supply of stools and settles, and attending to the music that we had heard from outside. The musicians were on a dais at the far end of the room. I noticed that the harp was a splendid affair, the height of a man, and probably a fixture.

There were plenty of seats, and small tables here and there as well. There was a good fire in the hearth, though every now and then, the chimney smoked, emitting puffs of woodsmoke into the room.

The Brewster sisters guided us to a vacant settle and then were accosted by a man with a list in his hands and an anxious query about when a certain item was to be played. He drew them away from us so we settled ourselves as best we could. Mildred, Joyce and I took the settle, while Brockley found two stools for himself and Dale. Sabina however, remained standing, looking about her. The piece that was being played came to an end and was applauded. Sabina said: 'That was by William Byrd. His music is the theme for this evening though everything won't be by him – one must have variety. Now I must leave you – I see friends I should greet.'

She went off to speak to a lean, grey-haired and grey-clad man on the other side of the room. Laetitia had gone to stand in front of the dais and now made an announcement, declaring that the next item would be a song composed by King Henry the Eighth himself. It would be sung by Master John Hudd.

She added that there were new guests to swell the numbers this evening, and please would everyone welcome Mistress Ursula Stannard, her ward Mistress Joyce Frost . . . And so on. Everyone turned to stare at us, so we stood up politely and returned their bows and curtseys. Mistress Laetitia observed aloud that two of us had brought lutes and that no doubt we could take part in the evening's entertainment a little later. Meanwhile . . .

Master Hudd sang his song, to which I listened with interest, since my father was supposed to have composed it. It was a love song, warmly sentimental, and I wondered if the man who had had two of his wives beheaded could possibly have written it. People could be very complicated, I thought. A galliard by William Byrd was announced, by Katherine this time, along with a smiling apology because we weren't going to dance. The galliard commenced. Then the lean, grey-haired gentleman came to ask if we would indeed like to join in and did we play any other instruments besides the lute, and before we knew it, Joyce and I had agreed to play a duet, with lute and spinet.

'It is not usual, of course, for ladies to perform in public,' he told us, 'but when music-loving friends meet in a private house, that's different. Now . . .'

The piece he suggested was another Byrd composition. It was well known and quite familiar to us for we had practised it together, with Joyce taking the major part on her lute while I accompanied her on the spinet. We would be invited onto the platform after the refreshment interval, which would be soon.

The lean grey gentleman departed and the interval was announced. The maid Deborah appeared with trays of snacks, followed by the Brewster sisters with tankards and jugs. We pulled a couple of the little tables towards us. Sabina came back for a moment but then said she had seen someone who had promised a donation to the charity for seamen's widows, and left us again to speak to him. He was sitting on the far side of the room and she sat down beside him. A moment later I recognized him as Pascal Bryers.

Mildred noticed too, and the longing in her face as she looked at him, was sad to see. She had no skill in hiding her feelings. I hoped he wouldn't recognize us and come over to talk to us. He would surely be indifferent to Mildred and that would hurt her. However, he didn't seem to notice us, and presently, we saw him rise and leave the room.

Mildred made an effort and began to make conversation about the music. I caught sight of Sabina again, now earnestly talking to someone who had taken Bryers' place beside her. We sipped our cider and nibbled our refreshments, which were fortunately quite substantial. After that ride through the chilly winter afternoon and the even chillier dusk that followed, we all needed something more solid than raisins and nuts. Happily, the snacks included chunks of cheese and slices of ham, and some big slices of a very good honeycake. I was much enjoying my honeycake when Joyce nudged me and said: 'Look, quickly, over there!'

Her nudge nearly sent my honeycake down the wrong way but when I looked, I saw that Sabina now had a third gentleman beside her, and it was Crispin Hanley. He was holding out an open purse to her, and Sabina was shaking her head.

'By the look of it,' I said dryly, 'she's refusing to contribute to his orphans. Very wise of her.'

Across the room, Crispin put his purse away and turned from Sabina to speak to a woman who had sat down on his other side. Sabina rose and moved away and for a moment I lost sight of her because my attention had been caught by the woman to whom Crispin was now talking. She had striking looks, for her hair, hardly concealed by the little black hood that she wore pushed to the back of her head, was such a vivid red. When I caught sight of Sabina again, she was in talk with a man I didn't recognize, but I noticed him pressing something into her palm. A moment later, she left him and came back to us.

'That man Hanley!' she said as she came within earshot. 'Wanting donations for his orphans again. Lucius is right. They probably don't exist! I've done well this evening for our own charity. I won't ask you to contribute, though; you're my guests. I wish Hanley hadn't come tonight. I get tired of his importunities.'

Lucius. At the mention of his name, a dreadful thought suddenly arose in my mind, inspired by the memory of something he had said.

I don't like to think what would become of us Protestant clergy if the Spaniards got here. Though I sometimes feel sorry for Mary. She's been shut away so long.

No, what was this nonsense? It had been a casual remark, a comment made out of kindliness, out of pity.

Or . . . could it be? Could fear of the Spaniards, of a Spanish invasion, gradually have grown in his mind? Could Lucius have decided, as it were, to insure himself – yes, and his sister too, against the danger?

That wasn't nonsense. It was perfectly possible. Fear for himself and Sabina, rather than a passion for Mary or for the Catholic faith, could be a strong motive for offering support to a plot. But it was a motive shared, by every vicar in the land. Why should I distrust Lucius just because of that casual remark, made, I said to myself, by a kindly man . . .

Kindly? Is he? No, he is not. You don't like him and that's why. Look at that very unkind homily he pitched at poor Mildred! And the way he talks about Sabina, in public, to her face! God knows what he says to her in private. Telling her that her plain face is the will of God, indeed! What if he is urging Sabina to collect money for seamen's widows and all the time the money is going to fund Mary? Is Sabina in it or not?

I contemplated these thoughts with horror. Then Sabina was saying: 'I think you're being called to play,' and yes, Joyce and I were being beckoned forward. It was time for our piece. Joyce took her lute from its case and left the case in Mildred's care. I massaged my fingers gently to make them pliant for the keyboard and took my seat at the spinet. My head was whirling.

Worse than that. I was so appalled by my own suspicions that I actually felt ill. To a tentative list consisting of Crispin Hanley and Miles Baines, I seemed to have added Lucius Parker and even Sabina, yet I had no real grounds for suspecting any of them. After all, people did collect for genuine charities. Thomasina had actually seen some of the clothes that Sabina had assembled so they were real enough. I was seeing bears in bushes and clutching wildly at straws. I wanted to go home to Hawkswood and choose new maidservants and worry about the increasing ages of John Hawthorn and Adam Wilder and buy an ambler for Dale and forget that I had ever heard the names of Gray and Reeves.

SEVENTEEN
The Uses of Indiscretion

Once I had started to play, I grew calmer. The spinet was a good one and my fingers knew the piece we were playing. But all the same, I would have liked to get away as soon as possible afterwards. However when Joyce and I had finished, which we did amid flattering applause, we were at once accosted by the woman with the red hair.

She drew us to a settle and smilingly asked us to sit down. We did so. Another piece by Byrd had begun and we mustn't disturb that. Also, our new acquaintance seemed very eager to talk with us, albeit in low tones. She addressed me by name.

'Mistress Stannard! You are the Mistress Stannard who has been talking to Andrew Reeves about the death of his son, are you not?'

I guessed that she was in her late thirties. Her ruff was small and she had no farthingale, while her gown, which had a closed front, was of plain brown wool except for a few yellow slashings in the sleeves. None of it was costly, and nor I thought, were the polished yellow stones in her earrings and necklace, though everything suited her. Like Sabina, I thought, she was a woman who could make the best of little. She had a local accent but not a strong one and her tone was a mingling of the shy and the eager. She was fiddling with her wedding ring and her attractive green eyes were anxious as she gazed at me, awaiting my reply.

'Yes, I am,' I said warily. 'And you are?'

Joyce, tactfully, fixed her eyes on the dais, where Sabina was playing the clavichord. In the necessary undertone, the red-haired woman said: 'I am Jane Leigh. Dare say you've heard of me. You was axing Master Reeves about me, not long since, axing if Gregory might have been led on to the moor, thinking he'd had a message from me, which he hadn't.'

'How do you know that?' I asked her. 'Did Andrew Reeves tell you that I . . .?'

'Lord no, not him. He wouldn't come anigh me! No, but I've a friend as works in his weaving shop and he heard what you was axin'.'

'Ah,' I said. 'Hal Gurney?'

'Yes. How'd *you* know?' A pair of eyebrows, darker than her hair, rose in surprise.

'A young man with wild black hair?'

'Why yes, that's him, but . . .'

'He spilt a basket of orange hanks of wool right at our feet when I was talking to Andrew Reeves the other day, and took his time over picking them up. If he'd wanted to hear what we were saying to each other, I dare say he could. What did he tell you?'

'He'm a good friend of mine,' said Jane with a smile that told me exactly how good a friend Master Gurney was. 'Hal said as you'd been there afore, with questions, so he decided to try and hear what you was after this time, and he said you was axin' would Gregory Reeves have gone up to the moor or to the old cottage where we'd sometimes met if he'd had a note axin' him to meet me there again. Seems you want to know what happened to him. Dare say Andrew Reeves wants to find out too but he don't have time to go hunting hisself. That leaves you. Well, I'll help if I can. You seen the cottage?'

'Yes.'

'Not much of a place but it weren't so bad in the summer. Oh, he liked little Sally well enough and he knew it were time he got wed and got a son to follow him in the workshop; he was no fool, young Greg. He were a decent fellow too; that's what I liked about him, apart from his smile and a gentleness controlling his passion like a bridle on a powerful horse; used to make me tremble with joy inside, feeling that ordered passion . . . reckon you know what I mean . . .'

Beside me, Joyce emitted a scandalized gasp but I said: 'Yes, I do,' because I did. I glanced at Joyce and whispered: 'Go and join the others. I won't be long.' Joyce slipped away, looking both shocked and astonished, and I turned my attention back to Jane.

'He had a real thing for me,' she said, 'and I for him though I knew I couldn't keep him. So there's the answer to what you was axin' Andrew Reeves. Greg wouldn't have gone up to the moor on a freezing January evening, of course he wouldn't. We never did meet on the moor, anyhow. But yes, he might of gone to the cottage if he thought he'd had word from me. I didn't send him one. But someone else could of used my name. Crowner suggested as much, at the inquest.'

I said: 'How many people knew about you and Gregory? Knew where you met, and so on.'

'Oh, any number,' said Jane casually. 'Not that we made any show of it but things get known. Men boast in their cups; even nice ones like Greg. And they say *women* can't keep secrets! Besides, I go to church like everyone else and I've had remarks aimed at me from the pulpit. The vicar of St James in Okehampton knows about me and Greg all right though I don't know who told him, I just know it means that every vicar for miles knows too. They talk to each other. Worse than gossipy old beldames, they are. And when he aims homilies at me, he *looks* at me, and then everyone in the church takes an interest, and once they're outside, they start chattering together.'

I nodded, recalling Lucius Parker's onslaught on poor Mildred. 'I believe you,' I said.

She glanced at the clavichord and, pointedly, at its player. 'That poor soul up there now. Sabina Parker. Time was, afore Greg took up with me, she come to Okehampton wanting to buy cloth from the Reeves and she took a bit of a shine to Greg. Worried him, it did, her making excuses to keep coming, all that way from Zeal whatever its name is. Then it stopped; likely her brother put a stop to it. But it got round and there was talk and Greg had people laughing about it and axin' him if he and Sabina had a date for their wedding, and I reckon it was vicar's gossip that set it all going, her brother talking to his fellow vicars, enjoying it as a joke or a scandal, and then chattin' to a favoured parishioner or two.'

Once more, I believed her. According to Lucius, who really should not have told me, Sabina had once taken a shine to Samuel Rossiter as well. Sabina was a normal woman trapped in a badly shaped body. It shouldn't be something for men to gossip about, but her brother had talked about it to us and no doubt to others.

Jane gave me a sharp look. 'You're thinking I'm a wicked besom myself. T'ain't wickedness. I don't do it for money; I'm no whore. It's need. My man's never home. He'd sooner be at sea than with me. When he does come back, it's a few quick pokes and demands for hot dinners, and then he's off again and I get lonely. And hungry and I ain't talking about food. And if you're thinking what if there's a child that ain't his, well, there's ways.'

'I know,' I said. Once, not wishing to bear a child to a man who had forced me, I had sought unlawful help from Gladys. As it chanced, the help wasn't needed. It was pointless however to pretend to virtuous ignorance. The green eyes looking into mine recognized that.

I said: 'I have wondered how many people knew about you and him and the cottage, but from what you say, it could have been . . . well . . . common knowledge. That's a pity.'

'Makes it harder to catch them as did for him, you mean,' said Jane frankly. 'But I hope you do. I'll pray for it,' she said. She rose, and quietly, with a soft swirl of her brown skirts, she moved away. She moved with grace, I saw. I also noticed that unlike Sabina, she did not despise lavender water.

And at that very moment, it came to me, what I must do. It was perfectly true that I had no genuine suspicions of anyone. Miles Baines, Crispin Hanley, Lucius Parker, poor Sabina, any of them could be secretly gathering funds for Mary or laying plots on her behalf but I only thought that because I chanced to know that they had spoken of Mary with sympathy or had hidden Catholic leanings. Thousands of honest folk felt the same, out of chivalry for a sad lady, or nostalgia for days gone by, but without meaning harm to any, least of all the queen. I didn't happen to know them, that was all.

It was not actually a crime to have Catholic symbols in one's bedchamber (Sir Francis Walsingham would have liked to make it illegal but the queen wouldn't agree), and it wasn't a crime either, or even especially unusual, to express vague feelings of sympathy for a foolish woman who had lost her crown, been separated from her son and been kept in semi-custody for twenty years.

In conditions, I thought with irritation, that might well be envied by many plain folk who kept food on their tables, clothes on their backs and roofs over their heads by working from daybreak to sunset, sewing or scrubbing floors or wresting a living out of unproductive land and struggling to rear child after child. They didn't worry about being separated from their offspring. As soon as they could, they sent them out in the world to support themselves. The Hethercotts – the carter Brockley had interviewed for me and his wife – dealt with their brood that way. There was a girl there who was just ready to be pushed out of the nest, wasn't there? I might be able to do something for her.

But my thoughts were wandering, avoiding the main issue. I returned to it, slowly and painfully facing what I now saw as my duty. It would either confirm or remove my suspicions of Parker, Baines or Hanley; and if they should be innocent, the real miscreants might be drawn out into the light.

Or I might be killed myself. I nearly had been, once. But all my attempts so far to find out who had murdered my agents, had led nowhere, and there had been no second attempt on me. Even that, however unwelcome, might have offered a lead.

And so . . .

A fresh piece of music had now begun. The lean grey man was playing the harp and singing. I didn't know the piece but liked it and would have enjoyed listening, except that I now had other things on my mind. I must speak with Jane Leigh again! She was now sitting at the far side of the room. I made my way quietly round to join her and sat down next to her. At that moment, a gust of wind made the smoking chimney belch clouds into the room and the singer had to stop in order to cough. Everyone was coughing, although the smoke at least smelt quite pleasant. Applewood, I thought distractedly. We often burnt applewood at home. We had some old apple trees now that were ready to be turned into firewood. I was homesick. Once again, I longed for home. Except that there

were two dead men who needed justice and I could not abandon
them.

The wind subsided after a moment and the smoke dis-
persed. The singer resumed. I let him finish and then I said: 'I
did not make myself quite plain just now. I have good reason
to seek out whoever killed Gregory Reeves. He was one of her
majesty's agents, paid to look out for signs of plots on Mary
Stuart's behalf. It was I who found him and made an agent of
him. Perhaps you find that hard to believe but it's true. I feel
responsible for his death and also for another, that of a man
called Peter Gray. I am not idly curious.'

'I know,' said Jane unexpectedly. 'Gregory told me you'd
chosen him for special duties – spying duties – in these here
perilous times. He said you were kin to the queen. I didn't
know whether to believe him but then he dies and you come
here, axin' questions . . .'

Gregory certainly had been indiscreet, and probably it had
killed him. 'I am her majesty's half-sister. Not legitimate,' I said.
'Old Henry?' I nodded. 'So you're a king's daughter.' Jane
looked me up and down, appraisingly. 'Yes. You have the air.'

'Have I? Did you mean it when you said you'd help? If so,
there's a way. It won't endanger you, at least I hope not.'

'That's honest, at any rate. What do you want me to do?'

'Simple enough,' I said. 'Just talk about me. Talk about what
I'm doing here. I haven't been able to find out anything helpful.
But not long ago, someone tried to murder *me*. I was lucky to
escape. Someone is prepared to go to great lengths to prevent
me from finding out the truth. If I know who that is, then I
know who killed Peter and Gregory. I want to draw them out
of the shadows, panic them into trying again – only this time,
I and my friends will be ready! I am making myself into bait. I
shall be talking unwisely to anyone I can. Pretending I *have*
found out a thing or two. You can help by spreading a rumour
like that. Will you do it?'

'Yes, if that's what you really want. But what if they do try
again and succeed?'

'I have to trust to being forewarned, and having friends
who are forewarned as well.'

'Good luck!' said Jane Leigh. 'I'll talk. But God keep you.'

I was committed now and if I had been terrified before, I was terrified now twice over. Indiscretion had killed poor Gregory and now I was trying to use it to lure his murderer into the light of day. It might so easily kill me.

EIGHTEEN
Living Bait

What happened next, I might have foreseen. All my life I had been subject to migraine headaches in times of fear or conflict. I woke next morning, in my bedchamber at the inn, feeling as though an iron band had been fastened round my brow and temples, and a hammer was being applied in rhythmic strokes to my left eyebrow.

'Now what has brought this on?' Brockley enquired, coming to see me along with Dale, who knew how to make the potion that Gladys made for my headaches, carried the ingredients with her at all times and had just come from brewing the potion in the kitchen of the Tavistock inn. Joyce had never witnessed me having a migraine before and was sitting with me, looking both helpless and worried.

I knew well enough what was wrong with me. I had not only determined on a plan that petrified me; I also had to tell Brockley and the others about it and ask them to cooperate. Brockley above all would be outraged. I drank the potion that Dale offered me and then, closing my eyes, so that although I would have to hear the chorus of protests, I needn't see anyone's expression, I made my announcement. There were horrified cries, and from Brockley, a predictable response.

'You are out of your mind. Madam!' He ignored my headache, remembered his station in life at the very end of the sentence, and then made the last word sound like an accusation.

'Not quite,' I said. I forced myself to think lucidly. 'Brockley, I know that my royal sister lives in continual fear of assassination, in case there's a plot that slips past her protectors. I can't refuse to help her. Whoever arranged those accidents for Gray and Reeves has to be, must be, a dangerous conspirator against her. She *is* my sister, as well as our queen. If she can live with that constant fear of death, then so can I. l look to you, my friends, to guard me until this is over.'

'How? We are to taste your food? Must I sleep outside your door!'

Still with my eyes closed, I said: 'In a way, my plan has already started. Andrew Reeves knows I am enquiring into the death of his son; Pascal Bryers saw me going through Peter Gray's papers. The Parkers and Miles Baines all know something of my purpose here. And Jane Leigh has promised to gossip. There have been no more attempts on me; perhaps those responsible think I have been frightened off. I want them to know that I have not.'

I let my eyes open in time to see Brockley raising his hands to heaven. 'You have done insane things in the past, madam, and drawn me into them. Of course I will guard you with all my heart and all my strength but what if I fail? Whoever arranged the deaths of Reeves and Gray was cunning. Whoever poisoned your cider in Okehampton was *very* cunning. You are pitting me – all of us – against magicians.'

'If I receive an invitation to meet anyone in the middle of the moor and to come alone, I promise not to go. Did you bring your sword with you from Hawkswood?'

'I *always* have my sword with me when we travel.'

'Good. And I have my dagger. We ought to be able to look after ourselves.'

'Neither sword nor dagger would have helped you in the Castle Inn, madam,' said Brockley and Dale put her hands to her mouth. Her blue eyes were popping in alarm.

'I will be more careful in future,' I said wearily. 'I don't expect to be poisoned at Ladymead, or by the Greshams, but even at their tables, I shan't sit next to guests from outside, and I'll make sure that whoever pours my drinks when I am at an inn is a real employee of the inn.'

'Even people who collect funds for Mary Stuart may have lawful employment, serving customers at an inn,' Joyce pointed out and in a trembling voice, Dale said: 'Ma'am, please *don't*!'

'I don't want to do this,' I said. 'But don't you see, all of you? We're not getting anywhere. We have suspects of a sort but no real reasons for suspecting them. We've got to start the quarry out of the covert.'

'May heaven protect you,' said Brockley, and he sounded so weary that I was stricken with guilt. He was in his sixties, and in my service he had endured much danger. He had probably had enough.

'Brockley, I'm sorry,' I said.

'I'll do my best,' he said. 'I hope I'm better at it than heaven.'

I said: 'I think I'm about to be sick.'

That was the usual end to a migraine attack. The three of them scrambled to find a basin for me and Brockley won the race. It was he who held the washstand basin for me while I vomited. And between us there was one of the strange moments that through the years had come to us now and then. We had had one when we both so deplorably wondered about the love-life of the Hethercotts. Now just as I finished and asked for a drink of water, it happened again. Our eyes met and all that we might have been to each other in another world, all that we so very nearly had been to each other even in this one, was there, unspoken but as vivid as a flash of light or a phrase of music or an embrace.

I drank the water and said: 'I will be better soon. The headache is already easing. Give me an hour to rest and I shall be ready to get up.'

While I rested, I leant back on the pillows to think. I had four vague and probably mistaken suspects. Since they were all I had, though, I thought I could begin by stirring them up. I couldn't think of an excuse to visit Miles Baines on my own account, nor could I find a reason for calling on Crispin Hanley again. But I could do something about the Parkers. Meanwhile, Jane Leigh would be doing her best among her acquaintances.

We were able to get back to the Greshams that afternoon, though it was a cold and muddy ride. It was March now but it still felt like January. That year, winter seemed to go on and on. But the weather wasn't allowed to stop me from doing what had to be done. Next morning, Joyce and I paid the vicarage a visit.

I asked Catherine if she had any of Mildred's outgrown clothes to spare, pretending that I had promised to collect some for Sabina, and Catherine supplied a patched chemise, two well-worn gowns of suitable size for a girl of twelve, some pairs of sleeves to go with them and a smallish cloak, scuffed about the neck. They were to be my excuse for a visit to the vicarage.

'Oh, how nice of you,' Sabina said, receiving the offering with approval and taking it into a small room where there was already a pile of similarly youthful garments, to which she added my gift.

'Is your brother busy?' I enquired. 'I should like to talk to him if possible.'

Sabina looked slightly surprised but said no, she thought he was only reading, and took us to the parlour. He stood up to welcome us, saying: 'Is this a social call or are you in need of a vicar?'

'There is something I'd like to ask you,' I said, 'and as I was bringing a contribution for Sabina's charity, I thought, why not take the opportunity.'

'Very well, be seated. Sabina, what about some refreshments . . .?'

'No, never mind about that,' I said. 'Sabina may be as helpful as you. Please let her stay. I can be frank with you, Dr Parker, for you already realize that I am here on the queen's business and you have offered to help. You are aware that I am looking into the deaths of Peter Gray and Gregory Reeves, are you not?'

'Yes, as I think I implied the first time we met. I must repeat that I cannot think it a suitable task for a lady.'

There was no point in entering into an argument about suitable tasks for ladies. 'I am sure now that those deaths were not accidents,' I said. 'Have you any idea who might have arranged them? You know so many people. If you think about it, does anyone come to mind?'

The answer, of course, from both of them, was no. But I had planted my arrow. I had made it clear that, undeterred by henbane, I was still hunting.

*   *   *

I was unsure what to do next but decided to visit Zeal Aquatio's solitary inn. Brockley could escort me there; we would dine and I would do some talking, in a voice a little too loud.

We did this. I had never entered the place before and didn't like even the outside of it. It was built of crudely dressed reddish stones and its windows were too small for its flat staring face. Inside, it had a cobbled floor and some benches but not much comfort. Brockley said he had once asked Bartholomew why the inn sign showed only a helmeted head, supposed to represent a long-gone Sir Somebody Marcher, and not the arms themselves. The answer was that the arms were something in silver on a black background and were too depressing. I doubted that. The inn was as depressing, it seemed to me, as it could possibly be already.

The evening was a fiasco.

Comfortless or not, the place was crowded when we entered and everyone seemed to be full of excitement over a game of Nine Men's Morris which two men were playing to the accompaniment of cheers and moans from the bystanders, and helpful remarks from some and shushes from others. The onlookers were crowding round the table and the players were hunched over their board with its black and white balls on their wires, looking like some peculiar form of abacus. Bets had been laid, Brockley guessed. I could have talked in as loud a voice as I chose but it would have been lost amid the babble and I doubted if anyone present would have cared a straw for anything I was saying, even if they had heard it. It was a wasted evening.

The next day was a Saturday and by then I had run out of ideas and doubted if any of my ploys so far were likely to produce results. I didn't have the courage to go out alone and see if anything happened. I felt safer staying on the Greshams' premises.

A week passed, and nothing happened, though it continued so cold. The following Saturday was sunny for once though there was a north-east wind with an edge on it like the edge of a sword. However, the horses needed exercise, so we all rode out that afternoon, and came back to find a considerable atmosphere in the house, because Miles Baines had arrived and not for the purpose of courting Mildred.

He had come to ask to be released from his betrothal.

In the evenings, we usually went across to the main house for supper. In such circumstances, I think the Greshams would probably have asked us to take supper in our own quarters, but they were perhaps too distracted by this unwelcome turn of events. At any rate, they didn't, and when evening came, just as usual, we went across to the main house that evening and walked into the middle of it all.

'. . . but my dear Mr Baines,' Catherine was saying as we entered the parlour, 'it is natural and proper for young girls to feel unsure of themselves when they first take over the running of their own homes. It is even a good thing; it shows modesty and allows the mother-in-law and the husband to train her in their ways . . .'

'There is no mother-in-law.' Because the weather was so cold, there was for once a fire in the hearth. Miles Baines was standing in front of it with his feet apart and blocking most of the heat from the rest of the room. He sounded assertive. 'And I have no wish to instruct a timid and inexperienced girl in the way to run my home and keep my accounts. I have not the mind of an instructor. There is also the point that Mistress Mildred does not like me.'

Joyce and I had been leading the way. We stopped short in the doorway. Dale bumped into us and I sensed Brockley pulling her back. I saw that Mildred was present, sitting in a corner, her hands clasped in her lap. Her eyes were two wide blue-green pools.

She was nervous and not without reason. Her father, who was standing in the middle of the room, was staring at her grimly. 'Is this true, Mildred? Did you actually *say* to him, to the man you are contracted to marry, that you *don't like him*? Did you say that, regardless of how a man might feel, indifferent to the pain you were inflicting—'

'No,' said Baines. 'Mistress Mildred said nothing of the sort. But I'm not blind or stupid or without experience. I don't need to be told when a woman doesn't care for me. And I am not really surprised. I am too old and too ugly—'

'Mr *Baines*!' Catherine gasped.

'—to be attractive to a young girl. Only, of course, many

young women would not mind; I have other things to offer; my good position, my beautiful home, and I would be indulgent. However, Mistress Mildred is not one of those young women and I can respect that. I . . .'

'I hope,' said Mr Gresham, 'that you will not rush away from here without further discussion of this. Mildred! Go to the kitchen and fetch the oatcakes you made this morning, and some cider. And then sit down beside Mr Baines and talk with him. We don't customarily take what are called appetizers before our meals, Mr Baines, but we relax our rules when guests are present. I beg that you will stay for supper. And you, Mildred, will sit beside him at the table and go on talking.'

He suddenly became aware that this drama had an audience. The four of us were still standing paralysed in the doorway to the vestibule.

'Ah. I had forgotten. Mrs Stannard, Mistress Joyce, Mr and Mrs Brockley. I regret that you should find yourselves in the midst of all this. Please come in. Be easy. There will be no more high emotion. Supper has been somewhat delayed. *Mildred!* Why are you still sitting there? Fetch the oatcakes!'

Mildred rose obediently, remarking as she did so that her mother had made the oatcakes. 'I am a poor hand at them,' she said, rather bravely, I thought. Her father went crimson.

Mildred vanished towards the kitchen and Henry Gresham relieved his feelings by asking impatiently why we were still clustering there, come in, come in!

We did as we were told and dutifully sat through half an hour of forced social chitchat in the parlour, while we nibbled oatcakes and sipped cider and unanimously wished ourselves elsewhere. Mildred, just as dutifully, sat beside Miles Baines and talked to him, mostly about the weather as far as I could make out.

When it was time for supper, she was obliged once more to sit beside Baines. All round the table, the unnatural, trivial conversation continued. At the end of it, Henry took Miles away to the small upstairs room that was his study. Dale, Joyce and I bumped into each other in our efforts to escape to the kitchen and help with the washing up. Mildred and Catherine followed. Catherine was full of anguished comment.

'They will be deciding, up in the study. How could you, Mildred? How could you so insult an honest suitor? To let him see that you think him ugly? When he doesn't care that you lack beauty yourself?'

'Oh, Mother, don't!' Mildred, overwrought, was now in tears and wiping them away with a dishcloth.

'Your father will do his best to persuade Miles Baines to honour his contract, and it will be a bitter shame if he does not, and all your fault, you silly, undutiful girl, throwing away a chance as good as this!'

'I couldn't help it!' said Mildred tearfully, pouring hot water into a tub and seizing a supper plate. She scraped it into a bin and plunged it into the tub. '*I don't like him!*'

Still sobbing miserably, she started to scrape another plate but plainly couldn't see what she was doing for the scrapings fell onto the floor. Joyce quietly took the plate away from her, finished clearing it and put it in the tub herself.

'You drop your tears into the water,' she said. 'Not on the plates!' Mildred didn't smile.

'Last time we went to his house,' she said bitterly to her mother, 'he took me round it and he tried to kiss me and I hated it; his lips were all wet and slobbery and there'd been onions at the dinner we'd just had and his breath reeked of them! And when I think what marriage means . . .!'

'Nonsense!' Catherine seized a cloth and began to dry dishes. 'That side of marriage pleases men; for you it is a duty and no one asks you to enjoy it. It will give you children, think of that.'

I had heard Lucius say the same thing. It annoyed me then and it annoyed me now. I dried plates with great thoroughness and handed them to Dale, who had found out which shelves and drawers were which, and was putting things away. But when the washing up was done, I could bear no more.

'The rest of you may please yourselves,' I said quietly to the others as we left the kitchen. 'Go and be sociable in the parlour, if you like, or go back to our quarters. I'm going to commune with Jaunty!'

I fetched a cloak and went out. The north-easter was still blowing but it was not yet dark. We were well into March now but spring seemed far away. The stable was as ever a peaceful place. Jaunty welcomed me with a friendly snort and I fetched him a handful of oats. He was soothing company after the embarrassments of the evening.

Eddie was not there; he hardly ever was, in the evenings, once he had fed the horses. He would look at them again when he returned but that wouldn't be yet. Will, the Greshams' groom, was on friendly terms with the two grooms who worked in the stable at the dyeworks, where there were three pack-horses, and two horses owned by the supervisors. On most evenings, Will walked over to see the grooms for a tankard of ale and a game of dice or cards and lately he had been taking Eddie with him. I wished I could stay there, crooning absurdities into Jaunty's flicking ears, for ever. Still, as that was not possible, I eventually gave him a final pat and went out. It was dark now, and starry, but the wind was bitter. I hurried, wanting to get indoors and sit at a fireside.

Then something struck me, on my head. There was an explosion in my brain, as if the stars that had been in the sky had plunged into my skull and were madly dancing. I had time to realize that the Greshams' premises were not as safe as I had thought. Then I fell into blackness.

NINETEEN
Without Hope

I surfaced first into a vague awareness of being alive, but unable to remember who or even what I was. My name returned to me after a while, which was a relief but with it came something quite otherwise: a blinding headache.

After that, I became painfully aware that I was in motion. Something beneath me was rhythmically moving and pressing into my stomach. In fact, I was face down, lying across whatever it was with my head and feet dangling.

Gradually, I understood that I was lying across a saddle on a steadily plodding horse, which was being led by someone on foot, whose shape I could dimly see.

I could see because my head was exposed except for the indoor hood I had been wearing when I was seized, and because the sky was clear and starry and there was moonlight. The moon was not very far past the full and was brilliant. I could see that I was being taken out across the moor. The rock outcrops caught the moonlight and looked stark, threatening.

Most of me, including my arms, seemed to be wrapped in fabric of some kind and I gradually realized that I was in a sack, with only my head outside. My wrists were tied. I tried to move my feet and made the surprising discovery that I now had boots on. My ankles were also secured in some way. My nose was bringing me the familiar smells of horse and leather saddlery, and the less pleasant smell of sacking. There was a trace too of something that reminded me of the Brewster sisters and the way their chimney smoked and made the singer choke. Applewood smoke, I thought. It dried my mouth and I had to clear my throat in order to speak.

'Where are we going? What is all this? Who are you?'

There was no answer and I suppose I hadn't expected one. The plodding journey just went on and on and the cold increased. I waggled my feet as much as I could, to keep them from going numb.

We stopped at last. My captor came to me, released some of my bonds and let me slide to the ground, feet first. For a few moments he was close to me and again I smelt that smoky odour, acrid and sweet at the same time, on his clothing. I tried to see his face but he had a scarf across it so that only his eyes could be seen, glinting between the scarf and his hood, which he had pulled low over his brow.

My ankles and wrists were still inside the sack and still bound. I was manhandled onto my knees and then pushed face down on the ground. He began to drag me along and for the next few moments, I was only concerned with holding up my head so that my face wouldn't be scraped along the ground, or through what I thought was heather. I wasn't dragged far however and as we stopped, I was aware of a rock outcrop looming above me.

My captor stooped and for one terrifying moment I saw a blade flash in the moonlight. But he merely pushed the point through the sack and started to rip it away, though without disturbing the bonds around my wrist and ankles.

Through cold, stiff lips, I said: 'Who are you? Why are you doing this? Don't you know it will all be in vain, it will only make things worse for you in the end?'

Once more, I was ignored. By turning my head, I could just make out the shape of the horse, which was placidly cropping grass. The man stood for a moment while he made the torn sacking into a bundle. Then he turned away and went to the horse. It raised its head and pricked its ears at him. The moonlight showed me that he was letting down the stirrups. Then he mounted and rode away, the sacking thrust somehow under his cloak. I was left bound and helpless on cold heathery ground beside a rock outcrop in the heart of Dartmoor and the dark, bitter night was only just beginning.

Brockley had wanted to protect me but it hadn't occurred to either of us that there could be danger on the Greshams' very premises. I went to see Jaunty every evening, after all.

Yes, and somebody had known it.

This, surely, was the fate that had befallen Gregory Reeves.

His killer had probably come back to him when he was dead of exposure, and removed the tell-tale bonds.

How long would it be before the cold killed me, too? The answer to that was frightening. The night was truly bitter. In both our cases, our assailant had taken advantage of winter weather to do much of his work for him.

The stillness was terrifying. The rock outcrop above me loomed like a dungeon wall; another outcrop, perhaps a quarter of a mile away, looked like a giant tombstone. The dark, piled-up hills beyond it could almost be . . .

. . . the mounds of excavated earth piled beside a monstrous grave. I was lying at the bottom of it and the moon, lopsided now at the start of its wane, was the face of an idiot, staring down at me. No, don't think of such things. *Don't*, or terror will send you mad. I must not go mad. I must think. I must notice. I must keep aware and keep alive. I must . . .

But what was there to notice? All I knew now was the cold. It drove into my head like a spear and made my headache worse. But it would soon be cured. By morning, I would be, literally, frozen stiff, my blood turned to ice within me. I would be like a washed sheet left on a line in freezing weather and rendered as stiff as board. I would be dead.

I began to struggle against my bonds. It made my head pound even more but at least, I thought, movement would keep me awake; let myself sink into unconsciousness and I would be lost. My hands were in front of me and I managed to reach down and feel the rope round my ankles. My fingers wrestled with the knot. They made no impression on it at all. I raised my roped wrists to my mouth and attacked the knots with my teeth. All in vain.

Why had I been put beside this outcrop? Why hadn't I just been left on the open moor? So that my captor could find me more easily, of course, when he came back to remove my bonds and make me look like the victim of accident. Though I wondered how much he really cared about that. Mine would be the third unlikely accident, after all. He could hardly expect anyone to believe that I went wandering on the moor of my own free will. Not even in the boots he had kindly provided. No, he just wanted to be rid of me and found this a convenient method, and he had made it resemble an accident, just for luck.

I was alone in this frozen world beneath a cold moon and stars like dagger points, and what were the chances of anyone finding me in time?

And even as I stared, I saw the silvered edge of approaching cloud. I watched it fearfully.

It came in slowly, but at length, it swallowed stars and moon. Darkness came down around me and the cold gripped my bones with hands of iron. I wondered if it would snow. If so, I would soon be buried in it, a little white mound in a white landscape.

I struggled again, but had to desist. I could not escape. I could not get up, could not walk. I was trapped.

The next part of this story isn't mine. I have put it together from what Brockley and the others told me, later on, when it was all over. It's a piecemeal narrative, for various people were doing different things. Lying there beside the outcrop, of course, I hoped that someone was looking for me, but could not suppose that out here, they would find me in time. I had made myself into living bait and the bait had been taken and by dawn it wouldn't be living any longer.

Someone, Jane Leigh, the Parkers . . . it hardly mattered who had set the trap for me and now I had sprung it.

I lay there, my wrists on fire from the ropes that I had wrenched to and fro in my struggles, and I wept, from terror and despair. I had no hope.

TWENTY
The Midnight Hunt

I t was Brockley who raised the alarm. When I didn't come back from visiting Jaunty, he sent Dale to see if I had been delayed by the Greshams. Dale stepped into their parlour in time to witness Miles Baines finally and firmly repeating that he wished to end his betrothal to Mildred and believed that Mildred also wished to end it, while Mildred, with hands clasped tightly together and a trembling but resolute voice, declared that yes, she did. Henry and Catherine had perforce to let Miles go. They then rounded angrily on Mildred.

In the middle of telling her daughter that she was an ungrateful, worthless, disobedient and foolish jade, Catherine noticed Dale and demanded to know what she wanted. Dale said timidly that she was looking for her mistress. Catherine snapped that Mrs Stannard was not in the house and Dale fled. As she did so, she heard Mildred crying.

Brockley, puzzled, went out to the stable, where he found Baines just leaving, along with his groom. I was not there and they hadn't seen me. Jaunty was there; evidently I hadn't ridden off anywhere. By then Brockley was becoming anxious. He came back indoors, wondering what to do next. Joyce, who by now was also worried, wondered if I could have gone to Ladymead to see my family. I might have gone on foot.

'Without *telling* anyone?' Dale demanded. 'The mistress would never do that! Least of all now, when she's courting danger!'

The three of them were still in anxious conference when there was a noisy hammering at the front door. They ran into the vestibule, in time to see Mr Gresham, a branched candlestick in his hand, opening it, to reveal Baines' groom, on his feet, looking distraught and grasping his horse's reins while his horse peered interestedly over his shoulder. Behind them was Miles

Baines, in his saddle, but sitting lopsidedly and so ashen-faced that it was visible even by candlelight.

The groom explained. They had been less than a quarter of a mile from the Greshams' house when a deer sprang from a patch of bracken on their left and leapt across the track in front of them, causing Mr Baines' horse to plunge in alarm, so violently that Mr Baines had lost a stirrup and been flung off, striking the ground with his left foot bent under him. He had sprained his left ankle badly and could only hope it was no worse than a sprain. His groom had grabbed the reins, so the horse hadn't got away. Baines had tried to stand but could put no weight on the injured foot.

However, with Baines clutching the saddle pommel while the groom, who was young and strong, heaved from behind with all his might, he was somehow got back astride the saddle, though he couldn't put his left foot into its stirrup. They had decided to turn back. The Greshams were much nearer than Miles Baines' own home.

My disappearance was not precisely forgotten but for the moment, Brockley felt called upon to assist as Baines was helped down and brought indoors. The groom took their horses to the stable but reappeared very soon, looking concerned.

By then, Baines was in the parlour with his left foot in a bowl of cold water, to bring down the swelling, which was already impressive, with blue bruising beginning to show. Dale and Tilly were in the kitchen, mulling ale for him, while Joyce and Mildred cut up an old sheet to make bandages. The ankle was out of the bowl and dried and the young groom, who was very deft, had bandaged it securely, before my absence was once again remarked upon.

When it was, by Brockley, Dale and Joyce in unison, Baines took it unexpectedly seriously.

'Mrs Stannard is the queen's sister! Relatives of Queen Elizabeth can't just be mislaid on Dartmoor on a freezing night! She does secret work at times – who knows what she is involved in now! And it's going to snow!' he said. 'Late in the year for it but I've known blizzards in April and we're still in March. I know moorland weather; I've grazed sheep on Dartmoor long enough to recognize that tang in the air. If

Mrs Stannard has vanished, then it's something to worry about.
A sister of the queen is a dangerous thing to be. And there
could be a reward for rescuing her.'

When, much later, I heard about that, I gave a wry smile.
Miles Baines was a man of the world, one who wouldn't miss
the chance of a reward. 'She's got to be found,' he said. 'Jimmy!'

'Sir!' said his anxious groom.

'Saddle up again and get yourself home as fast as you can
and get every able-bodied man in my employment out on a
search. Tell them to split into parties and comb the moors. The
moors must be searched first, because if she's out there long,
and lost, then she won't survive. Get Bryers to take charge;
he's the best man. Then you come back here. I might need you
later. And you!' He turned to Mr Gresham. 'Mrs Stannard's got
family here in Zeal Aquatio, hasn't she? Get them to start a
search in the village and round about.'

Miles Baines was behaving as though he and not Mr Gresham
was the master of the house but Mr Gresham, also taking my
disappearance seriously, didn't complain. He volunteered at
once to go himself to Ladymead and went to put on his cloak
and riding boots.

Brockley was relieved. A search was being mounted. He
would begin a search of his own, he said. He would find Eddie
– who was no doubt with his friends at the dyeworks stable –
and perhaps the dyeworks men, grooms and supervisors, might
join in. He'd be off at once.

Whereupon a new complication arose. Mildred announced
that she wanted to join the search as well and this of course
produced an outcry. Catherine exclaimed: 'You can do no
such thing!' and Mr Gresham, reappearing cloaked and
booted, declared decisively that no young girl could go
scouring the moor at night in the company of men. Mildred
retorted that if they found me, then I would be rescued *by*
a company of men, unless they had at least one woman
with them.

Joyce, still busy with the bandages, agreed with the Greshams
and said it would be best that she and Dale and Mildred stayed
behind and provided soup and hot drinks when the searchers
came back – 'and let us pray heaven that when they do come

back, Mrs Stannard is with them.' Dale bit her lip and said that
Mistress Frost was right.

Mrs Gresham then brought the whole argument to an unfore-
seen end by saying that it would be a good chance for Mildred
to get to know Mr Baines better, through looking after him.
'I think that the two of you haven't really made friends yet and
that's been the root of the trouble.'

Whereupon Mildred, suddenly and astonishingly resolute,
said: 'Mr Baines and I have agreed that we don't want to be
married, and for me to look after him now would embarrass us
both. I am going to saddle my cob and join the search and *no
one is going to stop me.*'

'Then,' Brockley told me later, 'though her mother shouted
at her and her father seized her arm and tried to hold her back,
she broke away and *ran*, just ran, out of the parlour, into the
vestibule where she snatched a cloak off a hook – it turned
out afterwards to be Tilly's cloak – and then on into the
kitchen, slamming the door behind her and turning the key.
There, she apparently snatched up a leather flask and filled it
from a wine keg, and then dashed out of the back door. And
Baines called out to let her go! *The more folk that hunt for
Mrs Stannard, the sooner she'll be found and I dare say
Mistress Mildred will be better at riding her cob across the
moors than she was ever going to be seeing to my dinners or
adding up my account books.*'

'Then Mr Gresham put his hands to his head and said, God
help us all, what is the world coming to, when young girls defy
their parents and ride out on manhunts as though they were
youths, and which was he to do first, pursue Mildred or get to
Ladymead and start them off searching, and I just left them all
and made for the stable to throw a saddle on my Firefly and
set out to find you, madam. Let Baines and the Greshams fight
all they liked; I had other things to do.'

And after that, Brockley's story blends into Mildred's.

When Brockley reached the stable, Mildred was in the tackroom,
fetching her saddle. There were lanterns on various hooks;
Baines' groom had probably lit them. Brockley caught her arm,
just as her father had, and she resisted, expecting him to say,

You can't do this and *I'm taking you back to the house at once.*
He said afterwards that he meant to say precisely that and had
even opened his mouth to say it, but Mildred spoke first,
and said: 'I won't go back to be bullied about Baines, I will
NOT!' so emphatically that he stopped short. He hadn't liked the
way they were treating her, anyway.

Then – his own words – he heard himself saying: 'You can't
go galloping over Dartmoor in the middle of the night, dressed
in long skirts and a farthingale and shiny shoes with buckles
on them! And a side saddle won't do, either.'

Mildred gaped at him in amazement, and Brockley said: 'Is
there a cross saddle to fit that cob?'

Afterwards, he said that even so, no matter how emphatic
Mildred was, he wouldn't have helped her as he did except for
his long experience of me. I had so often taken part in wild
rides, even at night, and sometimes I had done so in breeches.
For Brockley, it had become a commonplace. 'Alas,' he said to
me, with mock seriousness, 'association with you, madam, has
greatly changed my outlook.' Where most people would have
been shocked, Brockley was just practical.

There was a cross saddle, provided so that Will could sometimes exercise the cob. Brockley told her to put it on her cob
now, adding, 'Find a saddlebag for that wine flask you're
carrying,' and then scrambled up the ladder to the grooms'
quarters, to raid their clothes chests for breeches, shirt and
jacket, and grab a likely pair of boots. Then he ran down and
told her to change in the tackroom while he saddled Firefly.

Mildred said to me afterwards: 'He was brusque and matter
of fact and I hardly knew what to make of him, but he didn't
fuss. He just went straight to the point. So did I. I just did as
he said.'

Catherine and Henry had probably done a fair amount of
fussing, I suspected. Nagging, anyway. Mildred responded to
Brockley's straightforwardness. She changed quickly and came
out to find him holding the two horses.

'The dyeworks first,' said Brockley. 'Eddie and Will are
probably there. I want to collect them and the dyeworks grooms
too, if they'll come. The more of us, the better. Get mounted.
Do you know the dyeworks grooms?'

'No,' said Mildred. 'I've never been there. My father says it's not a place for women. I've ridden past it, that's all.'

'Your world is about to be widened,' said Brockley, who would once have agreed heartily with Henry Gresham.

The search party that was assembled in the end consisted of Brockley, Mildred, Eddie and Will, and the two dyeworks grooms. One was thickset and dark, while the other was mousey, short and wiry. Both were called John. 'So to distinguish us,' said the thickset one, to Mildred, 'we're Big John and Little John. I'm Little John. Just our fun.'

The supervisors were not there, as it chanced, but their horses were. 'They'm off to some friend's wedding,' Little John explained. 'On foot, as it's just into the village. Well, with me and Big John, and Eddie and Will, that's four. We'll borrow the packhorses – they're ridden at times – and one of the bosses'; that big chestnut's the strongest. Wouldn't do that normally but this here's an emergency.'

They did look doubtfully at Mildred, but Brockley said: 'Mistress Mildred Gresham will ride alongside me. She is coming in case Mistress Stannard needs another woman,' and Mildred said: 'Grey Cob will find his way home from anywhere. Whatever happens, I shan't get lost.'

After that, the packhorses and the big chestnut were saddled, and the party was mounted and away, taking what Big John said was a good clear track on to the moor, glad of the moonlight, as it showed them the path very plainly. 'We're lucky to have it,' Eddie said.

'But we'd best hurry and find the lady all the same,' Big John said. 'While the moon's still out. I don't trust this weather.'

TWENTY-ONE
Chance Met by Moonlight

The track that Brockley's search party chose led straight uphill to a moorland crest. Being moonlit it was easy to follow but once they were over the crest and descending on the other side, they met a dilemma, for it forked. The party pulled up. 'Which way?' Brockley asked.

'Lord, we'd forgotten that,' said Little John. 'None of us comes this way often. But that left-hand track bends and takes a line that's south-west rather than west and then forks again. I think.'

'Yes, that's right,' said Will. 'After about two miles. One path goes on south-west and the right-hand one goes off at a sharp angle and turns north. The right-hand fork *here* – this one in front of us – meanders a bit but it eventually crosses the one going north from the second fork. But that's far away, deep in the moor. We ought to split up.' He looked round, counting heads. 'There are six of us . . .'

Brockley said: 'I suggest that Mistress Mildred and I take the right-hand fork here. Eddie and Will can be another pair, and you two Johns. When the four of you get to the second fork . . .'

'Eddie can come south-west with me,' said Will.

'And we'll go north,' said Little John. 'We can all keep in touch with each other for a while. Like this.'

He then demonstrated a possible method, with a piercing whistle that made the horses start and snort. Grey Cob bucked and Mildred lost a stirrup, but hastily reclaimed it, hoping that no one had noticed. 'It'll carry a long way,' Little John said apologetically.

It emerged that Brockley could match it, and so could Will. Each party, in fact, had a man who could whistle. Between them they hastily devised a code. 'One steady whistle just to keep in touch. Two whistles mean a call for help. Three whistles mean that Mistress Stannard is found. If we don't find her soon, we'll eventually lose touch with each other but that'll do for the moment,' Little John said.

'I hope the moonlight lasts,' Mildred remarked as she and Brockley started along the right-hand track. 'It would be dangerous to lose the path. There are bogs!' She laughed, apparently made light-hearted by the sense of adventure. 'It's like those tales we were told when we were little, when people went on adventures and were warned not to leave the path through the forest, only they always did, and then they got into trouble from giants or wizards.'

'Don't be so cheerful!' said Brockley.

'Oughtn't we to call her name?' suggested Mildred. *'Mistress Stannard! Mistress Stannard! Ursula!* Like that?'

'Yes, we ought,' Brockley agreed. 'We can take it in turns. I'll begin. *Mistress Stannard! Ursula! Mistress Stannard!* Now a pause to listen for an answer. Quiet!' There was no answer. 'Nothing, so now it's your turn, Mistress Mildred.'

Shouting, turn by turn, they rode slowly on. The cold was intense and the biting wind tossed the horses' manes about. Grey Cob snorted with displeasure. 'He doesn't like the weather,' said Mildred. 'That's his disapproval noise.'

They lost sight of the quartet on the left-hand path but faintly, far away, they heard them calling my name as well. The sound faded after a while but then someone remembered about keeping in touch and a clear, steady whistle came across the moonlit moor. Brockley replied, emitting a truly ear-splitting signal through his fingers.

It sent Grey Cob into an outraged plunge. He bucked again and then jumped sideways off the track, all four legs as stiff as tree boles. Mildred gripped with her knees, noticing that having a knee on either side of her mount had much to recommend it, and clung on, hauling at his head and trying to use her legs to urge him back to Firefly.

Grey Cob would have none of it. He wanted to go home to his nice warm stall in a stable where all was quiet except for ordinary equine noises and the voices of human beings who knew they should speak quietly in the presence of nervous

creatures such as horses. He gave a final, furious buck and then
threw up his head, veered away in the opposite direction and
bolted.

Mildred held on and stayed in the saddle. She could hear
Brockley calling after her and galloping in pursuit but she was
too preoccupied with keeping her seat to answer. She sat down
hard and tried with all her might to drag Grey Cob's head
round to the left in the hope of slowing him down. Grey Cob,
who had a hard mouth, took no notice.

He had covered a good deal of ground before, at last, he
slackened speed of his own accord, partly because his wild
gallop had caused him to charge straight across a stream and
the cold water had shocked him out of his panic and partly
because he was out of breath. At any rate, he emerged from
the stream in a mere canter, which quickly sank to a trot and
finally a plod.

'Oh, dear heaven, where are we?' Mildred whimpered. She
could no longer hear Brockley's pursuit. He had been behind
her but he must somehow have taken a wrong direction.
Moonlight could be misleading. She called his name but there
was no reply. She was alone in an empty moorland, its rock
outcrops weird and pallid, its shadows inky, its silence so
intense that it pounded in one's ears.

At this moment, she realized that Grey Cob's plod was
remarkably purposeful. 'With every solid thud of his hooves,'
Mildred told me, 'he seemed to be saying, *You two-legged
human creatures think you're so clever but if you get off the
track you lose your bearings. You're afraid of the dark and
confused by the moon. But while your two legs go round in
circles, my four legs will get you home.*'

He would undoubtedly have brought Mildred back to the
Greshams' stable, except that before the cob's steady walk had
taken them very far, there was the snort of another horse and
a shape loomed up in front of them. Mildred gasped with fright
and then with relief, as the shape clarified and turned into Pascal
Bryers, on his mare.

'Mr Bryers!'

'Mistress Gresham! What brings you out here?'

'I was with Roger Brockley – Mrs Stannard's manservant

– but something frightened my cob and he bolted, and I lost touch with Brockley. We're searching for Mrs Stannard. She's missing.'

'I know. That's why I'm here. Mr Baines sent orders that I was to organize a search on the moor, using the men in his employ.'

'Yes, I heard him say that. But . . . you're alone?'

'I sent his men to comb a wide patch of moor – the part where his sheep graze and a wide swathe beyond. I told them to be methodical, work in strips as though they were ploughing a field, and I hope they're still at it. But as I was sending them off, I suddenly thought of something. Something I came across by chance – and then made sure of, because it interested me. Likely enough,' said Pascal, 'it was made by the ancient folk who once lived here. There's a queer sort of upright stone not a furlong from the edge of Mr Baines' further field. Take a straight line from that towards a rock outcrop on a hilltop ahead of you, and then from that, take a straight line towards another one, an extraordinary one, with a big stone like a flat pancake, balanced on top of another stone; get to that and then make for another upright stone, on a hilltop, like a finger pointing to the sky. There's a whole line of outcrops and stones and they lead straight across the moor towards the town of Launceston. I think they mark an ancient route to whatever sort of place Launceston was then, long ago. If Mistress Stannard has been taken out to somewhere on the moor, perhaps her captor knows about that trail of standing stones and he's using them as guides to wherever he's taking her.'

'And to make it easy to find her again,' said Mildred, shuddering. 'It's like what happened to Gregory Reeves. Mistress Stannard says that he was probably carried off to the moor with his hands and feet tied, but whoever took him wanted them untied when he was found, to make it all look like an accident, and came back later to remove them.'

'And you think Mistress Stannard has met the same fate? You could be right,' Bryers said. The moonlight showed her his grin: debonair and brave. Mildred looked at him and her insides felt as though they were melting.

'I'm so glad I met you,' she told him. 'I want to go on with the search. I seem to have lost Brockley but can I come with you?'

The grin disappeared. 'Certainly not. You should go home and at once. Does your horse know the way? Horses often do.'

'Yes, I think he does, and yes, I was going to let him because I can't search on my own,' said Mildred. 'But it would be different if I were with you. I could be useful.'

Mildred's account of her meeting with Pascal was factual enough yet I could sense what she had been thinking at the time. Her tone whenever she spoke his name told me that. I knew how pleadingly she had looked at him, and I knew the wordless message she had tried to send.

I want to come with you. I want to come with you and stay with you for ever and ever . . .

Cunningly, she said: 'I was in the original party because we thought that if Mrs Stannard were found, she might be hurt or . . . well, she might be glad of another woman. There were six of us to start with but we split up into pairs.'

'She'll be glad of anyone, I fancy,' said Pascal shortly, and gathered up his reins. 'No. You go home, my lady. I must be on my way.'

Mildred admitted to me that what she did then was outrageous. She followed him. 'I just wanted to stay with him,' she said.

When he realized that she was riding behind him, he twisted round and shouted: 'No! Go home!' but she took no notice and Grey Cob, pleased, now that he was calm, to have the company of another horse, merely lengthened his stride to lessen the distance between them. He was no longer trying to go home. Even though it meant once again splashing across that bitterly cold stream.

It was only a few minutes later when, faintly, they heard a voice calling, *Mistress Gresham! Mildred!* Pascal once more turned in his saddle. 'Who's that?'

'Brockley!' said Mildred. 'But he's a long way off.' And again, from her voice and her eyes, I could guess what she was thinking then. *I don't want to answer. I want to go on riding with Pascal Bryers for ever. Even though he doesn't want me, and even though it's so cold I can hardly feel my feet and my fingers are numb upon the reins, this is Paradise.*

'We're not going to change direction to find him,' said Pascal, drawing rein and allowing her to catch up with him. 'Unless I keep on following my landmarks, I would soon get as lost as anyone. It's hard enough to see them as it is. I think there's a drift of cloud coming up. But if we can hear Brockley, maybe he can hear us and then I can hand you over to him.' He raised his voice and bellowed: 'Brockley! I've got Mistress Gresham here!' More quietly, he added: 'You call to him. *Now!*'

Mildred couldn't well refuse. She raised her chin and shouted: '*Brockley! Brockley!*' several times. They waited for an answer and it came, though it was faint. '*Mildred! Mildred! Where are you . . . where . . . you . . . where . . .?*'

'*This way!*' Pascal shouted. '*Over here! This way! Come towards our voices!*'

'*Can't . . . bog!*' came the reply, nearer this time, but discouraging. '*Swamp in the way! Dangerous! Who's that with you, Mildred?*'

'*Pascal Bryers!*' shouted Mildred.

'*Can you take her home, Bryers?*'

'*Her horse'd know the way but she won't damn well go!*'

'*Go home, Mildred! Go home!*'

'Yes, you must,' said Pascal. 'For God's sake, turn your horse and let him take you home. Just turn him away, make him part company with my mare, and once she's out of his sight, drop the reins and let him go where he will, which with any luck will be his stable.'

Mildred tried, or appeared to try. It wasn't too difficult to make Grey Cob seem to turn obstinate and refuse to leave his new equine friend. He wanted to do just that anyhow. And besides . . .

'I'm afraid to be on my own,' said Mildred, trying to sound sorry about it. 'Please let me stay with you.'

'You'll hinder me! I don't want a woman along!' said Pascal angrily. Mildred flinched but persisted. 'It wasn't only that I wanted to stay with him,' she told me. 'If we found you, you really *might* be glad of a woman's help. That was *true!* And I told him so!'

'Seems I can't get rid of you!' Pascal snapped. 'Very well, we will look for Mistress Stannard together. But don't make a nuisance of yourself if it's a cold ride and a hard one. Come on.'

They rode on. Brockley's voice had ceased. It had, though, reminded her to call my name and she did so. The wind, which was strengthening, merely blew her words away and Pascal told her that she was wasting her breath. They went on for a time in silence, except that Pascal pointed out the next landmark, the silver finger of stone on top of a hill. Then, suddenly, the moonlight began to fade. 'Weather's changing,' said Pascal. 'There really is cloud coming over.'

So there was. It was flowing over their heads, and not far over, for they were on high ground. The stars towards the west had disappeared.

Pascal gave a snort of disgust. 'I think it's going to snow. Nice blinding snowstorm, just what we need. Dartmoor in winter is no place for you, madam, and I'm none too keen on it myself. Here's where we turn for home.'

'But your next landmark is just ahead! We're halfway up the hill to it, and we're on a deer track pointing that way!' Mildred said. 'Let's go that far, at least. We must *try*! Come on!'

'No, really, Mistress Gresham. We can't . . .'

'But we can!' Mildred was already urging Grey Cob forward. She said afterwards that she didn't quite know what made her so insistent on reaching the landmark before turning back. Perhaps it was the fact that Gregory had been found beside an outcrop, even though she wasn't aware at the time that she was thinking of Gregory. Pascal swore, but came with her. To placate him, Mildred reached down into her saddlebag and pulled out her leather flask. 'I have some wine here. Would you like a sip?'

'Wine? You have wine?' For a change, Pascal sounded pleased with her. 'Yes, let us both have a sip. By all means! It will warm us.'

Mildred sipped and handed him the flask. He took a long drink of it and passed it back to her. She returned it to the saddlebag and they rode on, somehow keeping themselves on the deer track. Then they were there, and the tall stone was there before them.

'This far and no further,' said Pascal. 'What did we come for, anyway? If it starts to snow, we'll have to trust the horses to find the way.'

'One more shout,' said Mildred. '*Mrs Stannard! Mrs Stannard!*'

'Oh, really, do you expect to be heard against this wind, even if anyone's there to hear you?'

'I must *try!*' said Mildred obstinately. '*Mrs Stannard! Mrs Stannard! Mrs Stannard!*'

I was half in a dream, an evil dream, made of despair, a black viscous substance in which I was drowning. No one would find me; how could they? Around me was only silence except for the sigh of that hateful wind. My body instinctively tried to curl up to conserve my own warmth, but I no longer seemed to have any. The wind was increasing and it was like having knives plunged into my back. But soon I would become unconscious and then I wouldn't feel the cold any more. The idea was tempting. I had only to let go . . .

Only, I could not quite let go, for surely, I could hear the sound of my name.

Someone, not far away, was calling to me.

'*Mrs Stannard! Mrs Stannard! Mrs Stannard!*'

My eyes opened. I lifted my head. With difficulty, for it felt huge, heavy. I took a deep breath. The icy air seared my throat and chest but it was air all the same. My captor hadn't gagged me. I tried to shout. At first I only managed a feeble groan. Then a louder one. And then, at last, words and something resembling, if not a shout, then at least a cry. '*Here! I'm over here! Help! HELP!*'

There were horses, trampling near me. I was afraid they would trample *on* me but no, their riders were dismounting, someone was bending over me. A voice I remembered, a female voice, said: 'Mrs Stannard! Oh, thank God, thank God!'

Another voice, a man's, said: 'She's bound. Here.' I heard the sound of a knife being pulled from its sheath and for a moment I was afraid again but then I felt the flat of the blade press harmlessly against my wrists. It was cold like everything else in this horrible world of knife-edged winds. My wrists were free and he was working at my ankles. I thought I knew his voice, too. Then the woman – surely it was Mildred – said: 'I'll bring the flask,' and the man answered: 'Yes, fetch it here.'

He tried to sit me up, but I was so inert that he couldn't. I flopped down and for a frightening moment my face was in the folds of his cloak and I had no strength to lift myself away and I couldn't breathe. I heard him curse and then he was pulling me free and propping me up and a flask was being held to my mouth. I swallowed, with difficulty, and then felt the warmth of wine in my gullet.

I couldn't stand, but somehow the two of them managed to pick me up, one holding my shoulders, one gripping my feet. I heard them panting as they strove to lift me. They did it somehow, up and up and to my own surprise I found myself being heaved onto a horse, shoved astride its withers, skirts bundled round me. The man was getting into the saddle behind me. The woman was mounting her horse, too. Was it really Mildred? But whatever was she doing out here, with . . . with *Pascal Bryers*? Yes, suddenly I recognized his voice too. How extraordinary, I thought, lolling against Pascal's chest. How . . .?

Pascal was saying something and Mildred was answering. 'Grey Cob will know the way.'

'I hope so! It's bloody well started to snow,' Pascal growled.

I didn't fear the snow now. Cradled against Pascal Bryers, drawing warmth from him and from the horse beneath me, I slept.

TWENTY-TWO
A Glimpse in the Distance

I slept nearly all the way home. My headache still throbbed but sleep was calling to me and I surrendered to it, because now I was safe, with rescuers.

Then, at last, we were there. I raised a heavy head at the sound of someone pounding on a door. I heard running footsteps and people exclaiming. Then torches spluttered amid the snow-flakes, lanterns were wavering about, hands were reaching to get me down. My knees crumpled and I heard Mildred saying, *She can't stand, she'll have to be carried.* I heard Brockley's voice, too, demanding to know what had happened to me, and exclaiming, *Thank God, thank God,* as he came to help with the carrying. I gathered later that all the others had given up the hunt when the snow clouds came up and had come back, one couple after another, just before us. They too had had horses with a sound homing instinct.

I knew nothing of that for the moment. I only knew that I was off the horse and being borne indoors. I heard myself cry out because someone had accidentally touched the back of my head, and I felt someone part my hair and Brockley's voice saying something about blood. I heard Dale ordering hot bricks. Mrs Gresham was saying: 'Pascal Bryers! How do you come to be here?' and Pascal was explaining, and Mildred was trying to tell everyone how they had been following a line of standing stones.

I was carried through to my quarters. Brockley had my shoulders. I knew the leather and horseflesh smell of him. I think Mr Gresham had my feet. Someone was following us with a lantern. I was being placed on my bed. Someone was busily lighting candles and Dale's face loomed over me in their light. I saw tears on her cheeks. 'Ma'am, we thought you were lost!'

I managed to smile at her. Then Joyce and Dale were peeling my clothes off and the boots were being dragged off my feet. Mrs Gresham came in with a steaming basin and washed the back of my head. It hurt me and I whimpered, but she hushed me, and laid me back, putting a towel beneath my head and saying something about a nasty bump. Somebody was lighting a fire in the hearth.

Mildred joined us, saying she had brought a woollen nightgown. 'Silk's no good to her; it's too cold.' I was being put into the nightgown. People were pulling it over my head, feeding my arms into its sleeves. A coverlet was put over me, and then another. Tilly came in with the hot bricks, wrapped in cloth. One was laid by my feet, one by my stomach. The fire crackled cheerfully. I was lapped around by comfort.

Nothing seemed real. I had been so cold. Now I was so hot. Too hot, and the people moving about in the room, feeding the fire, lighting more candles, talking in low voices, discussing who was to watch beside me through the rest of the night . . . they were becoming insubstantial, their shapes wavering, melting into each other, turning into beings from legend or nightmare . . .

I was becoming delirious. I was ill.

The following week was nearly as hazy as the ride home on the withers of Pascal Bryers' mare. I slid in and out of dreams. I was aware of cold compresses being put to the back of my head but the rest of me was hot, so hot. Voices came and went. I learned afterwards that so as to let me have the big bed to myself, Joyce slept for many nights alongside it on a truckle, while Dale had another one on the other side. The Greshams fortunately had several. I was never without someone near at hand.

I knew them only as phantoms and disembodied voices. I was vaguely aware of having my sweaty skin wiped, and being sat over a basin to relieve myself and I would resist, in a feeble, petulant, semi-conscious way. They brought cups to my lips and encouraged me to swallow milk, or wine or well water. Swallowing hurt. I had lost my voice. Food made me retch. Dale told me later that sometimes they despaired of getting any nourishment into me at all and feared I would starve. Joyce said: 'We tried you with bread mixed with milk and honey, and warm soups, different kinds. But you threw it all up.'

They persevered, however, and I dimly recall hearing Joyce and Dale, in unison, arguing spiritedly with a man – I learned later that he was a physician that Mrs Gresham had summoned – who wanted to bleed me. 'She's weak and exhausted enough as it is!' That was Joyce. And then Dale said indignantly: 'She needs comfort, not someone making holes in her! No, you may *not* bleed her!'

The physician did, however, recommend a medicine. Joyce said it was made from willow bark and was just like one of the medicines that Gladys used at home when people ran fevers. At any rate, mine began to subside after I had been given the medicine, three times a day, for two days. I began to sweat in earnest. It poured out of me and the day after that, I became lucid. I still had a sore throat but my headache had gone and I was cool.

On the eighth day of my illness, I woke to find my throat much improved. I was able to sit up and ask Dale for something to drink. 'Oh, ma'am! You've got your voice back!' Dale squealed, overjoyed. Then I had to say: 'Please be calm. That milk is for me, not for the floor!' For she was so delighted that her hands were shaking and she was spilling milk as she filled a glass from a pitcher by the bedside.

I took the glass from her tremulous grasp and smiled at her. 'Do you know, Dale, I think I'm hungry! Dale? You're crying!'

'Ma'am, it's been so long. We've been so frightened. We thought . . . we thought . . .'

'We thought we'd lose you. Again!' Joyce came into the room, carrying a basin of hot water. 'Ursula, you keep frightening us to death.' She set the basin down and began to minister to the back of my head. 'You still have a big bump there,' she told me, 'but it's healed up where it bled to begin with.'

'And by the grace of God, the sickness never took your lungs,' said Dale, wiping her eyes.

'It's all right, Dale,' Joyce said gently. I rested a hand on Dale's white-capped head and gave Joyce a smile. She looked down at me and as I looked up, into her light hazel eyes, I saw in them real affection, the affection I had so long tried to win from her. We had made friends, but never until now had she taken that further step, into genuine love. I was touched.

'I'm better now,' I said reassuringly. 'I'll be up before long.'

'You mustn't rush things!' said Joyce, sounding quite alarmed at the prospect.

'No, ma'am, you mustn't rush!' Dale agreed. 'If you were to slip back . . .!'

'I don't intend to slip back.'

Joyce said: 'Do you feel well enough yet to talk to Constable Rossiter? He has heard the story from Mildred and from Mr Bryers but he wants to speak to you as well.'

I said I would see Constable Rossiter. I hoped that by pointing out to him the resemblance between my near-lethal experience and the death of Gregory Reeves, and adding the details of my henbane poisoning, I might get him to believe in secret agents and people who might want to murder them. I was wrong. There is no need to repeat the wearisome nature of my interview with him, which greatly resembled the things he said when I met him at the Parker vicarage.

He pooh-poohed the poisoning episode; folk was having food poisoning all the time; it was a hazard of life. He also pooh-poohed the resemblance between my *mishap* as he called it and Gregory Reeves' death. Yes, someone had perpetrated a nasty joke on me but . . .

Joyce was present, sitting beside me, and at the word *joke* she and I burst out with so much indignation that he retreated from it and said that well, yes, maybe it did sound as though someone had tried to finish me off though they'd gone a mighty long way round to do it. So, who might have a reason? I was a lady of substance, wasn't I, now? Who were my heirs?

My only heir, I said angrily, was my son Harry, aged fourteen, now living at Hawkswood, my home in Surrey, in the care of his tutor, and studying double-entry accounting, Latin, Greek and how to play the lute.

Samuel Rossiter went away shaking his head and saying that he'd look into it all and talk to Master Bryers and Mistress Mildred again. They told me afterwards that he seemed to have got it into his round bald head that Mildred and Pascal had for some reason got together and played a dangerous trick on me. Mr Gresham, as indignant as I was, then ordered Rossiter out of his house forthwith, informing him that Mrs Stannard would certainly not want to accuse either his daughter or Pascal. Rossiter had gone away, looking resentful, Dale told me, but anyway, he had gone.

I put him out of my mind and concentrated instead on getting well. In two more days I was able to get up and walk about the room, and after that I insisted on getting dressed. I was thinner, though, and my clothes felt loose. I had brought a bronze hand mirror in my luggage and even the colour of the bronze couldn't conceal how pale I was. Dale, however, was overjoyed by my improvement and went down on her knees in my bedchamber to say a prayer of thankfulness. Thomasina came to see me too, and did the same thing. She did not stay long, however. She was very bulky and looked tired. I asked her when she was likely to be confined and she said it was probably in three weeks. She would be glad to be rid of the burden, she said.

I was well on the mend by the end of that week, and on the Friday, Mildred came to see me, a new Mildred, with eyes almost starry enough to light a room.

I had put on a loose gown and was resting on my bed. Mildred sat down beside me and took my hands. 'You are better, are you not? I am so glad. My dear Mrs Stannard, I just have to tell someone. After all, we were all three together in the snow; you are the right person to tell first. I am going to marry Pascal Bryers. When you were so ill, he came to ask how you did, and we had the chance to talk a little. Today, we met for a walk and he told me he means to ask my father for my hand!'

'Dear Mildred,' I said weakly. 'I wish you every possible happiness. When is Mr Bryers coming to see your father?'

'He's here now. Father is at the dyeworks, of course. Pascal is in the family parlour with Mrs Gresham, waiting for him to come home. But he would like to visit you. Will you let him?'

'Of course. Bring him in,' I said.

Mildred did so and then slipped away and I lay looking up at my other rescuer, who smiled at me shyly and said: 'I gather

that Mildred has told you our news. I think I have to be grateful
to you, Mrs Stannard.'

'Grateful to me?'

'But for meeting Mildred in the snow, but for having to
search for you, I would never have realized what a fine young
woman she is. She was lost out there on the moor, but she was
keeping her head. She had a flask of wine with her, so practical.
She kept her nerve, all the time, and she was so determined
to find you.'

'Yes. I think she was,' I said.

'She is exactly the kind of wife I need,' said Pascal lyrically.
'When we met on the moor, I tried to send her home, but
she wouldn't go; she said she *must* help in the search. And
when we found you; she knew what to do; knew to give
you the wine and how to help me get you on to my horse.
And then when we got back here, I saw her in the lamplight
with her curly hair fallen free of her hood, and her eyes shining
as she smiled at me and, well, I fell in love; and it's real and
I just hope I can make her happy.'

'I'm sure you will,' I said, feeling happy too. This was what
Mildred needed. It was probably what Sabina had needed,
once, though for her, that time had surely passed. 'Go on, go
back to her,' I said. 'And be tactful with her father!'

'He'll be glad to see her married, or so she says,' said Pascal.
'And I think she'll be happier in my cottage than in Baines'
House. I sometimes help lambs into the world but I won't ask
her to do the same. It's no task for a lady, in my view.'

He went out laughing, and five minutes later, I received
another visitor. Against all probability, it was Miles Baines. The
Greshams could not in decency have refused to receive him
when he was injured and theirs was the nearest dwelling, and
of course, they hadn't refused. But now that he was recovered,
as he obviously was, for he walked across the room without a
limp, I couldn't believe that he was welcome in their house.
He looked amused at my surprise.

'Mistress Joyce fetched me here,' he said. 'When everyone
else was rushing off to look for you, she stayed behind and
bandaged my ankle. She and I talked, and something I said has
been on her mind, it seems. Yesterday, she rode over to see me,

all on her own. She sent me here. She says I must tell you, myself, that it must come from me because I was the man who actually saw it. She says it's urgent, important. So here I am!'

'I'm surprised the Greshams let you in!'

'I said I had business with you, concerning your safety, because of something to do with your work for the queen. All your secrets are coming into the open, mistress. They let me in because they have the good sense to understand that because a girl has refused to marry the man her parents have chosen, that isn't a good reason for refusing help when a guest has nearly been murdered and the queen's welfare is concerned. I told them I must see you on business concerned with that and Mistress Frost came to the door to add her voice to mine.'

I blinked at him. 'Well,' I said, 'may I know what this matter is that's been worrying Joyce? Though why she couldn't tell me herself . . . well, what is it?'

'It's just – you know my road home from here takes a track that turns off the Tavistock road and goes over a shoulder of the moor?'

'Yes. I remember.'

'I had my fall just after the turn. But just before that – it wasn't yet dark, you see – I caught sight of someone else on the moor, some way away, someone on foot but leading a laden packhorse and taking a line that led into the moor. Into the heart of the moor! I wondered where they were going, taking that line. I've known the moor all my life, you see. I wasn't near enough to see what the horse was carrying, but there was something slung over its back, dangling down its side. The more I think about it, the more I think – I probably saw you!'

'You could well be right,' I said. 'But could you tell who was leading the horse? What did the horse look like?'

'Not a horse really,' said Miles. '*Pony*-sized, more like. A biggish pony, brown, I think. Couldn't make out anything about the man; cloak and hood, that's all I could see of him. But the horse had a white sock on its off fore. Funny. I caught just a glimpse of that and thought nothing of it, until Mistress Joyce told me what it might mean and said you must know of it.'

His eyes were steady and somehow appealing, as though he

wanted me to say it first but I couldn't say it, not outright, not yet.

'I know what you're suggesting,' I said. 'But I must think, confer with Joyce and the Brockleys. But thank you for coming, Master Baines. You did right. But let's not say the name out loud just yet. I must talk with my friends.'

Baines nodded. 'As you wish, Mistress Stannard.'

He turned to go, but before he reached the door, it was flung open, and Mildred burst through it. A changed Mildred, the starry eyes all gone, curls loose and tangled as though she had clawed them, the prettily flushed face streaked with tears. She threw herself on her knees by my bed, buried her face in the covers and wailed something incoherent.

'Mildred!' For the first time since my illness, I achieved a shout. '*Mildred!* What is the matter?'

'I will fetch her mother, or Mistress Joyce,' said Baines, embarrassed, and went hastily out.

'*Mildred!*' I repeated.

She raised her face. 'I'm sorry, I'm sorry.'

'Never mind that. What's wrong? Won't your father . . .?'

'No, he won't, and do you know why?'

'Of course I don't. Mildred, please tell me.'

'He says that Pascal's a *papist!*' she wailed. 'And Pascal doesn't deny it! He says what does it matter? But it matters to Father and he's ordered Pascal out of the house and told him never to come back! Pascal's crying as much as I am! He went out in tears. And it was that man Miles Baines who told my father, told him long ago, it seems, when he was talking to Father about arranging a marriage with me! Telling Father all about his home and the people who work for him. Well, thank God I'm not going to be made to marry Baines now because I'd rather die! He's ruined my life! I wish I was dead anyway!' howled Mildred, and once more buried her face in my coverlet. I patted her head feebly and was thankful when Joyce came in, to lift Mildred up and lead her away.

When she came back to me, some time later, saying that Mildred was weeping on her bed and her mother was with her, I said: 'Bring the Brockleys to me. Baines has told me what he saw, that evening when I was taken. Now I must talk to you all.'

TWENTY-THREE
Seeking Evidence

'So,' I said. 'What have we got? Where are we now?'

It was the afternoon of Easter Sunday. I was up, dressed, and more or less normal though I had not yet ventured to walk far, let alone get into Jaunty's saddle, and I could not go to the Easter morning service.

The house was quiet. On Sunday afternoons, after dinner, Mr Gresham liked to retire to his study to read the Bible, or so he said, though Brockley insisted that he had sometimes passed the study door on Sunday afternoons and had distinctly heard snoring, and did I know there was a couch in there? His wife and daughter were also supposed to spend the afternoon studying Holy Writ but they too, I was fairly sure, welcomed the chance for a little extra sleep. It was a good time for a secret conference. We were holding it in Joyce's and my room, gathered round a fire, for although it was now April, it was still as cold as ever.

'You mean what do we know now about the fate of Peter Gray and Gregory Reeves?' said Joyce. 'And what do we think about the brown pony that Mr Baines saw, with the white sock on its off fore? You told us about it but then you said don't discuss it, just think it over. But isn't it time we talked about it? Especially about that brown pony.'

'There are hundreds of brown ponies with white socks on their off fores,' I said. 'It really means very little. The pony that Tom Hillman has, has such a sock.'

'It's nearer a stocking than a sock,' said Brockley. 'And Tom's pony is a dark bay.'

'At a distance, with twilight coming on, there isn't much difference. And anyway, there are still hundreds of other brown ponies with white off fores,' I said and knew I sounded feeble.

'You don't want to say the names,' said Joyce. 'You hate the idea of saying them. That's why you've not wanted to talk about it but we must. Sabina Parker has a pony just like that.'

'But Sabina couldn't . . . ! Can you,' I asked her, 'imagine Sabina drinking in the Castle Inn and getting Peter Gray drunk – maybe putting something in his cider – and encouraging him out into the street for whoever is her partner to run over?'

'A fair number of the local women drink in the inn,' said Brockley. 'But yes, Sabina would stand out, would be noticed – a stranger, except that if anyone did recognize her, they'd be recognizing the sister of Lucius Parker, the vicar at Zeal Aquatio.'

'And vicars' sisters don't often go drinking in inns,' said Dale.

'Yesterday,' said Brockley, 'I went to the vicarage and asked Dr Parker to include a prayer of thankfulness for your recovery, during today's service.'

Startled by this non sequitur, I said: 'Thank you, Brockley.' I then waited for him to explain. He gave me his rare, broad grin.

'I was cunning as well as careful,' he said. 'I talked of your frightening adventure, madam. Dr Parker said he'd known nothing about it until two days later, after the Hillmans had been told. Then he got it from Mistress Thomasina when she called at the church – I understand, to offer private prayers that all should go well when the babe is born.'

'As we all pray it will,' said Dale, large-eyed with earnestness.

'Dr Parker,' said Brockley, doggedly sticking to his theme, 'apparently spent that Saturday evening – the evening when you were seized, madam – in his study with a sheet of paper on his knee, backed by a piece of board, trying to revise his homily for the next day. Or so he says. Sabina had already gone to bed. She still has her woman's bad times, it seems. He was quite alone that evening. Maybe he didn't stay in his study.'

'I do hate saying this,' I told them, 'but I keep remembering how kindly he spoke of Mary Stuart, the first time we met him. I don't like the man but I don't like to think that he might be the one who . . . But he has told us that he sometimes borrows Sabina's pony, Sock.'

'And he said he was afraid of what could happen to him

and those like him, if the Spanish ever came here,' added Joyce sombrely.

'I know,' I said. 'It could be. A kind of insurance against that. He could have used his sister's pony – Sock is probably a steadier pack animal than his own horse and my inert body might be an awkward burden, I suppose. I wonder why he led the pony and walked on foot instead of taking his horse. Perhaps he thought the horse would be conspicuous – the vicar's horse is usually well known in his parish and beyond. Or maybe he thought it could be hard to manage two horses and me, in my sack, all at once. There is no one who can confirm his story but equally, who is there to contradict it?'

'But who was his partner? Who *is* his partner?' Brockley said. 'We know he must have had one, because of Peter Gray. One driving the cart, one pushing Gray into the road. When I talked to the landlord he said he didn't think Gray had had that much to drink, and yet he was reeling and staggering as though he was very drunk indeed or else drugged. To me, that suggests that he drank moderately but it was tampered with. But if we're up against two, who is the other one?'

'Well, it wasn't Miles Baines,' I said. '*He* wasn't knocking me on the head and carrying me off into the heart of the moor. He was here, with a sprained ankle, being ministered to by you, Joyce.'

Joyce said slowly: 'Mildred is in despair because her father won't let her marry Pascal Bryers, all because he's a papist. Pascal was out on the moor that night, alone, until Mildred came across him.'

'Mildred says he tried to get rid of her,' I said slowly.

'He tried to reunite her with Brockley, only Brockley couldn't get to her,' said Joyce. 'Then he tried to make her go home alone – she'd said that Grey Cob knew the way. He was angry when she wouldn't go.'

'I did my best,' said Brockley. 'I called your name, madam, and you answered but when I tried to ride towards you, the way was blocked by a bog – a horrible mass of quaking mud with reeds at the edge. Firefly felt the ground under his feet going soft and he balked, and quite right too. I shouted to Mildred to let Grey Cob take her home.'

'But she wouldn't leave Bryers,' I said thoughtfully. 'And he couldn't harm her in any way, not once Brockley knew she was with him. That would swivel suspicion his way at once.'

'He apparently told her he was taking a line along a series of landmarks,' said Joyce. 'While the moonlight lasted, they could see one of them, straight ahead, a tall stone sticking up on a hill crest. They were on a track pointing towards it and Mildred insisted on going that far. Pascal didn't seem to want to. And that's where they found you, Mistress Stannard.'

'It could have been where Pascal was going in the first place,' I said. 'To undo my bonds once I was dead, or nearly. And couldn't, because Mildred was there. Then she kept shouting and I managed to shout back! Yes, it could be.'

And then I remembered, with a sick sensation in my stomach, how, just for a moment, one of my rescuers had muffled my mouth in his cloak – until Mildred brought the wine flask to me.

Joyce was working it out. 'He obviously wasn't your kidnapper – while you were being taken across the moor, Bryers was organizing Baines' men into search parties. But if there are two men involved in this nasty business, then maybe Parker was one and Bryers was the other. Parker to take you onto the moor and leave you, Bryers to untie you when you were dead, or nearly. Why did Pascal try to marry Mildred? She hadn't noticed anything amiss – he had no need to control her, to keep her silent about anything.'

'According to Bryers himself, he was looking for a wife, and suddenly, he fell in love,' I said.

'Just because they spent an hour or two together and he was trying to get rid of her?'

'It can take just five minutes,' I said. 'I speak from experience.'

Gerald, my first husband, whom I virtually stole from my cousin Mary. Gerald and I met for the first time and saw each other and that was that. And Matthew, Matthew with whom I knew such magical passion, who fathered Harry, it didn't take me long to fall in love with Matthew, either. Marrying Hugh was different, though. That was just practical to begin with. Love came later. Dear God, it's all in the past; let it go.

'Let us take another angle,' I said. 'Is it really possible that Lucius Parker is supporting Mary Stuart?'

Brockley said: 'We've searched Peter Gray's and Gregory Reeves' papers in case they'd left notes of people they suspected. They hadn't. But if Parker has been collecting money for her cause, might he not keep records of it of some sort? Shouldn't we try to get a look at *his* papers? If we don't find an account book, we might find something else – popish symbols, perhaps. Letters of thanks for donations. Anything!'

'You mean search the vicarage. But we can't . . .' Joyce began.

'I can think of a way,' I said.

'If that is what you really want,' said Bartholomew, 'we will do it. But am I right in thinking that after all, you have involved us in . . . your unusual duties?'

'I'm afraid I have,' I said.

'I won't waste time asking questions that you won't answer,' said Bartholomew dryly. 'We've asked the Parkers to dine before but they may be surprised to find that Joyce and Dale are invited but that you and Brockley are not.'

'You must make our excuses,' I said. 'Say that I should have been there but had a relapse that very morning. At first I insisted that I would still manage to come but at the last minute I admitted I couldn't but sent Joyce and Dale because I didn't want to waste all the trouble you would have taken. Say Brockley wished to remain at hand in case he was needed.'

Bartholomew, who had come at once in answer to my request, delivered by Brockley in the form of a note, looked at me gravely. 'You clearly want the Parkers out of your way. Do you suspect Lucius of something? Do you mean to search his home? Am I right?'

'I'm afraid so,' I said, reluctantly. Bartholomew was a difficult man to deceive.

'You might as well have said so openly,' he told me. 'And I suppose you want us to keep the Parkers with us as long as we can?'

'Yes.'

'I will have to see that Thomasina only gives orders and does no work herself. But I will agree, if you will declare, on oath as it were, that your business is the queen's business and therefore lawful?'

'I do declare it,' I said, matching his formal tone.

'Well, I left Thomasina considering our menu,' said Bartholomew, allowing himself to smile. 'There's a butcher in the village who sells ducks, ready drawn and plucked. Thomasina was talking of duck for as the main course, accompanied by a nice tangy sauce with ginger in it, and verjuice . . .'

'I truly loathe this business,' I said, as I carefully loaded dagger, picklocks and a purse of money into the hidden pouch inside the open skirt of a narrow brown gown. I had dispensed with a farthingale and my shoes had soft soles. Thomasina had sent me a note saying that the Parkers had accepted her invitation. The vicarage, therefore, would be empty. The Parkers probably wouldn't have locked their front door; few people did. But if they had, I had my picklocks.

Brockley and I saw Joyce and Dale on their way to Ladymead. They went on foot and when, shortly afterwards, we set out as well, we too were on foot. Two horses tied to the front gate of the vicarage would be much too noticeable.

One of the most unnerving things about tasks like this was the moment when you had to stop behaving innocently, and take that first step into doing something dangerous. The moment when you had to ask the first question about something that you weren't supposed to be interested in; the moment when you entered a house where you had no business to be, the moment when you started to search someone else's desk or document box. Every time I did any of these things, it gave me the shivers.

As we walked through Zeal Aquatio, Brockley and I were still law-abiding people, a lady and her escort, strolling in the April sunshine, glad that at long last there was real warmth in it. Law-abiding we would remain until we reached the vicarage. If anyone chanced to be passing, we would linger in the front garden, pointing things out to each other, and we would still be innocent. But when we raised the latch of the vicarage front door – or when I inserted a picklock into the keyhole above the latch – from that moment on, however admirable our purpose, we had left the official path of righteousness.

In the vicinity of the vicarage, there was no one about. We walked to the door and when Brockley tried the latch, it opened. We stepped inside and shut the door behind us and stood there, knowing that we would be hard put to it to explain ourselves, if challenged.

'If he has a study, we had best begin there,' I said. 'After that, his bedchamber, I think.'

We advanced cautiously. First of all, we went into the parlour. The rest of the house was unknown to us but we made a rapid search of the ground floor, discovering a second, larger parlour, a dining room, a kitchen and a stuffy little room where some children's clothes were piled on a table. Evidently Sabina's charitable hoard. There was no sign of a study. 'We'd better try upstairs,' I said, half whispering, even though there was only Brockley to hear me.

Upstairs, there was no landing. The staircase led straight into what was quite obviously the study and after that all the rooms just led in and out of each other. Hawkswood had been like that once but Hugh had alterations done because he grew tired of people walking through his bedchamber to get to theirs, or vice versa.

'This is the study for sure, madam,' Brockley said. 'But it will take some searching.'

He was right. To say that the study was untidy was to have a shaft fall well short of the mark. It was fairly big as far as floor space went but its ceiling sloped and massive beams cut off corners. These upper rooms were immediately under the roof.

The floor space, therefore, had limitations but the desk, on the contrary, was vast. It was also chaotic, strewn with papers and books and scrolls and quills. A pot of unused quills had been pushed to one end and was in peril of falling off; a half-unrolled scroll was being kept open by a metal ruler and an inkpot and the inkpot was partly hidden because a small picture had been propped against it. Presumably Lucius had a sander but if so, it was buried amid the confusion.

'Oh well,' I said, 'with everything in such a muddle, it won't matter if we move things. He's not likely to notice!'

We searched the desk as best we could. There was nothing suspicious on it. The picture was a miniature of a woman, and on the back the words *Lucy Parker, my mother* were engraved. Judging from the writing on a sheet of paper that lay squarely in front of the chair, Lucius had been writing, or trying to write a homily on the theme of the wedding at Cana. There was a small hearth, in which there had recently been a fire, and some twisted, half-burnt bits of paper suggested that he had been throwing bad efforts into the flames.

There were a few letters on the desk, all to do with entirely respectable things such as an invitation to stand in for a Plymouth vicar who had fallen ill, another invitation, this one asking him to dine with a friend in Tavistock, a long screed apparently from one of his cousins. That was all.

There was nothing at all in the way of figures. We gave up as far as the desktop was concerned and tried the two shallow drawers below. These contained spare sheets of paper, an unused notebook and a little box of nuts.

'The bedchamber?' said Brockley.

'Yes.' I closed the last drawer. 'Which way?'

There were doors on either side of the study. Our first cast, to the left, took us through an unused bedchamber with a stripped bed, an empty washstand, an empty fireplace and a cupboard containing bedlinen and towels. But the next room, in the corner of the house, was plainly Sabina's. It was furnished with a clothes press, a simple tester bed, a little dressing table with two drawers beneath it and a washstand with a pitcher and basin on it.

This room too had a dramatically sloping ceiling and numerous massive beams and I noticed that Sabina must always have to get out of bed on her left-hand side. Her nightgown lay across her bed, and her dressing table held a brush and a comb, a pot of ointment and a little bottle of perfume, either lavender or sandalwood, no doubt; I didn't trouble to test it. I pulled the drawers open one by one but found only under-linen and stockings and nightwear. The press just held gowns, sleeves and ruffs.

There was no further door so we went back to the study and tried the door to the right. And here it was, Lucius' bedchamber. It was a contrast to Sabina's room and also to the study, for instead of being untidy, it was bleak and empty of all but necessities. The bed had the framework for a canopy but the canopy itself was absent. A small whitewood table with a single drawer did duty as a dressing table. The top of it bore only a brush and comb and a silver hand mirror. The room had the usual low beams, of course. Brockley went to look more closely at the dressing table, banged his head on one of them and muttered something under his breath.

A washstand occupied one corner but in another, there was a little desk with a small crucifix hanging above it. We both looked at it thoughtfully. Then Brockley said: 'The drawers and cupboards next,' and threw open the door of a clothes press.

This contained only clothes and few enough of those. There were clerical garments, riding things, a couple of ordinary sets of doublet and hose; some shirts. Two pairs of boots and one pair of shoes were placed neatly on the floor. Some meagre piles of under-linen had been set on a shelf. While Brockley was still examining the press, I pulled out the drawer of the dressing table. Two ruffs on one side and on the other, a tumbled pile of stockings, handkerchiefs, gloves and woollen scarves. I moved the pile aside.

'Brockley!'

'Madam?' Brockley turned from the press.

'Look!'

'Well, well,' said Brockley.

Beneath the heap of gloves and scarves, Lucius had concealed two most interesting objects. One was a miniature portrait of Mary Stuart. It wasn't a good portrait. I would have said it was a copy of a copy and by an indifferent artist at that. But it was still recognizable. I had known her, and anyway, I had seen copies of that same portrait elsewhere. The other object was a statuette, perhaps six inches high. It had been wrapped in a scarf, possibly for extra concealment. It depicted the Virgin and Child. She wore her usual blue robe; He had a golden halo.

'It isn't proof,' I said. 'These things could be just sentimental reminders – playthings in a way.'

'But they're suggestive.'

'Yes, they are. Only I wish we'd found some accounts or letters or *something* definite,' I said. 'Well, let's see the other rooms.'

We did this but found nothing of interest. There were two more spare rooms, furnished like the first. One was the same size, the other much smaller. We found a lumber room with not much in it beyond a couple of ironbound chests containing moth-eaten coverlets and rugs and the like. We also found a room where there were shelves containing books, mainly history and travel, and maps, but nothing at all sinister.

'Lucius' library,' I said. 'The books seem harmless. I think we're finished. I wish we'd found *something* more than the kind of relics any vicar might have, but . . .' I stopped, raising my head, listening. 'Brockley . . .'

'Stand still. Not a sound,' whispered Brockley. 'I heard the latch go. Somebody's come in.'

TWENTY-FOUR
Strange Contradictions

t was Larkhurst all over again; just as we thought ourselves safe from interruption, an interruption there was. My heart was pounding. Downstairs, footsteps were moving about. A voice called: 'Is anyone at home? Dr Parker?' Not the Parkers themselves, then. And now, feet on the stairs.

There was nothing for it but boldness. Thrusting miniature and statuette back into the drawer with one hand, tossing gloves and scarves on top of them with the other and jerking the drawer shut, I called, 'Mistress Ursula Stannard and Master Roger Brockley are here. Who is that?'

Before anyone could answer, Brockley and I were through the door to the study. We could not now be caught in the act of searching Dr Parker's belongings. We got ourselves into the study just before the newcomer did. His identity was a surprise.

'Master Hanley!' I said. 'Master Crispin Hanley. Er . . . good afternoon.'

'Good afternoon!' said Hanley. He stopped in the doorway. He had a bundle under one arm and an aggressive expression. 'I see the Parkers are out. So what are you doing here?' His tone was rude.

'Dr Parker and Sabina are dining with friends,' I said. 'As for what we are doing here, we might ask you the same question.'

'I have a right to be here.' Hanley patted his bundle. 'I have brought some children's clothes for Mistress Sabina's charity. The Parkers don't mind me walking in with my gifts of clothing. Mostly, when my older orphans grow out of their clothes, we pass the outgrown things to the young ones, but sometimes I like my young orphans to have something new. Then I have a few cast-offs for Mistress Sabina.'

He gave us his yellow-toothed grin. It made him, to my mind, resemble a horse. 'You should see how my little orphan boys swagger when they have new breeches on, and how the little girls love a new gown. And now' – the grin disappeared – 'now that I've told you my business here; once more I ask you: what is yours?'

'Our business is our own. But it is lawful,' Brockley said coldly.

I said: 'We are here on the business of the queen.' I paused and then decided on frankness. 'We've searched the house. We have found popish symbols.'

'You were chosen personally and sent by the queen?' Hanley laughed, disbelievingly.

'Mistress Stannard,' said Brockley coldly, 'is a half-sister to the queen and one of those who perform secret tasks for her, usually on the instructions of Lord Burghley or Sir Francis Walsingham. She is here now for such a purpose. Mind your manners, please. *Extortioner!*'

'Did your nephew Robert, my steward, never tell you who I was?' I asked curiously.

'It's a long time since we exchanged any friendly letters. Can't recall that we ever did, really. Well, seems I'd better believe you, or you'll blackmail *me*, I expect.'

'That's possible,' said Brockley, his voice silken.

'I don't suppose you're here to steal valuables. You're not that sort and anyhow, I don't think there are any. Well, well. And now I'll tell you that although bringing things for Mistress Sabina was my excuse for walking into the house and I really have brought some, this time, it really *is* an excuse. What would you say if I told you I was on more or less the same business as you?'

'Are you?' enquired Brockley.

'It's quite a tale.' Hanley patted his bundle again. 'Let us go downstairs. I'll put this with Mistress Sabina's collection of smelly old garments, and then we can talk in the parlour. The bigger one. It's more comfortable.'

He stepped back in a tacit invitation to let us lead the way. As we walked past him, Brockley kept watchfully close to me. Hanley grinned at him. 'I am not about to pounce on your mistress, Master Brockley, either to ravish or to arrest her. I really am on the same mission as yourselves.'

We left it there until we were downstairs, had seen Hanley deposit his contribution to charity in Sabina's little storeroom and repaired to the larger of the two parlours. This had a diamond-paned window with a window seat, and overlooked the track that led to the village. By peering through the diamond panes, one could also glimpse the track towards Ladymead, and to the left, a stark shoulder of Dartmoor with a scatter of outcrops. I turned hurriedly away from that, and seated myself. This second parlour had cushions on its seats. 'Now,' I said. 'We don't understand, so please explain yourself.'

'I know the Parkers quite well,' Hanley said. 'I've never liked Lucius. Sabina's a fine woman, far too good for that disapproving brother of hers. There are regular musical evenings at a house in Tavistock – owned by a couple of sisters called Brewster . . .'

'I know,' I said. 'I have been to one of them.'

'Indeed? Mistress Sabina goes regularly. I often go as well. That's where I met her. Parker lets her go to them because he likes music himself, though he believes he shouldn't, and I suppose he has *some* conscience. He knows he's made use of her. He should have found a marriage for her years ago but if you ask me, he didn't want to lose an unpaid housekeeper. So he keeps her sweet by letting her have music. It's her only enjoyment. I'm sorry for her though she puts a good face on things. He's always preaching at her about accepting the will of God. Sanctimonious pig!' said Hanley with venom.

'Where is all this leading?' asked Brockley, to stem the flow.

'Why I'm here, using old clothes as an excuse? I'm here because of things I've lately heard – or overheard. They've worried me. Just three weeks back, one evening at Tavistock, I heard two fellows talking and one said to the other something about Mary Stuart and funds being collected for her. I couldn't hear clearly but I think that's what was said. Someone was playing the spinet at the same time. I didn't know the two men – they weren't regulars – and I didn't think I'd better ask. Thought about it afterwards and didn't like it but I didn't know what to do. Then, at a fair in Okehampton, a week or so ago, I heard something else. I was watching a ferret race and three or four fellows close by were watching it too but talking together and they said a couple of interesting things. You want to hear?'

'Go on,' I said. Brockley grunted assent.

'One of 'em said he'd heard as funds for the Stuart cause could be handed to that Dr Parker, but he didn't know if that was true. But if it was, what a way for a vicar to behave! Then they laughed, as if they didn't take it seriously. Then there was a bit more talk I couldn't hear properly and then one sentence I heard clear. *Some folk are saying that young Reeves was poking his nose.* Well, I know about Gregory Reeves and his peculiar accident; all of Okehampton does. I didn't like over-hearing that. It sounded like young Reeves might have been – got out of the way, so to speak.'

'Murdered,' said Brockley ruthlessly.

'Yes.' Crispin looked uncomfortable, as though he wasn't at ease with anything so downright. 'Well, that made me think even more,' he said, 'and think long. And then I heard that you'd nearly suffered the same fate as young Reeves, Mistress Stannard. Two of you getting lost on the moor by accident? I didn't think so. I kept recalling how those two men had mentioned Dr Parker's name and the Stuart cause, together. So here I am. Looking for evidence.'

'Gregory Reeves almost certainly was murdered,' I said. 'We are trying to find out who did it and why.'

'And you suspect Dr Parker, same as me.'

'How did you hear about my – accident?' I said.

'At that same fair at Okehampton, I got talking to a Mr Hart, as has a sheep farm adjoining Baines' land. He got it from Miles Baines.'

It seemed that here in this corner of Devon and especially in Okehampton, gossip travelled back and forth and sideways as though along the strands of a net.

Crispin was still talking. 'I know your constable, Sam Rossiter, a little and I thought of going to him, telling him there's talk of money for the Stuart cause being collected by Dr Parker, but it's all so vague and Sammy Rossiter . . .'

'We know,' said Brockley shortly.

'Well, it *was* vague. Things overheard that I couldn't hear properly. Once in a crowded room against the sound of a spinet, once at a fair, with a ferret race going on one side of me and a fellow bawling about how wonderful his pots and pans were on the other. But here's similar accidents to two people who have nothing to do with each other. No doubt about that. So I reckoned I'd best look into it myself. I'm free to walk into the vicarage any time I like. Anyone can, if they're bringing things – contributions to charity, or punnets of strawberries or a few pounds of apples, if someone has a surplus and wants to keep in well with the church. So I plucked up my heart and made a bundle of a few outgrown clothes and here I am, as I said.'

'So you've appointed yourself as a . . . queen's spy, more or less,' said Brockley.

'Yes. Why?' I said. 'You have no responsibility for Gregory Reeves, or for another victim of a curious accident, a man called Peter Gray. I have. Last year, I persuaded both of them to act as – spies, if you like the word – for the queen, on the lookout for Stuart plots in this district. I threw them into danger. I want to see their killers caught.'

'I heard about Peter Gray,' said Hanley. 'I drink in the Castle Inn. But I didn't link him with Gregory Reeves. Well, well. As for me . . . see here! Even if I'm an extortioner – and I didn't use the money myself; I used it for the orphans – I'm still a loyal subject of the queen and I did think that maybe there's a reward for someone pointing a finger at treachery.'

Another one with an eye to a reward! Crispin accompanied his mercenary confession with a leer and I wondered why virtue could sometimes seem more repulsive than villainy.

'The notion of that there reward got on my mind,' said Crispin. 'Helped me to decide, like. I've been at the Marchers' Arms for three days, waiting for a chance to get in here when both the Parkers were out. Maddening they are. First one goes out and after a bit, so does the other – and five minutes later, the first one comes back. Makes you want to scream. Then at last, I get to hear they're dining out today. With some folk called Hillman. They sent to the Marchers' Arms for a keg of cider and I heard their man telling the landlord about it. *Now's my chance*, I thought.'

'You are telling us all this,' I said, 'and it makes you sound innocent, but how do we know you are telling the truth? When we visited you in Okehampton, my maid, Fran Brockley, chanced to get a look into your bedchamber. She saw a crucifix there. And you were wearing a cross. Are you wearing one now?'

'No.' Crispin shrugged. 'There's too much talk of the danger from Spain. Folk are getting edgy and ready to be suspicious. I've taken my cross off and taken the crucifix down. I've hidden them. I've a liking for the old religion, Mistress Stannard. There is a sense of safety in it; saints to intercede for one, a beautiful virgin lady, the mother of God, who may perhaps listen to the little pleas of fallible mankind and understand them better than God the Father who is so great that He feels remote, most of the time. But I don't wish to hear Mass, not now it's illegal, and I don't want to push Queen Elizabeth off her throne, neither. I said I was her loyal subject and so I am. Seems to me she's kept this land more peaceful and more prosperous and a bloody sight *safer* than it ever was under Queen Mary Tudor. I remember Queen Mary's days all right. My family were Catholic; we were safe enough. But I remember the way so-called heretics were hounded; I remember the fear in the air; I remember the horror of the burnings . . . no, I don't want those days back! Ugh! I wonder if dear Dr Lucius could spare us a glass of wine? He keeps a keg or two in the kitchen as a rule.'

He sprang to his feet and left the room. We followed, protesting, but he ignored us. He made straight for the kitchen and began to look purposefully around it.

'Oh, really! Master Hanley, you can't . . .' I said, while realizing that, alas, he could.

'We can't stop him,' said Brockley, at my side. 'I dare say we can sort it out with Dr Parker. I admit my throat's dry.'

The kitchen was big, with a wide fireplace, two trivets, two stockpots, a spit and a little leather sack, open, full of silver sand for scouring. Hanley, with a pleased 'Hah!', had found a wine keg and was filling a flagon from the spigot. Brockley, wandering round the room, came across a further door which we hadn't noticed during our first rapid exploration. He vanished inquisitively through it and I followed because I was inquisitive too. I found myself in a combined storeroom and stillroom. Brockley was looking at the shelves. I did the same. And then froze.

'Do you see what I see, madam?' Brockley asked.

I did. In front of us were two long shelves holding jars of preserves, neatly labelled, evidence of much hard work on Sabina's part. *Plums, Raspberries, Strawberry Jam, Apricot Jam, Quince Jelly* . . . But below these shelves was another, narrower shelf, holding an array of little pots and jars which seemed to contain herbal brews and ointments. *Chamomile, Feverfew, Valerian, Hemlock, Henbane* . . .

Henbane!

'If Lucius is the one who somehow arranged to poison my cider in Okehampton,' I said, 'here's where he got the poison. The physician in Okehampton seemed sure I had had an overdose of henbane.'

'What's that?' Crispin, in the kitchen, had heard me. He came hurriedly to join us. 'Mistress Stannard, did you say you were poisoned? When? How? You were poisoned *as well as* being taken out onto the moor? I haven't heard about this!'

'Why should you?' I said sharply. I added: 'My drink was tampered with once at the Castle Inn. Fortunately, I recovered. My life has been attempted twice, not once, and I am convinced that it was to stop me from enquiring into the deaths of Gregory Reeves and Peter Gray.'

'And you say they were agents of the crown, on the lookout for plots in favour of Mary Stuart?'

'Yes, they were.'

'God's teeth! I *knew* something was going on; I was sure of it, only it was all just bits and pieces overheard, and guesses about you and Gregory and Gray. And folk are nervous, like I said. But now you tell me there's a real fear, in high places, that plots of that kind might be hatched around here? Conniving with Spain! Things like that?'

'It's quite a likely place, with all these inlets,' I said.

Crispin stared at me, giving off anger in waves. 'If they, the folk up top, the queen and Lord this and Sir That, think it's happening then it probably is and we can't be timid and watch our steps. *It's got to be stopped.* Mary Stuart can't be put on any throne, Scottish or English, without help from abroad. And that means Spain, for sure. Oh yes, the high ups are right about that. And who in his senses wants a Spanish army here, dragging the Inquisition after it like the tail on a horse? The pale horse of the Apocalypse. The horse named death,' said Crispin, revealing an imaginative, even a creative, side of himself which didn't fit at all with his rough speech and his yellow leer, nor yet with his treatment of his nephew. He seemed to be made of contradictions.

'I promise you,' he was saying, 'that I'd hate to have Mary Stuart as my queen. She's a wantwit. She hadn't sense enough to choose reliable husbands. She couldn't tell what her people would put up with and what they wouldn't. It is possible,' said Hanley in exasperated tones, 'to feel a kindness for the old religion without wanting to turn England upside down, soak her fields with blood and start hounding them as Spain calls heretics, all over again!'

I believed him now. Crispin Hanley was making sense, in a weird kind of way. He was apparently a man who could be two opposite things at the same time. He could create a charity for orphans and see no reason why he shouldn't help to finance it by blackmailing his own nephew. He could hanker for the old religion while still supporting Elizabeth. He could be passionate, in fact, about supporting Elizabeth and also calculate what kind of reward might be his if he uncovered a plot against her! Never before, and never since, have I come across another individual like Crispin Hanley.

Brockley said: 'I wonder how Dr Parker really feels about the Stuart lady? He *could* have taken the henbane from here and tried to poison you with it, madam, or got someone else to – I don't think he was there impersonating a serving man. But there's no proof. He has one small crucifix hanging on a wall above a prie-dieu, but the man is a vicar, after all. Hidden in a drawer, we found a bad miniature of Mary Stuart and a statuette of the Virgin and Child. That may mean something or nothing. There's no real evidence at all.'

'Just a few commonplace relics,' I agreed. 'We know that henbane's within his reach but not whether he ever used it. We know that someone, possibly him and possibly not, was seen from a distance, leading a heavily laden brown pony with a white sock over the moor. We know the man we're looking for had a partner. We're full of ideas but all we really have is theories, not solid evidence.' I was suddenly weary, still lacking strength after my recent brush with death. 'So where do we look now?' I said.

'Reckon there's only one way,' said Crispin. 'Well, two. Bring Sir Francis Walsingham here, breathing fire like some old dragon out of legend, or take Lucius aside some time, into a nice quiet corner, stick a dagger under his nose, and ask him.'

TWENTY-FIVE
Hidden on a Beam

I n the course of this discussion, we had drifted out of the stillroom and back to the parlour. I sat down, arranged my skirts with precision, and said: 'Please don't be absurd, Master Hanley.'

Crispin glared at me. 'I don't like being called absurd by anyone and least of all by a woman.'

Brockley bristled but I simply said: 'You know we can't do anything of the kind. Though we do have to do something. I think we can justify taking what we do have, tenuous though it is, to the authority at hand.'

'But, madam, that means Samuel Rossiter,' said Brockley. 'He couldn't even agree that there must be a link between what happened to Gregory Reeves and what happened to Mistress Stannard. He has no brains. Just a skull full of thick fleecy wool.'

Neither he nor Hanley had seated themselves, and Brockley now turned impatiently away from us and stamped over to the window, where he informed the diamond panes that Rossiter was a wantwit.

'Taking what we now know, Rossiter need only be our first step,' I said. 'If he won't take us seriously then there's the county sheriff or . . . yes, I could send a report to Sir Francis Walsingham. What I can't do is just walk past Rossiter. Ignoring him might offend him and that could rebound on the Hillmans in some way and . . .'

'I still reckon we'd do better to challenge Lucius Parker face to face,' said Hanley strongly. I began to shake my head and say no, if he laughed at us and said nonsense, we would just be back to Rossiter, when Brockley stiffened, peered closely at the diamond panes and then said: 'I think we may be obliged to challenge Lucius Parker face to face. Madam, please look at this.'

Hanley and I both went to join him and see what he was seeing. And there on the track from Ladymead was a remarkable procession. It was near enough for us to recognize the people in it. In the lead was Lucius Parker, with Sabina just behind him. She looked as though she was expostulating and being ignored. Behind the Parkers came Thomasina's cob drawing Thomasina's little cart, with Thomasina enthroned within. It was actually quite a smart affair, with glossily painted sides and a padded seat inside. The cob was being led by Bartholomew. Behind them came Joyce and Dale, side by side.

'They're coming here. They can't very well be going anywhere else, can they, madam?' Brockley said.

We met them at the front door, rather as if we were the hosts and they were our guests. Thomasina was just being helped out of the cart. She promptly pushed her way to the front where she burst into voluble apologies.

'I'm sorry, Ursula, I couldn't help it, time went on and on and I couldn't find any more excuses. Tom played and Ann sang and then I had more wine served, with little sausages and prawn patties but perhaps I showed I was nervous, anyway, Dr Parker suddenly started to say things like, *What's the matter, Mistress Hillman?* and frowning and then he said, *There's something going on; why do you want us to stay and stay and you not in the heartiest of health* and finally he announced that he and Sabina were going home . . .'

'And there certainly is something going on!' said Lucius grimly. 'I am let into my own house by a lady who is supposed to be on a sickbed elsewhere! A little odd, don't you think?'

'We insisted on coming too,' said Thomasina. 'To protect you. We feel we've failed you though we did our best . . .'

Bartholomew broke in. 'And I hope to heaven that sitting in that cart, that jolts with every stone in the road, even while I led you at the slowest walk I could manage, has done you no harm. You women!' He glared at me. 'When,' he said, 'I advised my wife against it, she just waddled out into the stable yard and ordered the cob to be harnessed up and finally I let her have her way; the physicians always say that in her condition a woman shouldn't be crossed. So here we are and can we now stop gabbling and go into the parlour with the cushions where Thomasina can sit down! I should never have agreed to this dinner party, never, and you shouldn't have asked it, Ursula!'

Bartholomew sounded angry but I thought it was worry and I could see why. I had last seen Thomasina only ten days before but then I had been too ill to look at her properly. Now I was shocked. She was so huge that as she came through the front door, she blocked most of the light. Lucius was just behind her. He had been trying to speak again and now seized his chance.

'I want to know what all this is about. You were supposed to be ill and unable to dine at Ladymead, Mistress Stannard, and now – as I had begun to suspect! – I find you here, in my house, you and your manservant together. And Crispin Hanley! Did you catch them here, Crispin? What *is* all this?'

'Let us do as Bartholomew suggests, go into the bigger parlour, and be comfortable,' I said. 'And then we can do the explaining.' I spoke calmly and turned to lead the way, while wondering frantically what form the explanations would take. They would surely amount to challenging Lucius. I could see no other outcome.

'I did find them here, sir,' said Crispin, addressing Lucius. 'But that ain't all the truth. And if you feared, Mistress Stannard, that I would back out and say yes, I caught you trespassing and deny what's followed, you needn't worry. You've told me enough to make sure I wouldn't leave you in the ditch now. We have words for you, Dr Parker. And you won't like them.'

We had reached the parlour. Bartholomew guided Thomasina to the cushioned settle, arranged her with her feet up and perched himself on its arm. The rest of us, except for the Parkers and Crispin Hanley, found seats too. Dale and Joyce took the window seat, and sat close together, as if for reassurance.

I was by now reminding myself that I had better remember who I was. I was an agent of Sir Francis Walsingham and Sir William Cecil, Lord High Treasurer and chief minister of the queen, who was both my sovereign and my sister, for my father had been King Henry the Eighth. A daughter of King Henry did not stand tongue-tied when to speak was a duty, no matter how appalling the circumstances. My friends knew that, too. Brockley was looking at me expectantly. It was my business now to take charge. Crispin Hanley had said that he had words for Lucius and was just opening his mouth to say them. I forestalled him.

'One moment, Master Hanley. I too have something I must say to Dr Parker. Dr Parker, I regret that you have found us here in your vicarage. Yes, Brockley and I have searched it. And yes, we asked Master and Mistress Hillman to invite you to dine, so that we could do so . . .'

'I see,' said Lucius frigidly.

'Master Hanley did find us here,' I said. 'He had come with a bundle of children's clothing to give him, so to speak, a right of entry. But he was really on the same errand as ourselves.' For the benefit of the Hillmans, I added: 'Master Hanley is the uncle of Robert Hanley, my steward at Withysham. As you know, I had business with him on Robert Hanley's behalf. And now, Master Hanley, forgive my interruption. Please speak for yourself.'

I had signalled that I was in command; I was ready now to yield the pulpit to him, as it were. He did so, in detail and with clarity, explaining how things he had overheard had aroused his suspicions, and then adding how those suspicions had now been strengthened by what I had told him of the deaths of Gray and Reeves, and my own nearly fatal mishaps.

He spoke well, working his way along the chain which had my recruitment of Gregory Reeves and Peter Gray as spies at one end, and led through their deaths and my narrow escapes to papist symbols, henbane and Sabina's pony Sock at the other.

After that, there was a terrible silence, then Bartholomew said: 'Most of this is new to us and I for one find it difficult to understand why you, Dr Parker, are being accused, as apparently you are – merely because a brown pony with a white sock and carrying a heavy-looking pack was seen from a distance at roughly the time when Mistress Stannard was being carried onto the moor. People do take pack ponies across the moor and how many ponies with white socks are there in Zeal Aquatio, I wonder? The Smithsons have one, and I think there's one in the Marchers' Arms stable. And the Lord knows how many elsewhere – it could have come from Plymouth or Tavistock.'

'I have not denied that,' I said. 'What Baines saw might mean little. But taken along with the things we found here . . .'

'According to Master Hanley, you found nothing incriminating at all. You came across a henbane potion, which I know is unusual in England as the plant isn't native here. I also know that it's imported sometimes and is a pain-killer. You have found some commonplace relics of the old religion. These are poor grounds for claiming that our good vicar is guilty of . . . well, what? Are you really accusing him of murdering these two spies of yours, Ursula? And attempting to kill you, and being involved in treason? Well, Lucius, what have you to say about all this?'

Lucius Parker was completely white. He stood there in the middle of the parlour like a statue in marble. But he could still speak. He could even smile. 'What clever people you are, to find out so much. And now, did you expect me to defend myself? To explain all the evidence away, to bluster and protest and call you names? I shall do none of those things. I am proud of what I have tried to do.'

He tilted his head back, chin raised, defying us. 'It's all true, I'm afraid, my friend Bartholomew. I don't dislike you, Mistress Stannard, but I needed to clear you out of my path and must regret that I failed. I am a Catholic. I was born in 1540, into a Catholic family. We hid our allegiance during the reign of old Henry and more still under the boy King Edward; we came out into the sunlight in the days of Queen Mary . . .'

'Into the sunlight? In the days of Mary?' Thomasina gasped.

'She only wanted to give her country the one true faith,' said Lucius. 'I think it was bitter pain to her, that there were those who refused the gift even in the face of death. Now, in the days of Elizabeth, I have to hide my faith again, if I wish to continue as vicar here, which I do. This is a pleasant place, an agreeable living. But if I could occupy it under a Catholic queen, under that beautiful, wronged, imprisoned lady Queen Mary Tudor, what heaven that would be! Yes, I have been gathering contributions to her cause. Bit by bit I am filling a coffer for her – which you did not find, Mistress Stannard, for it is hidden under the floor of – no, I will not say which room. I am not ashamed!' He stopped, holding his pose, chin still raised in defiance.

Bartholomew said: When you've filled your coffer, who will

then take charge of it? To whom will you pass it? Who is your master?'

'That is a secret,' said Lucius. His sly smile was horrid, and did not suit his strong features.

'It won't be a secret for long,' remarked Brockley. 'Have you ever heard of a man called Richard Topcliffe?'

'Topcliffe will learn little from me,' said Lucius, 'for I haven't planned ahead that far. I don't know myself who I ought to give the coffer to; that is something I have still to discover.'

'Of all the muddleheaded, haphazard plans I ever heard of . . .' Crispin burst out. He stepped up to Lucius and gripped him fiercely by an upper arm. 'Well, at least we have hold of *you*!'

'But this makes no sense!' Thomasina swung her feet to the floor, brushing aside Bartholomew's attempt to prevent her. She sat upright on the settle, looking round at us all. 'Dr Parker *can't* have tried to harm Ursula in Okehampton. I can perfectly recall when she was there, for she told me when she meant to go, and afterwards she told me that she fell ill on the evening of the day that she arrived there. I have been keeping track of dates, for an important one lies ahead for me, as you can all see. Ursula went to Okehampton on the twenty-sixth of February and was stricken down on that same evening. Well, on that day . . . Bart?'

'I know what my wife means!' said Bartholomew. 'I went to Plymouth on the twenty-seventh, to order wine. I use a merchant who lives there. Lucius, I met you on the way. You were returning from a church conference in Plymouth. You'd been there overnight and you told me there had been much talk at the conference about the danger from Spain. Sorry, Lucius. You were in Plymouth on the evening of the twenty-sixth. And I'm sure there were witnesses!'

'Of course there were! The Bishop of Exeter was there!' cried Sabina. 'He attended the conference. My brother told me he talked to the bishop himself. The Bishop of Exeter could confirm that my brother was in Plymouth on the twenty-sixth of February.'

'But we know that whoever killed Peter Gray had an accomplice,' said Brockley. And then hesitated, frowning, and withdrew. 'No. I am wrong. Dr Parker couldn't have learned of Mistress Stannard's plan to go to Okehampton soon enough to alert any accomplice.'

'There! It's all nonsense!' Sabina rounded on her brother. 'Lucius, why are you so willing to accept the blame for things you haven't done?'

'Could it be because he's shielding someone?' asked Bartholomew, apparently addressing the air.

'No,' said Sabina stoutly. 'Because none of it is true. The only true thing is that yes, we are secret Catholics, and my brother sometimes has fantasies about dying for the faith. But he has committed no crime. He has not tried to make converts, nor heard illegal Masses. But *you* . . .'

She marched over to me, her face suffused with anger. '*You* have to come creeping in here, imagining murder because of harmless trivialities, creating a story. You eat something that disagrees with you and imagine you are poisoned. You go for a moonlight walk on the moor and lose your way and perhaps you feel a fool, so you make up a tale about being kidnapped. *You . . .!*'

She was standing in front of me, pushing her face at me. She had dressed for a dinner engagement. Her over-gown was of peach-coloured wool; her kirtle was of linen, not good quality, but white, and embroidered – unevenly – with yellow flowers. Her sleeve slashings matched her kirtle. And she was wearing perfume. At such a short distance, it assailed the nostrils. It was exotic, exciting. She had been wearing it when she came to the musical evening in Tavistock.

It was sandalwood. The scent Thomasina had given to Sabina, the one she didn't want to use until she was her normal shape again. It had been handed round so that anyone who wanted could sample it. We had all done so. I had smelt it on Sabina in Tavistock. *And I had smelt it on the sacking when I was lying helpless across that horse!* I should have recognized it then! But it was so faint, and I was not familiar with it and my senses were swimming from that bang on the head. Today I was in full possession of them and I was certain. *This* was the fugitive scent that I had vaguely associated with the Brewster sisters and the applewood smoke. Someone wearing sandalwood perfume had handled the sack before they put me in it.

'It was *you*,' I said. '*You* kidnapped me and left me to die of cold, out on the moor. You've lived here all your life; you're like Miles Baines; you can read the weather. And you made use of that! And I don't doubt that somehow, with an accomplice, you managed the death of Peter Gray. Your brother is protecting *you*!'

'Nonsense!' said Lucius and Sabina laughed.

It was awful, that laughter. It had an insane edge. I saw Thomasina reach for Bartholomew's hand.

'How could it be me?' Sabina demanded. 'Since when was I a devoted follower of Mary Stuart? She was a damned silly woman and if I have a kindness for the old religion, as my brother has, I certainly have no kindness for her!'

I could believe that. There must be many, I thought, who felt like this. Walsingham always assumed that to have a tenderness for bygone rituals also meant a tenderness for Mary but it didn't. It . . .

But my thoughts were interrupted. Lucius was staring at his sister and there was something horrified in his expression. He began to speak, hoarsely.

'I have thought – feared – for some time that you might be . . . be collecting funds for her. There have been local rumours about funds being raised for the Stuart cause, and the name of Parker has been whispered. It worried me when I learned of that, for I knew you collected money as well as garments for your charity – or said that you did. I believe you keep it in that pretty embroidered purse you made. You hide the purse on top of a beam in your bedchamber. I have seen you putting it there. I wondered why you kept it so secret. You can't have thought I would steal it.'

I looked at Brockley. We hadn't thought of peering up at the beams.

Lucius paid us no attention. He was still challenging his sister, though with a plea in his voice, as though he were begging her to prove him wrong.

'Once, you were careless with that purse. My study is often stuffy, but if I open the window, a breeze may blow my papers

about and in summer in come the wasps and bluebottles while
in winter there's a cold draught. So if I feel stuffy, I open doors
– of my study and the spare room, and the door to your room
isn't always shut. Once, I saw that pretty purse lying on your
bed when you had gone to Plymouth with garments for children.
Out of curiosity, I went and picked it up. It was quite heavy
and I heard coins chink. I supposed you had had it down to
count what was in it. But if it was money for your charity, why
didn't you take it with you? It wasn't your own spending money
for you keep that in the leather purse that's on your girdle at
this moment. I stood there with that pretty red and blue embroidered purse in my hand and wondered why you had hidden
it on a beam. *And why hadn't you taken it to Plymouth?* I kept
on wondering; the mystery fretted me. I began to be afraid.
Gossip had whispered our name. Surely you couldn't be
collecting funds for *her*? I feared to ask you. Yet why else was
the purse hidden, except for some purpose I would dislike –
would forbid? You have always spoken against Mary Stuart and
I clung to that – but I knew you could be protecting yourself
that way, abusing her to hide your true opinions. And I never
dreamed of . . . of murder. Sabina, my very dear sister . . . tell
me the truth! Was Sock in his stable the night that Mistress
Stannard nearly died on the moor? Tell me that he was! I beg
you!'

'Of course he was,' said Sabina. 'Me collect money for that
woman Mary Stuart? Never!'

'But you dosed me with henbane and took me out onto the
moors to die!' I shouted it out. 'I *know*! Gregory Reeves died
of cold on the moors as I nearly did! He was one of Walsingham's
agents and so was Peter Gray. You killed them and you tried
to kill me. *I smelt your perfume on that sack you put me in!* If
the money you collected wasn't for Mary Stuart, then who was
it for?'

I had pitied Sabina, pitied her looks and her brother's
sanctimonious tactlessness about them, pitied her reluctant
virginity. Now I felt only rage. It choked me so that I fell
silent, unable to go on speaking. I looked at Brockley, who
said calmly: 'Mistress Sabina. You have been accused. What
is your answer?'

Sabina looked round. It was the look of a hunted animal, driven into a corner and seeking a way of escape. But there was no escape. The faces around her were intent, and accusing. Like Lucius, she threw back her head in a gesture of defiance.

And then the dam broke.

TWENTY-SIX
The Dam Breaks

I once saw a dam give way. My husband Hugh made the lake at Hawkswood by damming a stream with a strong stone wall. One day, during a storm, Hugh's chief forester, Jerome Billington, whose cottage was on the edge of the woods just upstream of the dam, sent his son running to tell Hugh that the dam was in danger of collapsing. I went with Hugh, the two of us in hooded cloaks, pulling our hoods on, hurrying heads down into the wind and rain. We reached the lake just in time to see it happen.

The dam was bulging. Just as we came in sight of it, a stone fell out. Another followed and then a shower of stones and then the imprisoned waters of the lake poured through, dragging most of the remaining wall with them, overwhelming the banks, uprooting trees, roaring and rumbling, with terrifying force.

We turned and ran, fearing the flood would catch us, but we were only pursued by the tumult of the waters and once on the safety of higher ground, we turned to watch the devastation below, and tremble. Hugh had the dam rebuilt more strongly later. 'It won't give way again,' he said to me. I hoped it wouldn't, for I had found the spectacle frightening. I didn't enjoy this, either, for what now happened to Sabina was another version of the same thing; the sudden breaking of a wall and an outpouring of something long repressed, and with a violence that terrified.

'Very well! You shall hear!' In Sabina's voice there was neither fear nor shame. 'I got rid of Gray and Reeves because they were finding things out, about to spoil everything, all my hopes!' She swung round to face Lucius. 'Yes, my hopes! I created them for myself because you should have done it for me and you didn't! What do you think it's been like, seeing youth and dreams all ebb away and no use made of them? A woman can't ask a man to marry her! Like cabbages on a market stall, we must wait to be chosen. Men are supposed to propose to us, or else our fathers or brothers must propose on our behalf. But when did you? What did you ever do to help me to marriage?'

'Sabina!' Lucius cried. 'I have always accepted your wish to make the best of yourself, even though I would have preferred you to wear modest colours . . .'

'Modest colours! To make myself invisible? *Bah!*' said Sabina.

'I'd have welcomed suitors for you but . . .'

'But I am six feet tall and I have a face like a horse with a roman nose! But a good dowry could overcome that. You collect money by the bucketful for *your* charities but you never collected a farthing for me! I could go to perdition for all you cared, as long as I went on saving you the price of a housekeeper. Well, to perdition I went! What you wouldn't do for me, I set out to do for myself! I'd always saved from the housekeeping so as to buy good clothing; but two years ago I started gathering funds. I told people they were for my clothing charity but I was the charity! When I had enough, I hoped I would, somehow, let it be known that I had a dowry worth something! Someone might have taken me, some widower; I might yet have children; I am barely forty even now. Why shouldn't I have my share of love? What have I done to be denied it? To be left hungry, starving, seeing others have what I can't; like an animal in a cage, looking through the bars at other animals running free? What God and life wouldn't give me, I planned to take! But first that man Peter Gray and then Gregory Reeves started sniffing round me. They'd both found out that I collected charitable money; maybe they'd overheard that silly gossip, that started somehow, about money being collected and ending up at our vicarage. I'd been careless at some point. Well, those two heard things and somehow they got together. They even questioned Lucius.'

Lucius gasped out: 'I told Gray that you collected clothes and a little money for the charity in Plymouth. But I had already seen that pretty purse left on your bed; that's when I began to

wonder what you were about, and the idea of Mary Stuart
crawled into my mind.'

'Yes, and that nosy Gray went to Plymouth and found that
I did now and then donate coins to the clothing charity – I did
that sometimes, to make it true in case someone did ask questions. Then, after Gray, it was Gregory Reeves; I heard he'd
been asking about me in Okehampton. I go there sometimes to
buy cloth from the Reeves' warehouse. And see a few people
who are my regular contributors. I found that Reeves had been
skulking round them. Him and Gray; they were like a pair of
bloodhounds. If they once worked out that the amount I collected
in Okehampton was four times the amount I doled out for the
charity in Plymouth . . . well! I'd be stopped – accused of
keeping money for myself or yes, perhaps, gathering funds
for Mary. So I got rid of that nosy pair. And I enjoyed it. Yes,
I did!'

She stared boldly round at us, challenging the world to do
what it would. I found myself able to speak again and said:
'How did you kill Peter Gray? You didn't drive those horses!
And I don't see you drinking in the Castle, either.'

'No?' said Sabina. Her strong features had changed. Her
mouth was hard and twisted; her eyes were full of malice and
contempt. 'My inches and my lack of good looks have one
advantage. I can pass as a man! I sometimes do, for amusement,
to enjoy the freedoms of men. I have collected men's clothes
for that purpose. I followed you to Okehampton the first time
you went. I knew what you were about. You wanted to find out
what really happened to Gray and Reeves. My brother had told
me that, naming names, and then I was horrified. I thought; if
you found anything out, you would spoil everything – as bad
as those two prying creatures. Then I took you to the Greshams
and while Mrs Gresham and I were struggling with that damned
key, you whispered something to your friends. You didn't think
I could hear, but I did. *We will go to Okehampton tomorrow. I
must see this Hanley and he's the perfect excuse for going there
at all. I shall start enquiries about Gray as well as Reeves.
Three birds with one stone!* That's what you said, and that was
when I made my mind up. You were losing no time and you're
the queen's sister and one of Walsingham's spies; you'd be good

at finding things out – better than Gray or Reeves, very likely.
So I followed you. You went into the Reeves' workshop. Just
as I thought you would. And then you went to Robbs Lane to
call on someone . . .'

'On me,' said Crispin.

'I heard you talking,' said Sabina. 'You noticed me. I was
the man in the homespun jacket and breeches, looking at a tray
of earrings.' Joyce suddenly stiffened and turned red. '*She*,' said
Sabina, pointing, 'called me unattractive, even as a man, and
doubted if I could have a sweetheart. And *he* . . .' this time her
attention swung towards Brockley, 'made a nasty joke at my
expense.' Brockley also reddened.

'I don't forget,' said Sabina, and now her features were
entirely taken over by malice. 'I did indeed drink in the Castle
Inn, a man among men. I drank with Peter Gray, and I slipped
something into his glass, a henbane tincture, just a drop . . .'

'As you did to me?' I asked.

'I tried to finish *you*! You'd been to see Andrew Reeves, you
were on my scent, I was sure of it. My God, when you survived
after all, I hardly knew what to do. I hoped you'd be frightened
enough to stop. But then the vicar of Okehampton rides over
to see Lucius and tells us that Okehampton is all abuzz with
talk of you being about to reveal that Gray and Reeves were
murdered, and reveal who did it as well . . .'

Thank you, Jane Leigh, I thought.

'. . . Well, I know the moor. I can read the weather. I thought:
there's snow coming. What worked for Reeves might work
again. Oh, I wasn't fool enough to think anyone would suppose
your death was an accident, not after Reeves' death, and Gray's
and your unfortunate stomach upset. But with luck, no one
would connect it with me and meanwhile, you'd suffer. You'd
know terror and despair. I wanted that for you. Oh, how I wanted
it! That's why I didn't just bludgeon the life out of you when
I attacked you in the Greshams' stable yard. I wanted you to
know what was happening to you. The time for accidents was
past. Though I made a good job of creating Peter Gray's accident,' said Sabina, with a certain amount of pride. 'I just wanted
him to seem a little unwell, to stagger so that I could urge him
into the fresh air, saying it would make him feel better. It worked

like a dream. The team and cart and driver were ready and
down under the hooves and wheels went interfering Gray.'

Her pleasure in what she had done made me shiver and look
away, but Brockley was bolder. 'Who was the driver?' he
demanded.

Sabina shook her head. 'That I will not tell you.'

'Richard Topcliffe will get it out of you,' said Bartholomew
and for once, I saw her whiten. The name was known to
her and now, it seemed for the first time, the true horror of her
situation was coming through to her. 'So you may as well
tell us now and save yourself some trouble,' Bartholomew
told her.

She was still full of hate. She glowered at me but didn't
speak. Until Crispin stepped forward and seized her arm. She
cried out as he twisted it. 'Tell us or I'll wrench your arm out
of its socket!' Crispin shouted.

Some of us were gasping but no one rose to help her. We
watched and let Crispin tear the information out of her. She
cried out: 'No, stop! I won't tell you. I won't! I won't! Let go
of me . . .!' But Crispin did not let go and I think her shoulder
probably was in danger of dislocation when at last she screamed
and broke down into sobs and then gave in.

'I suppose you'd find out anyway. You're as nosy as Gray
and Reeves were! It was that fool Pascal Bryers. We know Miles
Baines and his people well. I know Bryers. *Let go! Let go!*'

Bryers, I thought. Yes, of course. We had guessed at Bryers
already, just after my kidnapping. We had been right.

'Release her!' said Brockley sharply. 'She'll talk more easily
then.' Crispin eased his grip but still kept hold of his victim.
Sabina gulped but then continued to talk, as though, having
started, she couldn't stop the torrent.

'I've often talked to Bryers. Master Baines makes gifts to
the church now and then; he's given us a communion cup and
a set of candle stands and other things and Pascal always brings
them; I would watch my tongue, pretend I agreed when, after
a time, he let fall that he prayed to the Virgin Mary and adored
Mary Stuart as well. He knows I collect money and he believes
it's for Mary, because one day she'll need it to pay her soldiers.
I got him to understand how dangerous Peter Gray was. And

then he was willing to help. He drove the team that ran down Gray.'

'How did you manage to poison my cider?' I said it quietly, reining myself in. It was horrible to be physically near to this woman, to this hell-brew of malice and pitiful frustration. Though part of me did still pity her. She had once been a normal young girl, wanting to marry and have children, but an unlucky star had shone upon her birth, for she was so very plain, and had no big dowry to compensate for it. And, very likely, she was passionate. I think she was among those women who cannot do without coition, for whom celibacy is truly a hell. She had sought a way out, saving the housekeeping money to buy pretty clothes, collecting apparently for charity and holding on to that to create a dowry big enough to be bait. I could half understand what had driven her. But to let herself be driven to murder, to . . .!

'I dressed in black,' said Sabina. 'Doublet and breeches. I rode astride on the way to Okehampton. I went into the inn at dusk. I had tied up my hair and put a dark cap on to hide it. I went into the dining chamber. I saw what you were drinking. I had seen the jugs of cider set out on a sideboard. I took a cider jug and a flagon of wine and went round topping up drinks. There were people coming and going and all in flickering candlelight. I picked a moment when you were a little distracted and then I filled your tankard, but slipped the contents of a little phial into it as well. It was quite easy. No one noticed that I wasn't the usual waiter.'

Bartholomew suddenly stood up. 'Enough! We have heard enough. Master Brockley, would you be so good as to go in search of Master Rossiter, our constable? He lives in the main street, two doors from the Marchers' Arms, in a cottage with a blue door.'

'I wonder if he'll listen this time. But I'll fetch him,' said Brockley and went.

Sabina said angrily: 'I had nearly put together enough to make a fair dowry. There are respectable men who only earn a hundred pounds a year. Well, I have nearly a hundred pounds in that purse. If I talked about it, let it be known, there might be takers. I thought of Master Baines, who has been so generous

to the church. Lucius, I was going to ask you to approach him
for me.'

'I would have done so, willingly,' said Lucius. '*Willingly!*'

'Except that it would have been in vain,' said Joyce.

Everyone turned to her and she smiled on us all. 'It was
settled when I rode over to see him, about the brown packhorse
he had mentioned, with the white sock. We talked of other
things, too, and we agreed together so well that finally he asked
if I would wed him and I said yes. Only, then he said I must
think about it for a while and say nothing to anyone until I was
sure, and then he would speak to you, Mistress Stannard. But
I am sure. Please, when he comes, will you tell him so? Will
you wish us joy?'

We were all gazing at Joyce in utter astonishment, when
Sabina suddenly moved, not to flee, but simply to jerk herself
away from Crispin. She spun round, fumbling frantically in the
open front of her skirt. By the time we had grasped that – like
me – she had a hidden pouch inside it, she had snatched out a
phial, pulled out the stopper and swallowed the contents. Crispin
understood one second too late. He wrested the phial from her
but she had already swallowed whatever was in it. She looked
at him and smiled.

'I always knew that I might need it. I have carried it with
me for a long time. And now that I've betrayed Pascal . . . you
shouldn't have made me do that! Tell Pascal I'm sorry!'

Lucius wasn't standing where he could have seen the phial
and cried out: 'What is this? What are you saying, Sabina?'

'She's taken venom, Lucius. Someone get some salt water!'
Crispin shouted. I rose and took the phial from him and smelt
it. It wasn't henbane. I recognized it, though. Others, standing
in the same danger as Sabina, had used it. Anyway, Gladys
Morgan had once told me that hemlock smelt like cat's piss.
So did this.

Lucius was obviously bewildered but he ran from the parlour
and fetched the salt water. Crispin tried to administer it but
Sabina resisted violently. Lucius and Bartholomew both went
to help him and while they held her, Crispin seized her nose
so that she had to open her mouth to breathe and he tried to
pour the salt water into her. She kicked his shins and twisted

her head away. I watched, my mind churning, and then I leapt at Crispin and jerked his arm, so that all the water spilt.

'What in hell's name are you doing?' Crispin shouted.

'Letting her die,' I said. 'Better than leaving her to the law. The law may not content itself with beheading or even hanging, not for two murders of Walsingham's agents. That could be seen as treason. She could burn. Do you want that? Do you want that for your sister, Dr Parker?'

'I . . . no, but . . .' Lucius was stammering.

Crispin thundered: 'So what are we supposed to do?'

'Let her go,' I said. 'It's hemlock. Let Dale and Joyce take her to her bedchamber. Take a couple of basins as well,' I added.

'Yes. Do that!' Thomasina cried out. 'It's best! I couldn't bear to think . . . Oh!' Her final exclamation was a cry of distress not connected to Sabina. Bartholomew turned quickly towards her and so did I. Thomasina tried to smile but didn't succeed.

'I'm so sorry. But I think . . . *oh!*' She pressed a hand against her bulging abdomen. Then I saw the puddle round her feet.

'Your waters have broken,' I said, as I ran to her. Over my shoulder, I shouted: 'Dale, Joyce, get Sabina to her room, *go on!*' and saw them hurrying away. 'Thomasina, you can't get home now. Lucius, we shall have to use a spare room here.'

'Has the world gone mad?' said Lucius, but added: 'There are three spare rooms. Help yourselves. There's linen in all of them. The one next to the study is the nearest.'

'Good enough,' I said. 'Come, Bartholomew. Help me to get Thomasina upstairs. Joyce and Dale are up there already. Joyce can watch over Sabina; Dale can help us.'

'Is my sister dying?' asked Lucius, bewildered.

Bartholomew, fiercely, said: 'Yes, she is. So go to her, hear her confession and give her absolution. Isn't that what you're for? Since you're a secret Catholic.'

'I'm not! I just said that to save her!'

'Go to her just the same! See what you've made of her!'

Lucius looked as if he might be about to faint, but started out of the room, only to halt in the doorway because someone was banging on the front door. He stumbled away to answer it and came back with Brockley, Constable Rossiter and a young girl of about fourteen at whom we all looked in surprise.

'Thomasina!' said Bartholomew distractedly.

'Ursula and I know all about this. Don't worry. Just get me to a bed,' said Thomasina and between us, Bartholomew and I steadied her out of the room and up the stairs, leaving the unexpected situation downstairs to look after itself. We had just got Thomasina settled, aided by Dale who came gladly when we called, saying that Sabina was sneering at them and laughing, but looked terrified just the same and she, Dale, hated being in the same room with her, when the downstairs situation pursued us. Brockley, Rossiter and the girl came up the stairs.

Brockley and Rossiter looked at Thomasina in alarm. Brockley said to me: 'This young lady wants to see you, madam,' and then he and Rossiter went on into Sabina's room, shutting the door behind them. Lucius came heavily up the stairs and went after them, paying no need at all to Thomasina. Bartholomew said: 'I'll go for the midwife. Kate Evans, she's in the village,' and departed. He looked as though his world were dissolving round him, but he was a practical man. I thanked heaven for Bartholomew.

And now, I must cope with the girl.

'Look,' I said to her, 'who are you? Why are you here? As you can see, we have no time or attention to spare . . .'

'If you please, ma'am, I'm Bess Hethercott. Would you be Mistress Stannard?'

'Yes. But . . .'

Bess curtsied. 'Master Brockley said as you might have a place for me.' She looked past me, to the bed where Joyce was anxiously asking Thomasina what needed to be done for her, and Thomasina was talking about hot water and towels. 'Is the lady having a baby?' Bess enquired. 'Can I help? I've helped my mam, time and again.'

Brockley reappeared, eyeing Thomasina nervously and visibly embarrassed to be in the room but also aware that explanations were required. 'Rossiter and I met Ned Hethercott on the way here,' he said. 'The carter who lent his cart, madam, if you recall.'

'Of course I do, but what . . .?'

'He was bound for Plymouth with a cart-load of something . . .'

'Wine casks, half a dozen bags of silver sand, some earthenware, all landed at Exeter, and meant for Plymouth,' said Bess. 'Should of landed there instead. Someone made a muddle but it was business for us, us being carters for hire. My dad took me along 'cause he had a notion that someone he knows in Plymouth might take me to work in his kitchen. Time I was leaving home, he and mam say. But Master Brockley here, he said he thought you was needing a maid, Mistress Stannard, so dad let me come with him. I could help that lady, really I could.'

'Then go and fetch the hot water and towels that Mistress Hillman needs,' I said. 'That's the lady's name. Towels in that cupboard there, hot water in the kitchen downstairs.' Another pair of hands could be useful while we waited for Bartholomew to come back with Kate Evans.

'I'll leave her with you, madam,' said Brockley, and virtually fled from this roomful of feminine mysteries. We heard his footsteps recede down the stairs.

In this room, new life was coming forth. But in the next room, a life was ending and I, through my investigations, had set Sabina on the path to oblivion. I didn't want to see her but wondered if I should – to ask her forgiveness, perhaps. For a while I stayed with Thomasina, but nothing much was happening and presently there were cries from the next room and Joyce probably needed some female support. With dragging feet, I went in.

Joyce was sitting by the bed. Rossiter stood on the other side, gazing dispassionately at the woman who lay there and wrinkling his nose at the stink of diarrhoea. Sabina was crying out in pain and saying that she was going blind. Lucius was bending over her, wiping sweat from her forehead, and trying to soothe her.

Rossiter glanced at me and said: 'I'll be wanting a full report on what's led to this. Shocking business!'

'You shall have one. So will Sir Francis Walsingham,' I said.

The end was still some way off. Rossiter looked at the suffering figure on the bed and then, quite kindly, said: 'No need for you to stay, madam. No use talking to her, if you come

here to say summat. She don't know you're here. She's escaped
the law, right enough. Still, the law might do things I wouldn't
care to witness. Worse than this. I'll call you when the end's
near. And you go, too, Mistress Frost. Don't you linger here.
No need. Nasty business all round.' If Rossiter was in some
ways dim-witted, he wasn't cruel.

The dismissal relieved my conscience. I beckoned to Joyce.
'We'll just kneel for a moment and I'll say a prayer for her,' I
said. We did so, and then I took us both away.

I had prayed for Thomasina too and was glad I had, for when
we returned to her, we found her having violent pains. Dale
was holding her hands while the girl Bess was offering her
drinks of water and recommending that a pair of scissors should
be placed under the bed as it was a time-honoured charm to
aid delivery. Thomasina, in between her pangs, was saying it
had never been like this with any of the others.

Bartholomew came back with the depressing news that Kate
Evans was not at home and according to her little maidservant
had gone to Plymouth to help a client who was about to give
birth. We would have to manage without her.

It went on and on, into the evening, into the night, through
the hours of darkness. I was called when Sabina was near her
end, and I watched her go. She was unconscious by then; it was
finally a peaceful passing. She died and we covered her and left
her. The men gathered downstairs to keep out of our way and I
think they started drinking. I went back to Thomasina. I found
that Bess, the stranger I had never seen before in my life, was
behaving as though she were an established part of the household,
and I noticed that despite her faith in charms (a faith that I didn't
share) she was quick and deft, fetching towels and water when
they were needed, suggesting warm oil, and finding her way
about the house as if she had always known it.

As dawn was breaking, the moment of crisis came. The baby
was trying to emerge and it seemed that something was wrong.

I had had children and had some knowledge; Dale had helped
me and Joyce had been present when one of her nephews was
born. But this situation was beyond us. Dale resorted to prayer.
In the end it was Bess, fourteen-year-old Bess, who said she'd
seen this afore, with one of her baby brothers. It was Bess who

said: 'It b'ain't a breech birth. Baby's the right way round all right. But Mistress Hillman is so tired, and I think the little 'un might have an arm placed wrong.'

And it was Bess, whose young, slim hands could do what none of ours could do, who oiled her fingers and slid them into Thomasina and set the infant's arm right, and said encouragingly: 'One hearty push, mistress . . . and there you go!'

Thomasina screamed, just once, and then it was over. A new baby boy was in the world, rather a small one, but he soon made it clear that if his body was small, his voice was not. His roars of indignation at being cast out of his warm, dark fastness made even the exhausted Thomasina smile. Then she screamed again, with an air of surprise, and a second little boy slid into the world, and also began to roar. No wonder she had been so enormous. Twins.

We made Thomasina as comfortable as we could, and Bartholomew, weary, unshaven, and smelling of ale, was brought in to congratulate her and meet his new sons. He was still a little standoffish with me, until Joyce, now my ardent defender, said: 'Master Hillman, none of this is Ursula's fault. She has only done her duty. She's the queen's sister. And this is Bess Hethercott, Ursula's new maidservant, and Bess may have saved Mistress Hillman's life.'

It softened Bartholomew. He gave me a handshake, and made one of his unexpected jokes. 'She saved your life as well, Mistress Stannard! Saved it from me – I've been so angry! Now may I ask your permission to fetch your carriage from Ladymead so that my wife and sons can be carried home in comfort. I'll take the cob and the cart back at the same time. This house is no place for my wife, with *that*' – he jerked his head towards Sabina's room – 'next door.'

Kate Evans, a wiry, spry and businesslike woman in middle years, put in an appearance a few minutes later. She and Thomasina knew each other well, so we left them together with Bess to run errands. 'Joyce,' I said, as we went down the stairs, 'we shall soon be back at the Greshams. Once we're there, I wish for a word with you in private.'

TWENTY-SEVEN
Tying Knots

Thomasina and Bartholomew wanted to go home and later in the day, despite Kate Evans' indignant clucking, Thomasina actually walked down the stairs with Bartholomew's arm about her. He helped her into the carriage, which had been made ready with pillows, and she was taken back to Ladymead, her twins in her arms.

The first to be born was to be christened Ninian and the one whose arrival had been such a surprise was to be called Daniel because Bartholomew had noticed that nearly every young boy he knew was Henry or Robert or John and he wished his new sons to have more distinguished names.

Then I, and Joyce and the Brockleys along with Bess Hethercott, returned to the Greshams. We told them – and a somewhat puzzled Eddie – that our return had been delayed by the crisis that occurred when Thomasina Hillman suddenly gave birth to twins.

It made a good excuse and I hoped it would be enough. We were all too tired for complicated explanations. But when introducing Bess, I explained my need for another maidservant and the Greshams accepted this easily enough. Mrs Gresham obligingly provided a truckle bed. Presently, I told Bess, we would talk about the terms of her employment and her rate of pay. First, we all needed sleep.

And after that, just before supper, in our room, after warning the others not to disturb us, I had that private talk with Joyce.

'Joyce, why in the world have you agreed to marry Master Baines?'

'It grew by itself,' said Joyce. 'When I was tending his ankle, while everyone was out searching for you, Ursula, we made friends. He casually mentioned the pony with the white sock. I didn't take in at once what it could mean, but by the next day,

I'd realized and then I kept on and on thinking about it and in the end, the day after Miles had gone home – he went off as soon as he could, at a steady walk with his groom in anxious attendance and one foot not in its stirrup – I rode over to him to tell him that he *must* tell you as well. I would never have done such a forward thing – going there alone – except that I felt we had grown friendly enough so that he wouldn't take it wrongly. I was nearly there before I realized that I also wanted to see him again. Well, he was pleased to see me! I told him why what he'd seen was so important, and then he called for wine and as we sat over it, before we knew what was happening, we were talking of marriage. In general, at first. He became very frank about Mildred. He said that she seemed frightened of doing his accounts and helping with the lambing and frightened of him as well. He said he had kissed her and she'd recoiled and if she was going to shrink from him like that, what sort of wedding night would they have? And what sort of marriage?'

'Joyce, he really shouldn't have talked in such a way to you, a young girl, unmarried!'

'Perhaps not, but he did,' said Joyce. 'And I suddenly heard myself saying that I could do accounts and I thought I could learn to help with lambing if someone would show me what to do, and would he consider me? And I smiled at him and said I promised not to shrink.'

'And?'

'He smiled and he'd like to marry me instead of Mildred and did I mean what I'd said, and I said yes. But we couldn't go any further until you were really better, and when you were, everything crowded in; you wanted this dinner party to take place so that you and Brockley could search the Parkers' house. It was somehow the wrong time for Miles to come to you to ask for your formal permission to marry me. We wanted you,' said Joyce, 'to concentrate.'

'I am sure you did! But why Baines? He's middle aged and getting paunchy. I have introduced you to so many handsome young men, and some were very taken with you. Two actually did propose, but you refused them. You're hardly desperate for suitors!'

'They were all sons still waiting to inherit,' said Joyce. 'Well,

one had a house and land but I didn't like him. He was too
sure of his own attractions. Miles is established. He has a house
and a sheep farm; we would have each other's company and I
would have useful work to do, and children. I hope for that and
so does he. Very much so.'

'But Miles is so . . .'

'Physically unappealing? I wouldn't notice that in the dark,'
said Joyce in a practical tone. 'It is what one does to get children
and they're what matters.'

'*Joyce!*'

'Isn't that the way it has been, for thousands of women, all
down the ages? Isn't it the way Mildred's parents expected it
to be, for her?'

I was silent, for it was true. Lucius had said it. So had
Catherine Gresham. All the same . . .

'Joyce, he has a mistress, I'm sure of it. There's a maidservant
in his service who . . .'

'I know. My father did the same thing,' Joyce said imperturb-
ably. 'It's natural when a man is on his own. Miles talked to
me about that, too. He will pay the girl off – handsomely – and
she'll be out of his house before we marry. And, yes, I do truly
wish to marry Miles and I think I can be the kind of wife he
needs. I shall be as happy as most and happier than many, and
I want children very much. Please don't try to stop me.'

I looked at her in amazement, but she was calm and serious.
She meant what she was saying and suddenly I saw her father
Giles Frost looking out of her eyes. He was practical too.
He was able to regard three years in the Tower as a business
asset, since it would add to his credentials in the eyes of
the Spaniards, to whom he was being paid to feed inaccurate
information.

Joyce's twin Jane was all female, gentle and affectionate,
falling in love with a suitable man and going merrily off into
her own happy dream of marriage. Joyce on the other hand
was her father's daughter, all the way. All the same . . .

'Joyce,' I said, 'you are only twenty and Miles is about thirty
years older than you. And when he speaks his voice is . . .
thick. As though he's talking through phlegm. You may not
have him for long. Have you thought of that?'

'Yes, of course. I've noticed that thick speech as well. But I learned a lot from Gladys, about horehound cough linctus and using steam to ease mucus on the chest. I shall look after him and hope that he will live to see his children mature. But whatever happens,' said Joyce, 'if I do lose him, I may well still be fairly young and I shall be a woman of means. I can marry again, or not, as I choose. I think that either way, this could be a good thing for me and for him. He has been lonely, you know, and that's bad for anyone's health. I can at least discourage him from going out to tend sheep on freezing cold winter nights, because staying indoors lowers his spirits so. He's been doing just that,' Joyce said. 'Pascal Bryers used to play chess with him sometimes but I suppose Pascal will be arrested now.'

'Yes, he will,' I said, with some regret. It would be a sorry waste of a most attractive young man, the kind who would have made a good husband and father if only he had left politics alone and not surrendered to a romantic dream about an imprisoned queen.

'Miles and I had better meet,' I said. 'I'll visit him at his home.'

'Yes, that's best,' said Joyce. 'It's odd, that his house has no name. Everyone just calls it the Baines' House. Perhaps I can persuade him to give it a proper name. Oh, there is one other thing.'

'Yes?'

'Mildred is unhappy at home. And since – I trust – I won't be returning to Hawkswood with you, you'll miss having a woman companion, won't you? I think the Greshams might let Mildred become your companion and I fancy Mildred herself would like it. I've heard them telling her that they don't know what to do with her, and she can't expect them to search the world for a husband for her, not now that she's rejected such a good match, and she'd better try not to be a burden, and much as they deplore the old religion, it had one merit – girls like Mildred could go into nunneries.'

'Or stay at home to become servants when their parents got old,' I said thoughtfully. 'Well, well. I'll consider it, Joyce. Meanwhile, when shall we visit Miles Baines?'

*   *   *

We were on our way home. I had sometimes wondered if the moment would ever come, there was such a whirl of special occasions before we could in decency start out. We had to see Ninian and Daniel christened; Thomasina and Bartholomew insisted on giving us a farewell dinner at Ladymead; and of course, we had stayed for Joyce's wedding. The bride wore her favourite rose-coloured gown, with a chaplet of primroses in her hair, and she was married at St Ninian's church, to a Miles Baines bursting with pride and almost bursting out of his mustard-yellow doublet as well. Her attendants were Thomasina's daughters Ann, Alice and Kat. Mildred had wanted to attend her but the Greshams, still furious with her for, as they saw it, letting Miles slip through her fingers, indignantly forbade it.

Joyce seemed perfectly content with her bargain. At the last moment, when the pair had been bedded and I was kissing her goodbye, I probably looked anxious, because she smiled and whispered: 'All's well with me.'

I hoped it was.

When we finally left for home, through a world at last full of green leaves and birdsong, Mildred came with us. Her parents wouldn't let her attend Joyce at the wedding but they pounced joyfully on the suggestion that she should become my companion.

'Certainly,' said Henry Gresham. 'We have no wish to maintain a disobedient daughter. She could have had a home and a husband in Miles Baines, but all she can do, it seems, is pine after a papist who is shortly to die for treason. Catherine has heard her crying into her pillow and saying the name of Pascal. Have you not, Catherine?'

'Yes, I have,' said Catherine. 'Take her as your companion, or ward, or what you will, by all means and help her to forget him.'

Mildred (and Grey Cob) were therefore to come to Hawkswood and keep me company, now that Joyce was wed. When I told Thomasina about the plan, she said: 'From what I gathered from Joyce, you'll get Mildred married in five minutes. Joyce said that you have only to shake the nearest tree and young men fall out of it!'

At the last moment, when we were all mounted on our horses and Dale was in the carriage with the baggage, Bartholomew saw us off with one of his weird jokes. 'You keep chickens, don't you, Ursula? In future make sure you're the bane of hens, not the other way round.' So we started out with laughter, except that Mildred looked bewildered and had to be explained to.

I was able to start for home with a free mind. I had dutifully sent a report to Walsingham of what I had done and all that I had discovered. I gathered from his reply that he was now seeking fresh agents for the area to replace Gray and Reeves, but to my relief he hadn't asked me to find the replacements.

On the journey home, out of sheer curiosity, I decided to travel by way of Glastonbury, to find out if Crispin Hanley's orphans really did exist.

None of us had ever seen Glastonbury before and we were all impressed by it, especially Mildred, who had never before travelled further than a few miles from home. The tall tor, the ruined church of St Michael on top of it and the legends that surrounded the whole district, pleased us all but really delighted her. 'Did our Lord really come here when He was young, Mistress Stannard? And did King Arthur live here once? Do you know?'

I had to tell her that I didn't know – that no one knew – but they were lovely stories; she should just enjoy them. 'And meanwhile,' I said, 'let us find these orphans.'

They weren't hard to find. The landlord of the inn where we were spending the night knew all about them. 'Oh, ah, that'll be Hanley House you're wanting. Passed it on the way here, you did. There 'tis, just down the road, that tall house with the gables in front.'

When we knocked on its door, we were admitted by a maiden of about fifteen, dressed in serviceable dun, and with her hair drawn tightly back from her forehead and gathered in a woollen net, but with the most sparkling blue eyes imaginable. She took us to an office where we met an immensely dignified Principal, Mrs Boyce, dressed in a sweeping black gown, clean white ruff and white headdress. She had a set of clanking keys on her girdle, like a jailer. I explained that we knew Mr Hanley and had heard about his charity, and since we were passing this way, had decided to look in on it.

We had no letter of introduction, but the Principal, taking us in, noticing our well-dressed appearance and probably hoping for a donation, showed us round with alacrity.

Crispin's orphans were certainly real. There were twelve of them, nine girls and three boys. They were all, boys and girls alike, dressed in those practical dun-hued garments and they didn't seem unhappy but they were all very quiet, and the tutor and governess who had their day-to-day care had a stern air about them.

I whispered something of this to Mildred, who whispered back: 'Maybe it's better than living in the gutter and begging in the streets. But no, they're not cheerful.'

Their food was adequate, for we dined there and partook of fresh bread and mutton stew, with egg custard to follow, and the children had the same. The older girls served us, and one of them was the bright-eyed lass who had opened the door to us. After dinner, I asked the governess her name.

'That's Hannah,' the governess told me, standing before me with her hands clasped at her waist and a slightly defensive air, as though she feared I meant to criticize her, or send a dubious report of her to Crispin Hanley.

In answer to my enquiring look, she added: 'She is the daughter of a maidservant at a big house here in Glastonbury. A case, I fear, of a gentleman claiming *droit de seigneur*, though he let the maidservant and her child stay in the household. But the maidservant died and then the gentleman died too and his wife would not keep the girl. This place had just opened – it was two years ago. The chaplain of the family suggested that Hannah should come to us. We have taught her to read and write and she helps in the house and with the younger children and with the poultry, too. Next year, when she has turned fifteen, Mrs Boyce may employ her as a maid and pay her a wage.'

'What's her second name?' I asked.

'Her mother was called Alison Durley.'

'Hannah Durley, then. May we talk to her?'

It was permitted. We all liked the girl. I made the expected donation, and Hannah entered my service. And that is how I came to return to Hawkswood not only with a new companion to replace Joyce but also with two new young maidservants, Bess Hethercott and Hannah Durley.

'I did what I went to Devon to do,' I said to Brockley as we came in sight of the Hawkswood chimneys. 'But I'm thankful it's over. That outburst of Sabina's! She must have been brooding and fermenting for years and years.'

'She had been suffering for years, I fancy,' Brockley said. 'But when it came to her attempts to rid herself of you, I must say she had the devil's own luck. To follow you the whole day, as she said she did, and poison your cider in the evening, she had to be away from home all day and all night. She had to choose a time when her brother would be away as well, so that he wouldn't realize. He chanced to be in Plymouth on church business on the day we went to Okehampton, and it was a Wednesday – she had Tavistock as an excuse for being away all night, anyway. Devil's own luck, as I say.'

'Don't you remember an old friend of yours once saying that when in trouble, use what's there? I think Sabina did just that. The right conjunction of planets so to speak, suddenly occurred and she seized it. It's a miracle I am still alive.'

'That fall she had must have frightened her,' Brockley said, with a wicked chuckle. 'She had to reach home by mid-morning, at latest. Her brother would be getting home about then, I should think. She must have started at daybreak. If the horse had got away from her . . .!'

'Yes, indeed.' I reached under my hat and rubbed the fading bump where Sabina had hit me. I had been the lucky one then, for the headaches it gave me at first had died away and not returned. 'If the horse had run off and especially if she had her fall before she'd reached Tavistock, she'd have had to explain why she had apparently been riding in the wrong direction.'

Brockley remarked: 'Just for interest, while you and Dale and all the rest of you ladies were sewing your finery for Joyce's wedding, I rode to Tavistock and talked to the Brewster sisters. Sabina didn't attend their gathering on that evening. They were sure of it because they had meant to ask her to play an accompaniment for a visiting singer and had to find someone else.'

'We didn't believe Sabina could possibly have done it. We

weren't investigating her,' I said. 'Or there were things we should have found suspicious much earlier. But it's over now. She's dead. I think she hated me, you know. I have everything she wanted.'

'Madam, when you sent your report to Sir Francis Walsingham, did you tell him what Lucius Parker's cousin overheard at the meeting when Sir Francis was talking to Lord Burghley about the work of his agents? And mentioned the names of Gray and Reeves?'

'No,' I said. 'I carefully implied that Lucius did all his eaves-dropping in the Castle Inn. What Walsingham whispered to Burghley at that meeting may have done something to draw Sabina's attention to those two men. You could almost say that Sir Francis is partly responsible for the deaths of two of his agents. Ironic, in a way. I have often longed to crow over Walsingham but now I have the chance, I don't want to take it.'

'He's not a man to annoy, either,' said Brockley. Perhaps a little sardonically.

'Very true,' I said, refusing to rise to that and thinking of one or two alarming times when I actually had annoyed him. 'It wouldn't be safe.'

We were in sight of the Hawkswood gateway now and already the dogs had sensed our coming and were barking a welcome. I was safe. Safe among my own, free to be with my family, free of danger, no longer threatened by henbane and Dartmoor snowstorms, free of wearisome and difficult duties.

For the time being.